TARZAN
The Lost Adventure

EX·LIBRIS

EDGAR·RICE
BURROUGHS

TARZAN
THE LOST ADVENTURE

**Edgar Rice Burroughs
& Joe R. Lansdale**

Original Tarzan logo
J. Allen St. John
& Todd Klein

Dust jacket art
Dean Williams

Illustrations
Studley O. Burroughs
Gary Gianni
Michael Kaluta
Monty Sheldon
Charles Vess
Thomas Yeates

DARK HORSE BOOKS

original series editor
Peet Janes
specialty books editor
Lynn Adair
book designer
Brian Gogolin

Mike Richardson • publisher
Neil Hankerson • executive vice president
David Scroggy • vice president of publishing
Lou Bank • vice president of sales & marketing
Andy Karabatsos • vice president of finance
Mark Anderson • general counsel
Diana Schutz • editor in chief
Randy Stradley • creative director
Cindy Marks • director of production & design
Mark Cox • art director
Sean Tierney • computer graphics director
Chris Creviston • director of accounting
Michael Martens • marketing director
Tod Borleske • sales & licensing director
Mark Ellington • director of operations
Dale LaFountain • director of m.i.s.

Published by Dark Horse Comics
10956 SE Main Street
Milwaukie, OR 97222
USA

December 1995
Limited Edition
ISBN: 1-56971-128-3
Mass Market Hardcover Edition
ISBN: 1-56971-083-X

2 4 6 8 10 9 7 5 3 1

PRINTED IN THE UNITED STATES

A Preface

arzan: The Lost Adventure is what's known as a "happening" in the publishing world. Until now, nothing new from the pen of Edgar Rice Burroughs has been published for over thirty years. An unfinished and untitled Tarzan typescript of eighty-three pages was found in the author's safe following his death, and expectations soared as word got around. The author's popularity became even greater after his death, and pulp-magazine editors such as Ray Palmer of *Other Worlds* began clamoring for a successor to Mr. Burroughs. The fans, hearing of the newly discovered Tarzan piece, began speculating on who would finish the story and who would publish it. Likely candidates were hauled into the limelight and pitted against one another in the arena of public opinion. The fans clamored for a competition to finish the piece, with a prize going to the victor and awarded by a judging panel selected by the family of the late author. Like the rumble of waves on distant shores, the speculations rose and fell, but nothing happened for thirty years until Dark Horse Comics came up with a writer and a unique publishing plan. The writer was Joe R. Lansdale and the medium was a pulp-magazine format, highly appropriate since Mr. Burroughs is popularly known as "King of the Pulps."

What, exactly, has been the outcome of the Dark Horse venture? Holding this book in your hands is proof positive that the four-part comic-book version in soft cover was a resounding success, due in large part to the stable of competent artists whose drawings are so intentionally reminiscent of the pulp era: Arthur Suydam, Thomas Yeates, Charles Vess, Gary Gianni, and Michael

Kaluta. Their drawings are distributed throughout the text as head or tail pieces, marginal or half-page drawings, in short, providing the look and feel of pulp-magazine literature. Another and more obvious factor in the success quotient is the Burroughs name. It was not by accident that he was dubbed "Grandfather of American Science Fiction." Part of the privilege of reigning as "King of the Pulps" is that his name on the front cover of any magazine was guaranteed to sell copies.

But what of the writing? Earlier this year, an unpublished chapter of *Huckleberry Finn* was found among the literary remains of Mark Twain, and a new edition was hurried through the press to incorporate this new find. It may be that the author purposely excluded the chapter for personal reasons, or because of space limitations, but there is no doubt that it is a finished product, published or unpublished. The same cannot be said of Burroughs' *Lost Adventure*. It was not a finished product, scarcely more than an outline, and we have no proof that he lavished much time and care upon it. This task remained for Mr. Lansdale, and he has met the challenge head on and conquered. A few minor changes were made, but his prose reads fluently and the story now has a beginning, a middle, and an end that hold the reader's attention. Mr. Burroughs, I'm sure, could have asked for no more. The syntax is colloquialized for modern eye and ear, as in the following example from the opening line of the last chapter: "Tarzan used the flagpole like a pole vault." A pole is not a vault. The true meaning must be supplied by the reader who understands intuitively that Tarzan uses the flagpole like a vaulting pole. This sort of writing is the stepchild of Virginia Woolf wedded to the foster child of the television age. Our language is in a constant state of flux because it is a living language. We know what the sentence means, and it should be enough. Besides, there is every indication from Burroughs' last published Tarzan novel, *Tarzan and the Foreign Legion*, that the author was headed in this direction, adapting to the times and to more idiomatic speech patterns.

The plot spins upon a familiar wheel of intrigue and danger in which an archaeologist and his safari seek to penetrate the secrets of the lost city of Ur, a name well calculated to stir the imagination. It is believed that the ancient Sumerians' "cult of Ur" gave us the etymological foundation for the word "culture." Tarzan's alter ego, "Lord Greystoke," was originally called "Bloomstoke" in the author's first draft of *Tarzan of the Apes*; and "Ur" in *Lost Adventure* was originally "Sadeville," a decidedly unmagical name which Burroughs crossed out on his typescript in favor of "Ur." It was the only substantive correction he made in the entire piece.

It is true that the original fragment ends before the parties reach the city of Ur, but Mr. Lansdale has provided an effective story of his own, and we think you will enjoy this most unusual collaboration from both sides the ground (to paraphrase James Agee). Dark Horse brings you this limited-edition collectible knowing that no Burroughs collection would be complete without it. Nearly half a century has passed since Burroughs laid Tarzan to rest, so this resurrection is like icing on a cake. If this is your introduction to Burroughs, I hope it will inspire you to go back to his gold age (1914-1949) and discover the excitement of his original stories — not just Tarzan but the entire family of characters he invented. Mr. Burroughs remains one of the greatest storytellers America has ever produced, an achievement which grows more prodigious with time.

George T. McWhorter
Curator, Burroughs Memorial Collection
Editor, *The Burroughs Bulletin*

TARZAN
The Lost Adventure

I

Numa the Lion padded silently along the trail of the man thing he was stalking. Numa was getting old. Resiliency had gone from his muscles. When he sprang to seize his prey, he was too slow now, and often he went hungry. Pacco the zebra eluded him with ease, and so did Bara the deer. Only the slowest and weakest of creatures fell prey to his charges. And thus Numa became a man-eater. But he was still a powerful engine of destruction.

The man, naked but for a loincloth and his weapons — spear, bow and arrow, knife, and rope — moved as silently through the forest as did the man-eater behind him. He was moving upwind, and the scent spoor of the carnivore was carried away from him. But he had another keen sense always on guard to warn him of approaching danger, and when one of Numa's padded paws snapped a little twig, the man wheeled and faced the lion. He dropped the rope, bow, and quiver from his shoulder, let go of the spear he was carrying, and drew his great knife.

With only a knife, the man faced the king of beasts, and at this close range, that was the way he preferred it.

Discovered, Numa roared and charged. As he rose upon his hind feet to seize his prey, the man leaped to one side, turned and sprang upon Numa's back. The man's right arm encircled the beast's neck, and his legs locked around the small of its body, all with the speed of light.

Roaring in rage, Numa reared erect as the long-bladed knife sank to the hilt behind his left shoulder. Again and again the man struck, and Numa's rich red blood leapt in the sunlight. The lion threw himself from side to side, leaping and bounding in futile efforts to dislodge the creature from its back. And constantly the knife rose and fell, the man clinging to Numa as tight as an entwined ivy vine.

The lion hurled itself on its side and rolled about the jungle floor, tossing up dried leaves and leaf mold, trying to press its attacker into the dirt and dislodge him, but the man held and the knife struck repeatedly.

Suddenly, the lion went limp and sank lifeless to the ground. The man, gore-covered from the spray of Numa's life's blood, leaped erect, and, placing a foot on the body of his kill, lifted his face to the heavens and voiced a long and hideous scream that sent monkeys chattering in fear through the treetops. After five years, Tarzan of the Apes had returned to his jungle.

He was ranging the vast domain that had been his stamping ground since childhood. Here he had foraged with the tribe of Kerchak the king ape. Here the she-ape Kala, his foster mother, had been killed by Kulonga the warrior-son of Mbonga the chief. And here Tarzan had slain Kulonga.

These and many other memories, sweet and bittersweet, passed through Tarzan's mind as he paused to wipe the blood from his body and blade with leaves.

In most of this area, far off the beaten track, there were only the animals and the native tribes — savage and primitive, living as their forebears had for ages. The wilderness teemed with game. On the plains, the herbivores grazed; and there the carnivores hunted them by night, which was according to the laws of Nature.

But Tarzan had caught the scent spoor of creatures notorious as destroyers of peace and tranquillity, the one thing that stupidly upsets the balance of Nature. To his sensitive nostrils, Usha the wind carried the effluvium of humanity. And Tarzan was going to investigate.

Tarzan was always suspicious of humans in this district, as

there were far more accessible hunting grounds elsewhere; and, too, several of the native tribes here were dangerous, having learned from past experience that outsiders, or at least those they had encountered, had little or no respect for their way of life or for the natural laws of the jungle.

Tarzan could not imagine any reputable guide leading a safari into such dangers; any reliable guide or hunter would know that outsiders had not earned the respect of the natives here, and that to bring foreigners into this realm was to court death.

As the scent of the intruders grew stronger, indicating that he was approaching his quarry, Tarzan took to the trees, swinging through the middle terrace. So gently and naturally did he move amongst the limbs and vines of the great forest, the birds remained undisturbed. This silent, arboreal approach gave him an advantage when his quarry was man, as man is far less likely to detect danger approaching from above than at his own level.

Presently, he reached a point from which he could see those he sought. He looked down on a small, poor safari encamped in a jungle clearing. Tarzan's quick eyes and keen mind took in every important detail of the camp and its occupants.

Four tough-looking men moved about the camp with an assurance that told Tarzan they were the bwanas of this safari. Two of the men were white, two were black. All four looked as hard as tree bark and had the appearance of men accustomed to harshness. They wore .45s on their hips. Each of them wore battered military uniforms, probably the French Foreign Legion, though they were in such bad condition, it was impossible to tell at a glance. From that fact, Tarzan deduced that they were probably deserters. They seemed an impoverished and ill-equipped company, probably straggling through the jungle on their way to the coast.

Besides the four uniformed men, there were ten bearers, and two askaris — head bearers. Tarzan noted particularly that there was no ivory in the camp. That exonerated them from any suspicion of ivory poaching, which, with the needless slaughter of game, was a crime he constantly sought to prevent by any means or measure.

He watched them trudge along for a moment, then left them, but with the intention of keeping an eye on them from time to time until they were out of his domain.

Unaware that Tarzan had hovered above them and passed on, the four bwanas, who were preparing to break camp, uncorked a canteen and passed it around. The askaris and bearers behind them watched them intently, ready to take up their packs at a moment's notice.

When the canteen had made two rounds, one of the white men, a small, wiry man with a face that had seen it all and not liked any of it, turned to the large black man walking beside him, said, "There's only two of 'em, Wilson. And they're picture-takers, and one's a girl. They got lots of food, and we ain't got none."

The other white man, large and sweaty, great moons of sweat swelling beneath his armpits and where his shirt fit tight over the mound of his belly, nodded, said, "Gromvitch is right, Wilson. Another thing. They got plenty of ammunition. We ain't got none. We could use it."

Wilson Jones, whose black face looked to have been at one time a great and avid collector of blows, said, "Yeah, they got food, and they got ammunition, Cannon, but they also got what shoots the ammunition. Get my drift?"

"I get it," said Cannon, "but we don't get what they got, well, we're meat for the worms out here. We got to have ammunition and food to survive."

Wilson looked to the other Negro, Charles Talent. He was a tall man in a ragged uniform with too-short sleeves and too-short pants. The sides of his boots were starting to burst. He was leaning just off the trail against a tree. He didn't look like much, but Wilson knew he was amazingly fast and much stronger than his leanness suggested.

As always, Talent wouldn't look directly at Wilson, or anyone for that matter. He once confided to Wilson it was because his old man had beat him with sticks of sugar cane when he was young; he beat him every day and made Charles look him in the eye and say what the beating was for, even if he didn't know what it was for, other than the fact his old man enjoyed doing it.

Old man Talent had gone through a number of canes when Charles was growing up, but the last one he cut was the last time he did anything. Charles put a cane knife in him, spilled his guts in the cane field, happily kicked his innards around in the dirt, and departed and never looked back.

From that time on, Charles had never been able to look a man directly in the eye. Unless he was killing him.

Wilson studied Charles' slumped posture, his bowed head,

and said, "You got somethin' to say, Charles?"

It was slow in coming, but finally, "I ain't got nothin' against doin' what needs to be done. We should have done it then, when we come up on 'em. But then or now, it's all the same. That's all I got to say."

Wilson knew what that meant. Charles loved killing. For Charles, that was what always needed to be done. It was the only time he felt strong, in control.

The other two, they weren't much better. Gromvitch, though a bully, maybe didn't enjoy killing as much as Talent, didn't accept it as quickly as Cannon, but he didn't mind it. And Wilson knew he himself was only a hair's breadth better than any of them. He liked to think that difference made him slightly superior, but in fact he felt bad about how he lived, the choices he had made.

Cannon said, "We got ammunition, we don't need the food so bad. We can hunt game then. We don't get it, we won't last long. Anyone finds us, ever, there won't be enough left to pack a snuff box. Some chewed bones. I say we got to do something, even if it's wrong."

Wilson grinned some damaged teeth. "Hell, boys, wrong is all we ever done, ain't it?"

"That's the truth," said Cannon, "but now we got to do some right for ourselves, even if it is wrong for them pilgrims."

"They've talked to us and gone on," Gromvitch said. "I don't think they suspect nothin', and if they do, they don't care. They're just glad to be shed of us. See how nervous they was? 'Specially that gal."

"I figure if they thought we was gonna do somethin' we'd have done it," Cannon said. "This way, we can surprise 'em. Swoop down on 'em like hawks . . . 'sides, I'd like to have me a little visit with that gal. See she's put together right."

"That's good by me too," Gromvitch said, and he shook the canteen. "And they might have some whiskey somewheres. I'm sick of water."

Wilson thought a moment, studied his companions, and hated them as never before. He couldn't figure how he had ever got himself into such a mess. He wished he'd never left the boxing game. Throwing that fight had changed his life. He shouldn't have done it. Not for money. Not for any reason. He should have fought his best. He should have gone on to be a manager, even a cut man. He should have done a lot of things, but he hadn't done any of them.

Wilson thought, if I had it to do over . . . He caught himself.

Yeah, *if*. And if wishes were horses, beggars would ride.

Wilson turned to Gromvitch. "You stay here, we'll go."

"Me?" Gromvitch said. "Why me?"

"Because I said so," Wilson said. "That isn't good enough, maybe I ought to remind you who's boss here. Without me, you'd still be a Legionnaire eatin' desert."

"No," Gromvitch said. "I don't need no remindin'. But that girl — "

"Get it out of your mind," Wilson said. "I'm not in for that. We have to kill them, we do it quick, and we're out of there. We do what we got to do, not what's fun for you."

"Well," Gromvitch said. "Whiskey then."

"Just mind the camp," Wilson said, then turned to his confederates. "Come on, let's get goin'."

Eugene Hanson stood up from the camp chair, adjusted the camera strap around his neck, wiped the sweat from his face, placed his hands on his hips, stretched his back, and studied the jungle. It was dark and green and rich with the sounds of animals and the buzzing of insects. It was humid and uncomfortable. His feet hurt. He'd been bitten by insects on nearly every part of his body, and he was weary and sore. Yet, he loved the jungle. His mission and the beauty of the jungle had driven him on this photographic expedition. He wanted photographs that had never been taken before. Photographs of the manlike apes that were reputed to live in this part of Africa.

Outside of legends, the evidence was thin, but Hanson was convinced these man-apes existed. Man-apes were most likely cousins to the Yeti and the Sasquatch. He had researched them for years. Made plaster casts of their footprints. Talked to eye witnesses. But this trip to Africa, he was determined to prove their existence; determined to push into the interior where no white man he knew of had gone before, and finally, with his cameras, prove once and for all that the man-apes of Africa were more than legend and that they lived near the ruins of an ancient city — the remains of a once-great, black kingdom called Ur.

Hanson grinned to himself, thought: this is a hell of a lot better than a classroom. He had never felt like a Ph.D. anyway. And since he was interested in such things as Sasquatch, the Yeti, and the Great

Man-Apes of Africa, his colleagues at the University of Texas were not always inclined to think of him as a Ph.D. either. He certainly didn't look like one. A fact he was secretly proud of. He was a little less trim at forty than he had been just five years ago, but he was husky, strong, and he still had some of what had made him an excellent fullback on the Lumberjacks football team at Stephen F. Austin State University. And he could still throw a punch as well as when he was an amateur middleweight fighting out of San Antonio.

He turned to locate his daughter, Jean. She was nearby, directing the four askaris and the bearers, showing them where she wanted camp set up. She was like that. Always in charge. One of her anthropology professors — Hanson refused to have his own daughter in his class — Professor Chad Oliver, referred to her as having the head of a bull, if the bull's head was made of steel.

He studied her, thought: My God, she looks so much like her mother. Her shoulder-length blonde hair was dark with sweat, and the back of her shirt at the small of her back was stuck to her skin. Her baggy khaki pants were pocked with burs, thorns, and sticky little plants, the .38 revolver dangled Annie Oakley-style from the worn holster and ammunition belt at her hip, but still, even though a bit lean and gangly, she was beautiful.

When she had directed the bearers properly, and they were about their work, she turned and saw Hanson smiling at her. She strolled over to him, said, "You look happy, Dad. I'd hug you, but I'm so sweaty."

"It's just you remind me of your mother," he said.

"Really?"

"Oh, yeah. But I can't say *you* look happy. Sorry you came?"

"Oh, no. It's those men. I didn't like the looks of them. They made me nervous. They looked like criminals."

Hanson hadn't liked their looks either. He had kept his hand near his .38 all the time they had been near. The words that had passed between him and them had been friendly enough, but he hadn't liked the way they studied him, his supplies, and especially the way that one man, the fat one, looked at Jean, as if she were a pork chop and he a starving wolf.

"They were a tough-looking bunch," he said. "Deserters, I presume. Foreign Legion most likely."

"I thought so too," Jean said.

"Wise you didn't say as much," Hanson said. "They might

have been trouble if you had. But they're behind us now and they were heading south."

"I know," Jean said. "But I'm a worrier."

He patted her shoulder. "You needn't be."

The brush crashed. Hanson wheeled. The two Negro deserters and the fat white man came out of the brush. Each carried a .45 service pistol in his hand.

"I believe the best way to put this is," Wilson said, "This is a stickup."

The lean black man walked over to the bearers. He pointed the gun at them without looking directly at them. He had an odd way of holding his head, like a dog, constantly listening for a sound.

"Tell those bearers not to pull any weapons," Wilson said, "otherwise, we'll have to put holes in them."

Hanson spoke to the askari, who understood English, and they transferred the message to the bearers in their language. Hanson turned back to Wilson. "Just take it easy," he said. "We don't want trouble."

"Neither do we," said Wilson. "Trouble's the one thing I don't want. Get their guns, Cannon."

Cannon came toward them grinning. "Get your hands up, and no funny business." He removed their revolvers, taking far longer unbuckling Jean's ammunition belt and holster than was necessary.

"You and me, we could have some fun, baby," Cannon said, and he slipped an arm around Jean's waist and whispered something in her ear. She slapped him. It was a fast, hard slap, and it left a huge red imprint on his face.

"You witch," he said, and drew back his hand to strike her. Hanson, oblivious to the guns covering him, stepped in and landed a short right on Cannon's chin that sent him down and caused him to drop his .45.

Cannon scrambled in the leaf mold for the .45, grabbed it, turned to point it at Hanson. "Good-bye, tough guy," he said.

Wilson stepped in and kicked Cannon's arm and the gun went off and sent a shell whistling through the trees. Monkeys screamed and chattered and leaves rained down on them like colorful snow.

"No killing necessary," Wilson said. "They hang people for murder even in Africa."

Cannon stood up slowly, rubbing his wrist. The look he gave Wilson was incredulous. "We've done enough to get hung already.

Two more, ten more, won't make a difference."

"Then don't do it because I say don't do it," Wilson said. Wilson turned back to Hanson and Jean. "We'll take your bearers, your supplies. Even those cameras. Things like that'll trade or sell good. I'll leave you with a little food and water."

"We ought to just go on an kill this bastard," Cannon said, waving his .45 at Hanson. "We could find use for the girl, though."

"No," Wilson said. "Leave 'em."

Wilson grinned at Hanson. "I'll tell you this, that wasn't a bad punch. I've seen some good ones, and that one wasn't bad."

"Yeah, well, I'm flattered," Hanson said.

"You go on and be tough," Wilson said. "It's no matter to me, but it was still a good punch."

Hanson didn't need a Ph.D. to size up these men, and he knew that nothing he might say would change things. Wilson seemed reluctant to kill them, but in a sense, he was doing just that, leaving them unarmed in the jungle. For them to make it out of this area of Africa, to safety, more than a bit of luck would have to be with them. Perhaps the sentence Cannon wanted to pass would have been the best. At least death would have been immediate.

A few minutes later, Hanson and Jean stood side by side, a container of water and food at their feet, watching their stolen safari disappearing into the jungle.

"The beasts," Jean said.

"You malign the beasts," said Hanson.

After a moment of silence, Jean said softly. "There was one bright spot in the whole affair."

Hanson stared at her. "And what could that be?"

"The big black man was right. That was one pretty right you landed, Dad."

Hanson rubbed his scraped knuckles. "Felt good, too," he said. "But I got to tell you, that slap you landed wasn't second-rate either. You rattled that ole boy's teeth."

"Good," Jean said.

TARZAN
The Lost Adventure

II

Four days passed. The Hansons soon ran out of their meager rations and had eaten some fruit and nuts, such as they had seen the monkeys eat with evident impunity. But they were half-starved. The future looked grim. They had trekked back in the direction from which they had come but covered little distance due to their failing strength and the delays necessitated by the need for building platforms in the trees to escape the lions who prowled incessantly at night. Hanson couldn't help but think one change of the wind might carry their scent below, and if it did, the lions might easily climb to their not-so-elevated height and take them for dinner. Certainly a leopard might. It was not a thought that allowed deep, comfortable sleep.

It was day now, however, and Hanson's spirits were lifted somewhat, though they weren't the sort of spirits one might proudly write home about. He was sitting on a fallen log by Jean, slapping at biting insects, considering all this. They had found it necessary to rest more often as they seemed to tire more easily each mile.

"I was a stupid fool to bring you along," Hanson said. "It was dangerous even if we hadn't met up with those thieving bastards. We may never get out of here."

"Sure, we will," Jean said. "And don't blame yourself. I made you miserable until you gave in. I knew the dangers as well as you. And there's Hunt and Small. We'll meet up with them soon enough."

Hunt and Small were head of the party they hoped to join soon, but at the moment, they might as well have been on the other side of the world. And furthermore, Jean was merely trying to lift his spirits. She had no faith in either Hunt or Small — especially Hunt, and that was probably because she had grown up with the boy and he was madly in love with her. Hanson knew for a fact she thought Hunt and Small incompetent, and together, doubly incompetent, and in his darkest moments, Hanson feared she might be right. He realized he should have chosen his teammates more on ability to traverse the jungle than an understanding of the nature of anthropoids or the culture of lost civilizations. Fact was, just one man or woman with expertise in simple woodcraft and a knowledge of directions might have been a wiser pick.

But it was of no significance now. Nothing could be changed. They were in bad shape, no matter how you sliced it. Hanson tried to smile at Jean, but she looked past him and blanched.

Hanson swung around and saw an almost-naked giant approaching them. A bow and a quiver of arrows were slung to his back across his right shoulder. A wicked-looking knife hung at one hip, and he carried a spear with a leather loop at its hilt. Across his left shoulder and under his right arm a crude rope was coiled. He wore a breechcloth of the soft skin of an antelope. His black hair was long and shaggy, and his skin was deeply tanned and crisscrossed with numerous thin, white scars.

Hanson stood up and tried to position himself in front of Jean. The man watched him, but neither slowed nor sped up. He finally came to a stop ten feet in front of them. His keen eyes appraised Hanson and the girl. "Where is your safari? How did you come to be alone here, without food and weapons?"

Hanson relaxed slightly. He thought the man had a commanding, non-belligerent attitude. His English, though good, was odd. Not quiet American or British. Formal and stiff. Accented, but with no influence Hanson could name. Perhaps here was some kind of help. Someone who could guide them to safety. His manner, his voice, even his appearance aroused confidence. And besides, there was nothing to lose. Hanson dropped his guard but stayed mentally alert while he explained who they were and what had happened to them.

"I have seen those men," said the giant. "I thought they might be dangerous. Stay here and I will get you food, then I will go after your safari."

"They've got guns," Hanson said.

"I know," said the man, and he took the leather loop on the spear, fitted it around his neck, grabbed the low limb of a tree, swung into its leafy denseness, and disappeared. Treetops rustled ahead and beyond where Hanson and Jean stood, and in a moment the man was consumed by foliage. He was gone.

"Well," Jean said. "I've gone whole weeks without seeing anything like that."

Hanson, stunned, nodded. "Kind of short on words, isn't he?"

"Do you think he can get food out here?" Jean said.

"I hate to say it," Hanson said, "but I think we've seen the last of him. A man who goes through the trees like that, he's bound to have fallen on his head a time or two. Probably one of those slightly 'teched' characters you read about — a wild man of the woods."

"Isn't that what we're looking for?" Jean said. "Wild men of the woods?"

"The ones with fur, Jean. The ones with fur. Did you see how he looked when I mentioned what we were doing? I think he was amused. Or amazed. I got the feeling he thought we were a couple of dopes."

"Well," Jean said, "considering we're standing out here without our safari and little more than the clothes on our backs, he might be right."

"Point."

"Did you see how he took to the trees?" Jean said. "Nimble as a monkey . . . and he's certainly a handsome devil, and he doesn't look 'teched' to me. And those weapons he was carrying, they didn't appear to be window-dressing."

"I'll give you that," Hanson said. "But what now? Do we trust him? Do we try to move on or stay?"

"I say we rest awhile, see if he comes back," Jean said. "If he doesn't, then I think we should build a platform for the night and move out tomorrow."

"I'm not sure I have the strength to build a platform," Hanson said.

"We can do it," Jean said, "with or without help."

Hanson put his arm around his daughter, smiled. "That's right, baby. Don't pay me any mind. I'm just tired. Be strong. We'll make it."

Tarzan, traversing the middle terrace of the forest, caught the scent spoor of Wappi the antelope, and presently saw it below him standing tense and alert. Then the ape-man saw what had alerted the little animal — a leopard, on its belly, was creeping stealthily toward it.

Tarzan seized his bow and fitted an arrow. It was just a matter of seconds before the heavy shaft drove into the antelope's heart, as, almost simultaneously, the ape-man dropped quickly to the ground between the carcass of his kill and the beast that would rob him of it.

With a coughing cry, the leopard charged. Tarzan sidestepped, grabbed the maddened leopard by the scruff of the neck and the tail, whirled about, and tossed the beast as if it were a stuffed toy. The leopard went spinning into the brush, landed tail over claw, rolled, slammed into a tree, and staggered to its feet. The leopard crouched and studied Tarzan. The man stood sideways, low to the ground, as if he might take to it in the manner of Hista, the snake.

Never had the leopard seen anything so fast. And it was a man too, the weaklings of the jungle. The leopard let out a defiant yowl, and Tarzan laughed. "Run along, my friend," Tarzan said in the language of the great apes. "Spare me an arrow. This antelope is mine."

The leopard turned, ducked through the brush and was gone.

Tarzan jerked the arrow from the carcass of the antelope, swung the animal to a shoulder, and took to the trees.

Hanson and Jean sat on the fallen tree, waiting, but with little expectation that the wild man with the stilted English would return.

"If he does come back," said Jean, "I suppose he'll bring us fruit and nuts. I'm fed up on fruit and nuts, even though we haven't had enough of those to keep a canary alive."

"He brings fruit and nuts," Hanson said, "I'll eat fruit and nuts. What I think is, he's probably forgotten about us."

"Maybe not," Jean said.

Hanson glanced up to see Tarzan swing from the branches of a tree with the carcass of his kill and land less than three feet from them. Hanson and Jean stood up. "That didn't take long," said

Hanson.

Tarzan grunted and tossed the antelope on the ground. "After you have dressed it and cut off what you want to eat tonight, carry it up into a tree where the beasts won't get it. Can you make fire?"

"I have a few matches left," said Hanson.

"Keep them," said Tarzan. He unsheathed his hunting knife and removed the viscera from the carcass. Then he turned to them with a question. "How much can you eat tonight? I'll carve it, then start your fire."

"How about the whole thing?" Jean said. "I could eat it raw."

The suggestion of a smile moved the ape-man's lips, as he cut a generous portion from a flank. Then he gathered dry leaves and grasses, tinder, and larger pieces of wood, carried it some distance from the viscera.

"You'll have visitors tonight," he said, "but by morning all the antelope's innards will be gone. It will keep them busy. Less interested in you. I suppose I need not suggest you get into a tree early — and stay there."

Tarzan arranged the leaves, grasses, and tinder and made fire after the manner of the jungle people, then he straightened up.

"I will go after your safari now," he said. "Stay here until I come back."

"Why are you doing this?" Jean asked. "Not that I want to discourage you, but why?"

"Because it needs to be done," Tarzan said. "Here, keep this until you see me next," he said, and handed her his huge knife. Then he swung into a tree and disappeared.

"How in hell does he do that?" Hanson said. "I couldn't climb that tree with a ladder, let alone swing through it."

"Who is he?" demanded Jean.

"I don't know," said Hanson, "but God must have sent him."

"How can he recover our safari by himself?" said Jean.

Hanson shook his head. "He can't."

"That's what we thought about his getting food for us," Jean said.

"Dealing with those men, that's another thing. In fact, I feel awful that he might try. If something happens to him in the process, I'll feel responsible."

"There's nothing we can do about it one way or another now," Jean said. "Let's eat. I'm so hungry my stomach thinks my throat is cut."

"You cook the meat, I'll build a platform," Hanson said.

The meat was partially burned and almost raw, but they wolfed it down. Jean's fingers and face were covered with burned meat and grease as she looked up at her father and grinned. "We're just like the lions at feeding time in the zoo," she said, wiping her face on her sleeve.

"You're a sight," said Hanson. "Last time I saw your face like that, you were twelve or thirteen, and you'd stolen jam out of the pantry."

"All I know is, that's the best meal I've ever eaten."

The sun was low, and Hanson knew the brief equatorial twilight would come and go with startling swiftness. He banked the fire in the hope of preserving embers for breakfast. In the distance a lion roared.

Hanson and Jean climbed into the tree where Hanson had constructed a crude platform of limbs, vines, and leaves. They sat on the edge of it, dangling their legs, looking down into the growing darkness. There was a slight warm breeze and it smelled of the jungle foliage, and faintly of rotting leaves.

Again, a lion roared, but much closer now.

"Where do you suppose he lives?" said the girl.

"Who? The lion?" asked the man.

Jean laughed. "No, silly," she said, "our wild man."

"Oh, probably in a cave with his mate, and a half-dozen naked dirty brats and an ill-tempered, one-legged dog."

"And why would he have a one-legged dog?"

"Because he ate the other three."

"That's not very nice, Dad."

"Get your mind off the loincloth, dear."

"Dad!"

"Good night, dear. Try not to think about your jungle man too much."

"I was just curious, was all."

"Of course," Hanson said, lying down on the platform. "Good night."

It was suddenly quite dark, and below there were a multitude of noises — rustlings, a growl, and then the weird, uncanny yapping of hyenas.

"They're fighting over the entrails of the antelope," said Hanson.

"It's nice to be up here where it's safe," said Jean.

Hanson thought of the python and the leopard, but he did not mention them. The lion roared again. He was very close now, almost directly beneath them. Then he moved on, growling. Hanson could hear the hyenas scattering. The king had come.

TARZAN
The Lost Adventure

III

Tarzan went to the camp where he had discovered Wilson and his gang. From there he could easily follow the plain trail of the safari even though he was traveling through the trees. Presently, he caught scent of a lion, and a few moments later he saw the great carnivore on the trail below — a splendid, black-maned beast.

Tarzan dropped to the ground behind the lion, and as the beast heard him, it turned upon him with a savage growl. Tarzan stood perfectly still, a faint smile on his lips.

The lion approached, and rearing on its hind feet, placed a forepaw on each of the ape-man's shoulders. It was Jad-bal-ja, the Golden Lion, which Tarzan had raised and trained since cubhood.

Tarzan twisted its ears, and the great cat nuzzled its nose against his neck. A moment later, Tarzan pushed the lion from his shoulders. "Come," he said, "You and I have something to do."

The four renegades had selected a campsite after a hard march. It was off the trail near a break in the trees. The bearers were about setting up camp, and Cannon, whip in hand, was lashing at the carriers of his safari and Hanson's as well.

"Snap it up, you lazy bastards," Cannon yelled. "Quit loafin'. I say jump, you say how high. You're working for _men_ now." He laid the lash across the back of a carrier who was working diligently and took delight in watching him jump.

Satisfied for the moment, his arm tired, Cannon paused, his belly heaving beneath his sweat-stained shirt. The whip gave him pleasure. It made him think of the lashes he had gotten at the Legionnaire post. And for nothing — stealing food. God, but he liked to eat, and there was never enough to eat there. And the heat. And the marching and the drilling. What had ever possessed him to join the Foreign Legion?

Just as Cannon struck his last blow, Wilson came back from the concealment of the jungle where he had been hiding some of the weapons, ammunition, and a few supplies. He had taken to doing that at night, lest the safari take off with their supplies. Now, seeing what Cannon was doing, he was more certain than ever that the safari deserting them was inevitable. The askari and the bearers were silent and sullen, but he could see hate and murder on their faces. He beckoned Cannon to him.

"Lay off those fellas, Cannon," said Wilson, "or we'll wake up some morning with our throats cut. Or at the least, all our supplies gone. Besides, I get the feelin' you like hittin' black hide too much."

"It ain't like that," Cannon said.

"I'm not sure what it's like," Wilson said. "But lay off."

Cannon was about to respond, when his mouth fell open. "Who in the hell is that?"

Wilson turned, amazed at what he saw.

Tarzan was approaching, followed by Jad-bal-ja. The two looked to be out for an afternoon stroll.

"Look out, man!" cried Wilson. "A lion! Behind you!"

Tarzan continued toward the camp. As Tarzan came near, the lion walked at his left side, and Tarzan's fingers grasped the black mane. Tarzan and the lion stopped before the four men, who shrank back in fear.

"That your lion?" Wilson asked.

"Yeah," Gromvitch said. "He bite?"

"He's a friend," Tarzan said. "And yes, he bites. I will make this short and direct. I want the safari you stole."

Cannon pushed forward slightly, carefully eyeing the lion. "You what?"

"I am not in the mood for questions," Tarzan said. "In fact, I am an ill-tempered sort. You heard me."

"You can take a flyin' leap, brother," Cannon said. "Just because you come in here in your skivvies with a lion beside you, that don't give you no juice with us. I'll wring your damn neck, shoot the lion, and stick you in him."

"He's right," Wilson said. "You've got two minutes to get out of here. And take your cat with you. You do that, nobody gets hurt."

"And get on some pants," Cannon said. "I can't stand to see no man without pants. It ain't civilized."

Tarzan didn't move.

"The clock is running on that two minutes," Gromvitch said, snapping the cover off the holster of his .45.

Talent, though not looking directly at Tarzan, inched forward, his hand next to his holster. Tarzan sensed immediately, that though all of the men were ruthless, Talent was the most deadly, determined, and in love with killing. He had faced men like him before, and he knew their body language. He knew you gave them absolutely no quarter.

"How are we for time?" Tarzan said.

Cannon exploded. "Time's up!" He jerked his .45 from its holster and pointed it at the ape-man's heart.

Blinding. That is one way to describe the movements of Tarzan. To say that he struck swift as Ara the lightning is another. But neither do him justice. Even as he moved, he spoke a few words to Jad-bal-ja in the language the lion understood, and simultaneously grasped Cannon's pistol hand and his throat as Jad-bal-ja leaped upon Gromvitch.

Tarzan flung Cannon as easily as he had flung the panther. But not as gently. Cannon flew backward, high and hard, and hit his head against a tree trunk with the sound of rotten timber falling into a pond. He hit the tree and then the ground and didn't get up.

In the same instant, Wilson and Talent moved, came at the ape-man from two sides, drawing their pistols. They were fast. Real fast. But Tarzan was faster. His right leg shot out and kicked Talent in the stomach. As Talent bent forward, Tarzan slapped the .45 from his hand with the ease of a cobra striking a paralyzed rodent. Then Tarzan spun toward Wilson, dealing him a slap along the right side of his head, just behind the ear. It was a tremendous blow, dealt with the palm slightly cuffed; a technique Tarzan had learned in the Orient. It sent Wilson to his knees.

Talent had recovered enough to pull a knife from his boot, and now he came at Tarzan, thrusting. Tarzan sidestepped, caught the man's arm, swung under it, and pinned Talent in a hammerlock. He switched his grip and spun away from Talent, still holding the arm. Suddenly, Tarzan pulled it, as if the black man's arm was something he was about to toss over his shoulder. The move was so swift, sharp, and violent, that Talent's elbow snapped, the shoulder popped free, and his clavicle shattered. By the time Tarzan let go of him and turned to kick Wilson — who was trying to rise — full in the face with the ball of his foot, Talent was lying on the ground in a heap, his destroyed arm wriggling like a snake with a spear through it. Before the arm stopped its movements, Talent was dead of shock and Wilson was out from the kick to the face.

Tarzan turned to see Jad-bal-ja standing with both paws on Gromvitch's arms, pinning him to the ground. The terrified man lay trembling, looking up into Jad-bal-ja's snarling face, the lion's saliva dripped down on him. "Don't let him hurt me," he said.

Tarzan glanced up to see the safari was gawking at him, shocked. Everything had happened in less time than anyone could have thought possible. Now, with the action finished, Tarzan staring at them, his lion holding down its prey as if deciding which cut of meat it would consume first, they concluded they were next, and started to flee into the jungle.

"Stay where you are," Tarzan ordered. "I am not your enemy. I am from Hanson and his daughter Jean."

The bearers stopped their flight, but seemed ready to fade into the jungle at a moment's notice. "Hanson," said one the askari.

"Yes," Tarzan said. "Hanson."

Tarzan bent and took the gun from Gromvitch's hand, not that it might do Gromvitch any good with Jad-bal-ja's large paw holding his arm flat against the ground. Tarzan spoke again to the askaris and the bearers, speaking in their language.

"Hanson's bearers will pack up everything that belongs to him, and I will lead you back to his camp. Hanson's askaris will come over here, and guard these two men."

The bearers moved now with enthusiasm — all but Hanson's four askaris. They came forward slowly, for they were afraid of the lion. Tarzan understood and spoke to Jad-bal-ja. The lion strolled off a short distance, sat on its haunches, watching, awaiting his master's

Hanson's bearers were happy. They talked and joked. Sometimes they sang. Eventually, realizing they were not going to be slain, Wilson's bearers joined into the festivities with them; they had been under Cannon's whip long enough to doubly appreciate the humane treatment they had received at the hands of Tarzan of the Apes — a living legend of the jungle. They began to move down the trail.

Wilson, Cannon, and Gromvitch were tied, hands and feet, sitting on the ground in the middle of the trail. Wilson and Cannon had come around, but they still had confusion in their eyes.

Tarzan squatted down beside them. He removed the spear from his back and used the blade to cut them free. "Start for the coast, get out of Africa," he said. "And don't come back."

"But we haven't got a safari," Gromvitch said. "You've got to leave us food, some weapons."

"No, I do not," Tarzan said.

"Next time," Wilson said, rubbing his blood-starved wrists where the bonds had held him, "maybe we can tango a little longer. I like to think you got lucky."

"Think all you want," said Tarzan. "But do not cross my path again, or I will kill you."

Tarzan turned then and trotted after the safari.

Cannon rubbed the back of his aching head as he stood. "Man, I think maybe he dropped that whole tree on me . . . You know, there's some guys you don't like, then there's guys you really don't like. That guy, I like less than either of them."

"Yeah," Gromvitch said, shaking his legs out as he stood. "Me too. How we gonna bury Talent? We ain't got no shovels or stuff."

"You heard the wild man," Wilson said moving toward the jungle. "Animals will take care of him. Right now, what we got to do is get those guns I hid. And get that safari back."

"Oh, yeah," Cannon said with a smile. "Wilson. I take my hat off to you. You was thinking ahead . . . That wild man, he ain't so smart as he thought, is he?"

The great apes of the tribe of Zu-yad, the king, moved about in the early morning searching for food. Grubs. Nuts. Berries. Whatever came their way. They moved silently through the jungle, examining holes in trees, overturning logs, prowling the branches for orders.

Tarzan turned Gromvitch over to an askari, a little man with a jaw that had been broken and grown back crooked. He had a lump on the right side of his face, like a frog hiding under a blanket. "If he makes trouble or tries to escape, kill him," Tarzan said.

"I hope he tries to escape," said the askari. "I will whip him first, shoot his toes off, then cut his hands slow and all over, and maybe, when all the blood is out of him, I will cut his throat."

Tarzan stepped over to where Cannon lay. The man was still breathing. He would be out a while. "Tie him up," Tarzan said to the askari with the lump. "Make sure he is completely unarmed." Tarzan waved a hand at Wilson. "And tie that one up, quickly. I believe he will come around soon."

"What about the other one?" asked another of the askaris.

Tarzan glanced at where Talent lay. "Being tied or untied is exactly the same to him."

"Do we bury him?" asked the askari.

"The animals will see that he has a funeral crowd," Tarzan said.

The askari who had asked the question grinned, turned, saw Jad-bal-ja watching him. He stopped grinning.

"Do not be afraid of the lion," Tarzan said to the askari. "He will attack no one in this camp unless I tell him to. Take all the weapons from these men's askaris and bearers. Tell them they may come with us if they wish, or stay. Tell them that if any of them feel loyal to these men and do not wish to go with us, and should they attempt to follow us or rescue them, I will kill them."

"Anyone loyal to these men can be taken care of right now," said the askari.

"Let us do it my way," Tarzan said.

The askari, disappointed, nodded, and went to do as Tarzan had suggested. Hanson's bearers made quick work of repacking the loads and relieving Wilson's safari of its weapons and ammunition, but the sun was very low when they had completed their work and were formed in a single file, ready to march. None of Wilson's safari had remained loyal.

"We will need to march all night," Tarzan said. "I will march at the head with the lion. Hanson's askaris will carry rifles and bring up the rear. There is to be no straggling. Start out. I will catch up momentarily."

nests of bird eggs.

Zu-yad was feasting on an egg one of the tribe had brought him, when he smelled smoke, a sign of the tarmangani. His dark nostrils flared. Yes, he could smell the tarmangani as well. A male and a female. He licked his yoke-stained lips, gave a short, soft bark to his tribe, and they went still. All except Go-lot. Go-lot, a young bull of the tribe, purposely made a bit of noise before coming to rest. Zu-yad eyed him long and hard.

Day by day, Go-lot was becoming bolder. In time, Zu-yad knew he would have to deal with him, lest Go-lot take over his position as king. Dealing with Go-lot was not something Zu-yad wished to think about. Go-lot was younger than he, and strong. And in the end, strength, not wisdom, would decide who was king.

But for now, this day, this moment, Zu-yad was king.

Zu-yad moved like a shadow through the brush, climbed into a thick-limbed tree, and spied down on the two tarmangani. Zu-yad's tribe moved carefully forward, watching unseen from the brush.

Hanson was rebuilding his fire. Jean was cutting some flesh from the carcass of the antelope with the knife Tarzan had left her. She was scrunching up her face, holding the meat away from her as she cut. "This stuff is starting to smell like your socks," she said. "Then again, you always did like your meat aged, didn't you, Dad?"

"Aged," Hanson said, dropping small sticks onto the fire. "Not ripe. If our wild man doesn't return pretty soon we'll have to go back to nuts and fruit."

"I'm willing," Jean said. "Another day of this, and we'll be poisoned."

"He's been gone a week," said Hanson. "Those scoundrels probably killed him."

Jean pulled a strip of meat free from the carcass, and said, "I think he might be more of a challenge to them than you think. He was traveling very fast by the trees. Like a monkey. If he's returning with the safari by foot, having to slow down to bring them here, well, it could take a while."

"Could be," Hanson said, coughing from the smoke. "But I doubt it. Seems to me, now that we've regained our strength from the meat he left, we should consider smoke-drying some of it, and heading out."

"Our water is almost gone," Jean said.

"I think we'll have to chance a spring," Hanson said. "Things will only turn worse if we stay here. It's not like water is going to come our way while we wait."

Zu-yad, watching from the tree, appraised them. He sniffed the air. They were alone, and he neither saw nor smelled the sticks that belched smoke, that thundered and killed. The apes of Zu-yad were not naive. They had met tarmangani before.

From the concealment of the brush, Go-lot watched the tarmangani curiously. He knew of them, but he had only seen them before from a great distance. It was a great prize and status symbol to have a tarmangani slave. It had only been thus a few times — Zu-yad had owned two — and of course the slaves did not last long — but it was still prestigious, and Go-lot wanted this female for his slave. A tarmangani slave would give him prestige in his ongoing attempt to become king. But he was still a little afraid of old Zu-yad. He felt that his youth would give him the edge on the elder king, but he could not quite will himself to challenge Zu-yad. Perhaps, if he waited, a more opportune moment would present itself. Already, many of the tribe were looking to him, following his lead, and in time, when he had gained their complete confidence, then, and only then, he would strike at Zu-yad and claim his position as leader of the tribe.

Go-lot moved forward, and, as though it were a signal, the other apes did likewise. For the first time they made real noise — a rustling of the undergrowth through which they moved. At the same moment Zu-yad shot Go-lot and the tribe an angry look, the sound attracted Jean's attention. She looked up, hoping to spy Tarzan. What she saw pushing through the brush was Go-lot, and behind him the tribe of Zu-yad.

"Oh, hell," Jean said. "And us without a camera."

But what she thought as the apes rushed forward was: "Oh, hell, and us without a gun."

TARZAN
The Lost Adventure

IV

At the moment the apes burst forth from the brush and Jean spoke, Hanson looked up from the fire and saw what he had been looking for. The man-apes of Africa. They were huge beasts, more gorilla than man, but not quite either. If ever there was a direct link between man and ape, this was it. Hanson, because of his anthropological background, knew all this at a glance; from the way some of them chose to stand upright, to the size and shape of their craniums. A hundred little things.

But upon seeing them, realizing who they were, the enthusiasm he thought to have for such a discovery vanished. The man-apes sprang forward, beating their chests, running on their hind legs, and as Hanson grabbed Jean's wrist and pulled her away from the carcass she was carving, the creatures took to all fours and came springing after them.

Go-lot, ahead of his fellows, pursued the two and decided Jean was the one he wanted. Something about the way her hair flashed in the sunlight, the fact that she was easier to reach than Hanson, made his decision.

Hanson, glancing over his shoulder, saw Go-lot groping for Jean, and he swung around behind her and struck a hard right at Go-lot's jaw. It was a good blow, and Go-lot felt it, but it was as if he had been bitten by a stinging fly. He backhanded Hanson, sent him tumbling off the trail and into the brush like a tumbleweed.

Jean whirled then, the expression on her face like that of a wild beast. She still held Tarzan's great knife, and she thrust it at Go-lot. But Go-lot turned, and as he did, the blade sliced along his leathery stomach. Though it brought blood, it was not a straight contact wound; it only angered the beast. He slapped the knife from Jean's hand and grabbed her. He tossed her over his shoulder like a sack of meal and bolted into the jungle.

Behind Go-lot, worked into a frenzy, Zu-yad's tribe pursued him, anxious to examine his prize. Zu-yad, angry, and slower, followed. He passed where Hanson lay, eyeballed him, but left him there. If the prize had not been good enough for Go-lot, then he would leave it. To assure his position in the tribe, he would have to take the female tarmangani from Go-lot. If not, his time as king had come to an end. And so had his life.

Hanson struggled to his feet. The blow that Go-lot had struck him had nearly put his lights out, for good. He felt dizzy and sick to his stomach. He glanced in the direction the apes were taking, and he could see that one of the brutes had Jean slung over his shoulder, and he was bounding into the brush, followed by a horde of other apes, one of them bringing up the rear and making poor time. A moment later, all the apes, and Jean, were out of sight.

Hanson's heart sank. He looked about for some sort of weapon, snatched a broken branch from the ground, and set off in pursuit of Go-lot.

The day was still young when Tarzan arrived with the safari at the location where he had left Hanson and Jean. While Jad-bal-ja raced about sniffing the ground excitedly, Tarzan read the very recent events of the morning with his nose and eyes. Hanson and Jean's scent spoor were still fresh, and also that of a number of great apes.

Near the edge of the trail, Tarzan found his knife and the tracks of great apes, a man, and a woman. There was dried blood on the blade. Tarzan smelled the blood. It was that of a great ape. Since there was no pool or gush of blood on the ground, or in the brush, he determined that the wound had been a minor one, and from the way the tracks looked, it had probably been delivered by the woman, Jean.

Tarzan sniffed about until he found where Hanson had been thrown. He determined Hanson had followed after the apes, obviously in pursuit of his captive daughter. Tarzan snorted. "Good man." But he had about as much chance against the apes as a baby might, wrestling a crocodile.

Tarzan returned the huge knife to its sheath and took one of the askaris aside. The one with the lump on his jaw. A man who went by the name of Billy because he had found his name too difficult for foreigners to pronounce. And since he made his living being hired as a guide and askari, he wanted to be remembered, even if it meant changing his name.

Tarzan trusted him. His trust was based on the way Billy had handled his duties on the trail and in camp, and it was also based on Tarzan's instinct. Having lived more with beasts than with men, Tarzan had learned to observe men carefully, and therefore understood them even better than their fellows.

"Billy. Stay here and make camp," Tarzan told him. "I am uncertain when I will return. If I do not return within a few days, go to your homes and divide the supplies amongst you as a reward for yours and the bearers' service — both Hanson's bearers, and the others. If you should decide to leave when I am out of your sight and divide the goods, I will hunt you down and make things most unpleasant for you."

"I do not work that way," Billy said.

"I did not think you did," Tarzan said. "And you must pardon my bluntness. I am rarely among men, and when I am among them, I always feel it is too long."

"No offense taken. Until you walked into that camp back there, I thought you were nothing more than legend. As soon as I saw you, and that lion, I knew who you were. I have known men who claim to have seen you, but I thought them liars. Now *I* will be thought a liar."

Tarzan almost grinned. "Take care, Billy."

Tarzan turned, and with Jad-bal-ja at his heels, he raced into the jungle, hot on the recent trail of Hanson, Jean, and the great apes.

Jungle, brush, limbs, vines, all of them seemed to work against

Hanson. Thorns tore him, vines tripped him, limbs slapped his face. Then suddenly, he was aware of something behind him. He wheeled with the stick ready to strike, and was shocked to see a great lion in his path. And then he saw, standing slightly behind the lion, Tarzan.

Hanson eyed the lion, then Tarzan. Tarzan said, "Do not fear him. He is a friend. We are here to find your daughter."

"Thank God," Hanson said.

"Go back to camp — "

"No!" Hanson said.

"You must," Tarzan said. "I am more capable than you. You will slow us down. Go back to camp. Your bearer Billy is there, and the others. Go back to camp, and in time, I will join you with Jean."

"But — "

Tarzan was no longer interested in discussing the matter. He moved past Hanson swiftly, followed by the lion. Hanson turned, determined at first to follow, but so rapidly had the ape-man and the lion taken to the jungle, there was no sign of them.

Hanson thought a moment. So far, the wild man had done all that he had promised. And there was no way he could keep up with him and the lion. He had no choice but to return to the safari and wait.

The other apes overtook Go-lot at the edge of a small open space where Go-lot stopped to rest. They reached out and touched Jean, to see if the nearly hairless tarmangani were real. She fought and struggled as best she could, but it was useless against the strength of the great apes. So persistent were they in their curiosity, Go-lot was forced to drop and straddle her, and face his fellows. He growled at them and beat his chest and cursed them in the language of the great apes. He whirled this way and that, snapping and biting the air, flicking foam from his lips.

But Go-lot could not watch all directions at once. Zu-yad had arrived, and he reached out and grabbed Jean by the leg, pulled her from between Go-lot's legs, tugged her behind him. He beat his chest and snarled. Jean lay still on the ground, waiting for a moment in which she might escape.

She watched the apes bark and growl, not knowing that they

were speaking a language.

"I am the king," Zu-yad said. "The prize is mine."

Go-lot snarled and bared his fangs. "You are weak. I am to be the king. The female tarmangani is mine!"

"Come and take her," Zu-yad said.

Go-lot charged. The two came together with a great grunt and a slapping of chests, and then they grabbed each other and rolled about in the leaves. Members of the tribe formed a circle, awaiting the outcome.

Go-lot was strong, but Zu-yad was experienced. It wasn't the first time he had defended his leadership. He knew better how to grab Go-lot. How to twist his head down so that he might bite him in the back of the neck.

For a moment, Go-lot felt lost. His neck was aching with Zu-yad's bites. He considered submitting, hoping for mercy. Then he felt Zu-yad weaken, felt his youth and strength take hold, and that was all it took. Go-lot ducked and grabbed one of Zu-yad's legs and caught him around the neck with the other, lifted him high above his head, and dropped him face down across his extended knee. Something cracked in Zu-yad's chest. Go-lot drove his forearm against the back of Zu-yad's neck. Once. Twice. This time, the cracking sound was even louder. Zu-yad rolled off of Go-lot's knee, onto his back. His legs twitched and his mouth frothed blood. The scene held for yet another moment. A fly came out of the jungle and lit on one of Zu-yad's open eyes. The ape did not blink.

Go-lot leaped into the air suddenly, came down on his hind legs beating his chest, bellowing. "I, Go-lot, am king!"

The other apes, grunted and clapped.

"I, Go-lot," continued the great ape, straddling Jean again, "am the strongest. The best."

"You are lucky."

Go-lot wheeled. A bronze man with a great lion beside him was pushing back the brush, stepping into the clearing. Jean turned, saw that it was her wild man, but he was barking and snarling like the apes. She thought it might be best if she just carefully crawled off, leaving the whole lot. The world had gone mad.

Go-lot could not believe his eyes. Who was this man who spoke the language of the apes? Who was this man who walked with the jungle's most deadly killer? Go-lot could not decide what he felt most. Surprise at the man, or fear of the lion. Surprise finally ruled, then

turned to anger, when, again, in the language of the great apes,
Tarzan said: "You are lucky to beat an old one who had but a short
time to live anyway. I'm surprised he didn't die in your arms before
you struck a blow."

Go-lot's jaw dropped. "Who are you? How is it a tarmangani
speaks the language of our tribe?"

"I am Tarzan. Tarzan of the Apes."

Go-lot bared his teeth. "I have heard of you. I thought you
were but a lie of the elders."

"I am of a people like yours," Tarzan said. "And I tell you now,
let the woman go, or I will kill you."

Go-lot snarled. "You mean you and your beast will kill me."

"No," Tarzan said. "I want the pleasure for myself. Stay, Jad-
bal-ja."

Tarzan pulled his great knife, moved toward the circle of apes.
Jad-bal-ja sat on his haunches, waiting. He wondered if Tarzan would
let him eat the dead ape, or maybe the one Tarzan was about to kill.
He certainly hoped so. The meat of a great ape was very tasty.

Suddenly Tarzan charged. "Kree-gah!" he shouted. "Tarzan
kill." Tarzan's body loosened, and he came forward, bent, running
with the backs of his knuckles on the ground, growling, hooting.

Jean was astonished at this display. The man looked more
beast than human. She did not know how to feel. Once again, she
thought slipping off would be the ticket. But there was no opportuni-
ty. No way to get through the circle of apes unnoticed. She could do
nothing more than watch, mesmerized.

Go-lot pounded his chest in defiance, then, dropping to his
knuckles, Go-lot charged. Go-lot was astonishingly quick. He leapt like
a panther, his long arms reaching out for Tarzan's neck, closing on it.

Then Tarzan was not there. He ducked low and hit Go-lot in
the ribs with his shoulder, brought the knife up quickly, and buried it
in Go-lot's belly. Go-lot charged past, wheeled, hurled himself back at
Tarzan. Tarzan sidestepped. The knife flashed again. Go-lot made two
long steps, stumbled, stood, wheeled, his belly opened up, and his
innards began to roll out in a smelly, steamy heap.

Go-lot looked down at his insides. Instinctively, he grabbed at
them, as if to gather them up. Then he looked at Tarzan, turned his
head to one side quizzically, and fell forward on his face, smashing the
oozing contents of his body with a loud squish.

The great apes sat silent. Astonished. They looked at Go-lot, lying in his own guts. They looked at Tarzan, crouched, ready to fight, the great claw in his hand, red with blood from its point to the ape-man's elbow.

While the apes remained amazed, Tarzan slipped the knife in its sheath quickly, darted to where Jean lay, and pulled her to her feet. He said, "Come. Now."

No sooner had Tarzan wheeled with Jean toward the jungle, his arm around her waist, then the apes, frozen for the moment, came undone, let out a bellow and pursued them in mass. When Tarzan darted past Jad-bal-ja, the lion snarled.

"Too many," Tarzan told the lion in the language of the apes. He tightened his grip on Jean's waist and took to the trees.

"Hang tight," he said.

This was not a command Jean needed. She clung with all her strength. As they rose into the trees, carried by the arm and leg strength of Tarzan, Jean let out a scream, but a moment later she was silent. There was no air left in her lungs. She was too terrified to scream.

Limbs rushed by, and Tarzan grabbed at them and swung from them. Just when it seemed they would drop to the ground, another limb fortuitously appeared. He moved in such a way that he was sometimes high in the trees, perhaps fifty feet high, then, by dropping great distances, grabbing at a limb with one hand and swinging from it, they were sometimes only ten feet from the ground. It was like a roller coaster until they reached a mass of great trees from which hung thick liana vines. He grabbed those and swung way out, let go, grabbed another, and moved on; the treetops came down to meet them, then the ground grew tall, then the treetops were back again. Monkeys scattered through the trees all around them, scolding, chattering with fear. Birds rustled to flight. Once, Jean saw a great python raise its head from a limb and watch them pass with its cold, dark eyes.

Below, running on the ground, darting between trees, Jean could see the great lion. Once Jean looked back, saw the apes on the ground, looking up, trying to keep sight of them. The next time she looked, the apes had taken to the trees themselves, but even though they were born to the jungle, designed for it, they could not catch her wild man.

As they progressed through the treetops, Jean's confidence increased until she began to enjoy the strange adventure. It wasn't quite what she preferred to be doing this bright and sunny morning, but she presumed it was better than being kidnapped by an ape. And why had that ape wanted her? Was she supposed to feel flattered?

A week ago, life had been a lot less confusing.

Below, she saw her father and the safari. Tarzan let go of the vine they were swinging on, dropped rapidly through the brush. Limbs touched her, tore at her clothes, and just as it looked as if they might dash themselves to pieces at her father's feet, Tarzan snatched at a supple branch, swung way out, twisted, grabbed another, then dropped them to the ground next to her father.

When they landed, Hanson leaped back, bringing up both hands to fight. Then he saw who it was. Jean stepped into his arms and Hanson held her. Over her shoulder he spoke to Tarzan. "Thank you . . . Whoever you are."

"They call me Tarzan," the ape-man said.

"My God," Hanson said. "I thought you were a legend."

Jean turned from her father then, smiled at her rescuer. "Thank you, Tarzan."

"Can you believe this, Jean?" Hanson said. "I came to Africa to prove the existence of the man-apes, and they kidnapped you. Then you were rescued by a legend I didn't believe existed. Tarzan, the ape-man."

"Will the apes come after us?" Jean asked Tarzan.

"No," Tarzan said. "There are rifles here. They know what rifles do. They lose interest rather quickly, as well. They will be fighting amongst themselves to establish a new king."

Jean considered what Tarzan had said. She began to understand what all the fighting had been about. One ruler had been usurped, only to be defeated by Tarzan.

At that moment, Jad-bal-ja entered into the campsite. He padded over to Tarzan and lay down at his feet, and put his great head between his paws.

"He looks mopey," Jean said.

"He wanted to fight the great apes," Tarzan said. "That and eat one. He is hungry."

"Then it would not be a good idea to pet him right now," Jean said.

"It is never a good idea," Tarzan said. "He is a lion, and a lion is always a lion."

"I've never seen anything like it," Jean said. "You were actually communicating with those apes, weren't you?"

"Yes," said, Tarzan. "I was raised by a tribe not unlike them."

"You're kidding." said Hanson.

"No," said Tarzan. "I am not kidding."

Hanson studied Tarzan a moment. "No. I can see you aren't."

"You communicate with the lion, too," Jean said. "Do you think he fully understands you?"

"I know he does," Tarzan said. "I speak to him in the language of the great apes. My first language."

Hanson thought that explained Tarzan's stiff almost formal use of English. His strange accent — the accent of the beasts.

Jean was warming to the subject, excited. "What about other animals?" she asked. "Can you speak with them? Are they . . . your friends?"

"Animals in their native state," replied Tarzan, "make few friends in the sense that humans do, even among their own kind. But I have friends among them." Tarzan waved a hand at the golden lion. "Jad-bal-ja here would fight to the death to protect me. And I him. Tantor the elephant is my friend, as is Nkima."

"Nkima?" Jean asked.

"A small monkey that is usually with me," Tarzan said. "Where he is now, I can't say. He often wanders off. But when he gets in trouble, or is afraid, he often comes racing to me for protection. He is a coward, and an outrageous braggart, but I'm fond of him."

"You seem to prefer animals to humans," Jean said.

"I do."

"But that's because you've had unpleasant experiences with men," Hanson said. "Am I right?"

"You are," Tarzan said. "But let me remind you that you, as of recent, have had some very unpleasant experiences with men."

"That's true," Jean said. "But I wouldn't call my experience with the apes a picnic."

Tarzan smiled. "Ultimately, man and beast are not all that different."

Hanson said, "It's amazing. Everything they say about you . . . the legends . . . they're true."

Tarzan smiled, and this time it was a true smile. "Nothing is ever completely true about a legend," he said.

TARZAN
The Lost Adventure

V

Wilson laid the bundle on the ground in front of Gromvitch and Cannon and removed the oilcloth from the rifles, ammunition, and supplies. There were four rifles, two handguns, a limited supply of ammunition, some basic rations, and a canteen of water.

"We do some hunting, find some water, there's enough ammunition there to get us to the coast," Gromvitch said.

"I'm not going to the coast," Wilson said. "You do what you want. I'm going after this guy that kicked my butt. I don't take kindly to it. I was a heavyweight contender. I figure I can give him a little more for his money next time."

"I don't know," Gromvitch said. "Way I look at it is, what the hell? We got some guns, some food. We didn't desert the Legion post just to hike around in the jungle."

Wilson said, "We were going to check out that story Blomberg told us, remember? Make some dough, pool our resources. That way, we left out of Africa, it would be with more than what's left of our uniforms."

"Yeah," Cannon said, "and now we don't got to split nothing

with Talent."

Wilson glared at him. "That makes you pretty happy."

"Well, we won't," Cannon said. "I didn't kill him. It's just he's dead and now we get everything. We split three ways. I didn't like him anyway. Way he held his head and stuff, kind of gave me the creeps."

"I say we're splittin' nothing," Gromvitch said. "We haven't got anything to prove Blomberg wasn't nothin' more than wind. That talk sounded pretty good back at the Legion post, but now, with him dead and just having general directions, and us being in the actual jungle, I don't know."

"He got himself killed 'cause he was a fool," Cannon said.

"He got himself killed cause Talent killed him," Gromvitch said. "Carved him like a turkey."

"That was unfortunate," Wilson said. "But I still believe Blomberg's story."

And he did. Wilson had listened to Blomberg talk about the lost city at the Legion post. Blomberg claimed to have been there before becoming a Legionnaire. He wanted to desert and go back there, plunder the place, and become rich. He claimed there were people living there, mining gold, and had been for well over a couple hundred years.

Blomberg said he had been on an ivory-hunting safari, and had gotten lost and stumbled upon the city, had been taken captive by the natives who were mining it, but escaped. He had a handful of gold nuggets to prove it.

That's why Wilson had been eager to leave the Legion post. Blomberg was going to lead them there and they were all going to become rich together. But then Talent and Blomberg had gotten into it over a can of beans — a can of beans! And Talent, in a moment of mindless savagery, had cut Blomberg from gut to gill. Their living map had bled out his knowledge on the jungle floor.

"You got to think about it," Gromvitch said. "That story of his. A lost city of gold, mined by natives. How many times you heard that one? How come we got to believe this story? Blomberg, he didn't strike me as a man that got his feelings hurt when he told a lie."

"What about them nuggets?" Cannon said.

"Man can come by gold lots of ways," Gromvitch said.

"I believe him," Wilson said again. "I got nothing outside, or inside Africa 'less I come out of here with some jack. I don't find any city, I can maybe hunt some ivory. Make enough to get to the states, maybe have a little in the kitty when I get there. I go out now, all I got is the rags on my back. I might as well go back to the Legion post."

"Since I figure they'll hang me if I do go back," Gromvitch said, "that's an option I'm rulin' out. But the way I see it, we got nothin'. Don't know there's nothin' out there, and nothin' split four ways or three or two, it's all the same. It comes up nothin'. Nothin' plus nothin' times three, that's nothin'. Right now, we got a little food, and guns to get some more, and I say we head for the coast."

"It's not just the gold," Wilson said. "I want this guy who kicked my face. And I want to kick his face. Maybe stomp it a little."

"No offense," Gromvitch said, "but havin' been there, I'd just as soon we not see that guy again. He tore us apart like paper, and I don't even think he was good and mad."

"I'm with Wilson," Cannon said. "That damn wild man and his lion. Who does he think he is, ordering us out of Africa like he owned it? Besides, I don't like no guy in his underwear beatin' me up. Somehow that ain't decent, you know?"

Wilson took some dried meat from the oilcloth wrapping, passed it around to the others. He said, "What I know is this. All the landmarks Blomberg talked about . . . Ones I remember. We've come to 'em. And the land's slopin' like he said. It's such a gradual drop, unless you're lookin' for it, you might not notice it right away. It's just like Blomberg said."

"Maybe," Gromvitch said.

"Other night," Wilson said, "before all this bad business, I climbed a tree and looked, and I tell you, the land's slopin'. It's fallin' in the north. That makes me think Blomberg wasn't just tellin' us a windy. And I don't think he'd have stumbled around out here with us all that time if he hadn't been tellin' the truth."

"I don't know," Gromvitch said.

"Here's the deal," Wilson said. "It's not subject to discussion. You want to go your own way, Gromvitch, we give you a rifle, some ammo, but we keep the bulk of the ammo and all the grub. We feed you, you take the rifle and go. And good luck."

Gromvitch considered the suggestion. He wondered if Wilson really meant it. And if he did, he wondered if Cannon would honor it. What if he agreed, and then Cannon got to thinking nothing divided by two was even better than nothing divided by three?

No. Gromvitch figured he ought not chance it. And besides, Wilson was right. What was there for him on the coast — if he made it to the coast by himself? And he wasn't sure he could. Wilson was, if nothing else, a good leader.

"I'll stick," Gromvitch said. Wilson nodded, and so did Cannon, but Gromvitch thought the look on Cannon's face was one of disappointment.

Tarzan and Hanson's party, after a moment of reunion, started to move. They moved briskly, making good time, heading north. Tarzan decided to stay with them until he felt they had left the great apes far behind. Not that he thought they would pursue, not with the smell of guns in the camp, but insurance was a good policy. And he and Jad-bal-ja were good insurance.

After a time, they stopped to rest. Tarzan squatted on the ground and Jean came over to join him. She said: "Where is your lion?"

"He's his own master," Tarzan said. "He's gone off to hunt. One of the great apes, most likely. He had the thought of their flesh on his mind. He likes it. He says it is very tasty."

"Oh," Jean said.

"He comes and goes as he pleases. Sometimes I do not see him for months. This time, he has left because he does not approve of my association with strangers. Jad-bal-ja is something of a snob."

"Probably the result of royal blood," Jean said. Then: "I don't know that I've thanked you properly. Without you, and Jad-bal-ja . . . Am I saying that right?"

"Close enough," Tarzan said.

"Without you and him . . . well, I might be an ape's mate."

Tarzan grinned. "More likely a slave. You'd be gathering grubs for the tribe to eat."

"Slaves?"

"They are more manlike than apelike. They have many of man's bad habits. Slavery, for example."

"I don't think I'd like gathering and eating grubs," Jean said.

"They are actually quite tasty," said Tarzan. "Filled with protein. But you would not have eaten them anyway. They would have made you give them to the king, and they would have given you leaves. You can live on leaves, some are quiet succulent, but you cannot live well. The great apes, they do not understand humans. They sometimes take slaves of humans, and the humans do not last long.

They do not understand what is expected of them, they are fed poorly, and if they do not die in a short time from lack of nutrition, one of the apes will become angry and kill them."

"I suppose I should thank you double," Jean said.

"Not at all. I have to ask, though. Where are you going? Why are you in this part of the jungle?"

"It's like Dad told you. He's trying to prove the existence of what we now know exists. The man-apes."

"We are going away from them, not to them."

"That's true. But only because Dad is supposed to meet other members of his expedition soon, coming from the other side of Africa, moving to meet us at the place where he believes an ancient city to be. We hope to come back this way, get photos of the great apes — or man-apes. Whatever they might be."

"I know of no city," Tarzan said.

Hanson, chewing on a piece of dried meat, came over and squatted down beside them. Tarzan said, "Jean was just telling me of your plans."

"And what do you think?" Hanson asked.

"I think if you take back proof of the great apes, photographs, that hunters will come in and kill them," Tarzan said. "That is what I think. I would not want that. I would not want to be any part of that."

"We're a scientific expedition," Hanson said.

"It makes no difference," Tarzan said.

Hanson was quiet for a moment. He said: "Jean told you about this lost city? Legends refer to it as Ur. If it exists, it would be a wonderful find."

"I've heard of Ur," Tarzan said, "as a legend. But again, I know of no such city in that part of the jungle."

"I have a colleague, back at the university," Hanson said. "Professor Barrett. During the war he was a navigator on a heavy bomber that flew across this terrain several times. Twice he saw ruins of what appeared to be an ancient city. Later, when he got back to the states, got his degree in archaeology, eventually a doctorate, he could not get the city out of his mind. He began to research the area, found out there were legends of a lost city in that part of Africa. Ur. Supposedly a city of gold. Of course, in the legends, they are always cities of gold, aren't they?"

"There are legends of lost cities all over Africa," Tarzan said. "Some of them are true."

Tarzan was thinking of Opar when he spoke. Of the land of Onthar and the twin cities of Cathne and Athne — one a city of gold, the other of ivory. The Lost Roman Empire he had discovered. This, and others, but he didn't let his face show his thinking.

"All the more reason to explore this one," Hanson said. "My colleague, Professor Barrett, he's too old now to come, but I was his student, and I want to discover the city not only out of my own curiosity, but because I want to validate his life's work. The great apes, that is my own personal passion. I have another expedition coming at the city from the other side. We hope to meet in the middle. It seems like a sure way of at least one of our group reaching the ruins."

"Not with Hunt leading it," Jean said.

"Hunt is a good boy," Hanson said.

"That may be," she said, "but he can't read a subway map, let alone one of the jungle."

"Small is with him," Hanson said.

"Small can read a map," Jean said, "but he doesn't know north from south."

Hanson looked at Tarzan. "Hunt is my professorial assistant back at the University of Texas. Small is a talented student. Both are good boys. Hunt is a bit infatuated with Jean, I think."

"A bit?" Jean said.

"And she with him."

"Oh, for goodness sake, Dad. I find Hunt about as interesting as calculus — and you know what kind of grades I made in calculus."

"They've known each other a long time," Hanson said, "and they have this love/hate thing going. Another few months, I think the hate will come out of it. Now that they're both grown, packed with hormones."

"Dad, you're embarrassing me."

"Sorry," Hanson said, but he didn't look like he meant it.

"How will you profit by this expedition?" asked Tarzan. "Do you expect to find gold in the city?"

Hanson smiled. "This may sound hokey to you, but the purpose of this expedition is just what I said. Purely scientific. We'll be poorer when we return to Texas than when we left — poorer in financial resources, but richer in scientific knowledge and experience."

Tarzan was not sympathetic toward people who came from other continents to kill the animals he loved, nor was he sympathetic to those who would plunder the riches of Africa. The Hansons did not seem to fall into either category.

Tarzan said, "You said you had a map?"

"Yes. My old professor, Dr. Barrett made it years ago, from memory. It could be off a bit, but he believes it's generally correct."

"In Africa," Tarzan said, " a general mistake can make a big difference."

"I'll get the map," Hanson said, and went away.

Suddenly, in the trees there was a loud screaming of monkeys. Jean and Tarzan looked up, and presently a little monkey leaped into sight, fairly flying through the trees, pursued by a larger, very angry monkey.

"Nkima," Tarzan said. "He's gotten himself into trouble. As usual."

Nkima flung himself from a tree, landed on the ape-man's shoulder, shook his arms loosely, began howling belligerently at the monkey pursuing him. The pursuer, upon seeing Tarzan and Jean, halted at the end of a swaying branch and began to chatter viciously upon discovering his quarry had found sanctuary.

After a moment of ferocious cussing, the pursuing monkey turned, leaped away, and was lost in the foliage.

Hanson returned with the map as Nkima jabbered into Tarzan's ear and leaped about on his shoulder. Hanson said, "What have we here?"

"Nkima," Tarzan said. "He tells me that the other monkey was terribly afraid of him, which explains why he ran away. He didn't want to hurt the monkey."

Jean laughed. "He's terribly cute."

"There's not an ounce of truth in him," Tarzan said, stroking Nkima's head. "It is fortunate for the other animals he is not as large as he talks. As tough as he thinks he is . . . We were discussing your map."

Hanson squatted on the ground, unfolded the map for Tarzan to see. Tarzan studied it for a moment. He said, "It's not a very good map. I know portions of this area well." Tarzan put his finger on the map. "There is a mountain here. An extinct volcano. I have never been to it, but I have seen it in the distance." Tarzan touched the map again. "The forest depicted here, it is very dense. Almost impenetrable."

"That makes it all the more likely that the city might be there," Jean said. "Sort of tucked away in a pocket of intense foliage."

Tarzan studied Hanson for a long moment. "I wonder if you know what you are getting into. Even if there is not a city, there are certainly wild animals, wilder men. The forest itself, the terrain, can kill you. Neither of you seem well enough prepared."

"I've been to Africa before," Hanson said. "We've just had hard luck, is all."

Tarzan pointed. "You go north, you will have more of it."

Hanson folded up the map. He was very calm and polite, but Tarzan could tell that he was angry. "You're probably correct. But we're moving ahead. We can't disappoint our friends."

Then, abruptly, Hanson went soft. "But you could do me a favor. I've no right to ask. Not after what you've done. And I've no way to pay you. But you could take Jean back to civilization."

"Dad! Don't treat me like a girl. I'm a grown woman."

"You're my daughter."

"That may be, but I'm grown too, and I'll make my own decisions. I'm going. No matter what you say, or Tarzan says. I'm going."

Hanson sighed. He knew it was useless to pursue the matter. Once Jean set her mind to something, she was going to achieve it, come the proverbial hell or high water. As Professor Oliver had said, she had a head like a bull, if the bull's head were made of steel.

"I will go with you," Tarzan said.

"I can't pay," Hanson said.

"I do not hire myself out for money," Tarzan said. "Do not insult me."

"Sorry," Hanson said. "But why the change of heart?"

"I suppose I have been among men too much," Tarzan says. "I am developing a sentimental streak for the stupid and the ill prepared."

Hanson and Jean checked Tarzan's face to see if there was humor there. There didn't seem to be.

"You go north without a guide, you will die," Tarzan said. "You do not strike me as a man intent upon doing something to harm the animals here. You seem to be honestly interested in research. I am not. But I am interested, as I said through fault of association, in decent human beings."

"I suppose," Hanson said, "that is some kind of compliment. To be stupid, but decent."

TARZAN
The Lost Adventure

VI

Hunt and Small fought mosquitoes while they finished lunch. Hunt's pale, white skin was sunburned on the neck and forearms, and the mosquito bites were driving him crazy. Small, a Negro, was not so burned, but the mosquitoes seemed to love him. He had long gotten past making jokes about how sweet the dark meat was. After a while, mosquito bites ceased to be funny.

Hunt, finishing up his food — hardtack and canned meat — rose from his camp stool with the excuse he needed to leave camp to relieve himself. He went into the tent, got his .45 automatic and strapped it on, walked past the bearers who were sitting in a circle eating. They eyed him coldly. The way they looked at him made his stomach sour. It wasn't that they hated him, it was just they didn't respect him. Not that he blamed them.

Hunt went out into the bush. When he felt he was far enough away from camp, he leaned on a tree and cried. Not big savage boo-hoos, but hot, wet tears he had been holding back for days.

He was lost as the proverbial goose. He and Small had proved to be little better than a Laurel and Hardy expedition, even if neither of them resembled the comedians. Hunt decided if he were any more lost, he might turn up at the University of Texas, where this whole mess had begun. He had not wanted to go into the jungle anyway. It was hot. He had wanted to be near Jean, and then he had discovered Professor Hanson wanted to split the expedition up, as he was uncertain if the valley containing the lost city could easily be reached from both sides. He thought it might be better if one small group made it and made scientific studies, than if one large group did not make it. Hunt had volunteered to lead the second group, and Hanson had eagerly agreed.

Hunt realized now that Hanson's confidence in him had been vastly overrated, for he was definitely not going to make it. He had just about decided they should turn back, but he didn't know how to turn back. The map had turned into nonsense. Nothing fit out here. It wasn't like there were road signs and such. And Small, he read the map well enough, but he couldn't follow it. Neither of them had any business in the jungle, and he realized now that Jean had been right about him all the time. He was an idiot. And he had been right about Small. He was an idiot, too. They were both idiots. And they were lost.

Hunt wiped his eyes, found the trail, and was about to start back to camp when he saw three men with rifles walking toward him. They startled when they saw him, same as he did when he saw them.

One of them, a big black man with a face that looked as if it had been chewed real good and spat out, said, "This is supposed to be the jungle, not Grand Central Station . . . Who are you?"

"Who are you?" Hunt asked.

Wilson studied Hunt. He was an average-sized man, in his middle twenties. Very blond. Very smooth-faced. And quite sunburned.

"Our safari has run off," Wilson said. "Couple of the askari convinced our bunch to rob us. We've gone after them."

"To shoot them?" Hunt asked. The whole prospect excited and terrified him.

"Not if we don't have to," Wilson said. "We just want our stuff back. We're hunters."

"I don't hunt animals," Hunt said. "Unless for food, and we have plenty of food."

"We?" Gromvitch said.

Hunt studied Gromvitch. He wished suddenly he hadn't said anything. Gromvitch was a small, weasel-faced man, and the mention of food seemed to excite him. Of course, that could just be because he was hungry. Then again, these men, they didn't exactly look like great checker companions. And the fat one, Hunt didn't like that one at all. He wasn't as tough or confident looking as the big black man with the chewed-looking face, but there was something about him that made Hunt's skin crawl.

Then Hunt thought: Come on, man. You're being judgmental. If there was one thing you learned in Sunday school, it was that you shouldn't judge others. That you couldn't tell a book by its cover. These men are lost, probably hungry, and that accounts for their savage appearance.

"My companion, Elbert Small," Hunt finally answered. "Our ten bearers."

"You have askaris?" Wilson asked. "Guides?"

"They sort of ran off." Hunt said.

"Sort of ran off?" Wilson asked.

"They didn't like the way we were running things, so they sort of ran off."

Wilson thought about that a moment, concluded this man was most likely a fool. He was lost, but wouldn't admit it. The young man's bearers could lead him out of the jungle if they so chose, but perhaps they were having the time of their lives, following this idiot about. In the end, when supplies got low, they would desert, taking what was left, or they would lead the boy into their village and insist they be paid handsomely for bringing him to civilization. Wilson had seen that sort of thing before, back when he hunted big game. Back before the Foreign Legion.

"If you're not a hunting expedition," Cannon said, "then what are you?"

"A scientific expedition," Hunt said. "We're supposed to meet up with some comrades." He started to admit to being lost, but held back.

"Whatcha doing out here away from your safari?" asked Cannon.

"Heeding the call of nature," Hunt said.

"We're hungry," Wilson said. "We've been without food, for the most part of a day, and we figure we don't bring down some game soon, we're gonna be hungrier. I'd rather not wait to bring it down, if you can spare a little food."

Hunt wasn't sure he could spare anything. He wasn't sure how to get out of the jungle, how far the coast was. The desert. Civilization. He might as well have been blindfolded and parachuted into the jungle, confused as he was. But he said, "Come into camp and eat."

Small, was sitting on his camp stool, leaning over the camp table, turning the map this way and that. All right now, he thought. The top of the map is north, the bottom south. But where am I on the map, and if I knew, would I know if I was facing the bottom of the map, or the top? Or the sides? Can you go through the center of a map?

He broke out his *Boy Scout Handbook*. He reread the part about the sun setting in the west, rising in the east, being overhead about midday. But it didn't say anything about the sun falling down behind the jungle when it grew late, or that you could proceed on what you thought was a straight line, only to find yourself back at the spot where you started a day or two later. The *Handbook* didn't mention that. That was a kind of secret it kept to itself. The part about going in circles.

So far, they had managed to do just that, at least a half-dozen times. Small couldn't decide if they were near their destination, closer to where they started, right in the middle, spinning around, or if they were in the midst of a nightmare.

What he did know was this: they had plenty of food and water and ammunition, but the askaris had deserted with a couple of their packs, leaving only the bearers, who had so little English at their command, Small wasn't sure how to communicate with them properly. He could manage to get them moving, but they merely followed him and Hunt blindly about.

Small put the *Handbook* away, folded up the map. He fiddled with some of the hardtack and canned meat, but found he wasn't very hungry. He got out a deck of cards. He was pretty good at solitaire. He liked that. It was one of the few things he did in life that resulted in him winning. At least occasionally. And, as far as Small was concerned, all things considered, occasionally was good enough.

Small had just laid out a row of cards on the table, when he turned his head to the sound of Hunt returning. He saw the three men with him, and at first he thought it was Hanson and his party, then his hopes were immediately dashed when he realized it was not.

He stood up slowly from the camp stool, studying the three

men as they approached with Hunt. They didn't look like the friendly sort.

"I found these folks in the jungle," Hunt said.

"You don't say?" Small said. "Well, small world."

"Yeah, ain't it?" said the fat one.

Hunt told Small what they had told him, about their bearers running off. Wilson studied their camp and said, "Seems to me you boys are a little lost."

"Bewildered," Hunt said.

"Lost," Small said. "You fellas wouldn't happen to know this part of the country?"

Wilson leaned over and helped himself to what was left of the hardtack. He dipped a piece of it into an open can of potted meat. He ate it hungrily. "How about we get some grub from you, boys?"

"Well, yeah," Hunt said. "I guess so."

Hunt went into the tent and came out with a pack. He opened it, passed out provisions. Wilson took Hunt's camp stool, sat at the camp table eating. Gromvitch and Cannon squatted nearby, scooping in the meat tins with their fingers, smacking.

"You do know the country, then?" Small asked.

"Yeah," Wilson said. "We know it. Some. But we ain't got any supplies. You know what I'm saying?"

"I think so," Hunt said.

"What I think we got to do, see," Wilson said, "is, you know, team up. We share your grub and ammo and stuff, and we point you in the right direction. Where you want to go? The coast?"

"No," Hunt said. "Not really. Like I said. We're a scientific expedition. We're supposed to meet up with another party, and, well, I think we've gotten turned around."

"Maybe more than once, huh?" Gromvitch said.

Hunt tried to smile, but only the corner of his mouth worked. "Few times, actually."

Gromvitch chuckled.

"You got anything to smoke?" Cannon asked. "Cigarettes? Cigars? Pipe?"

"No," Hunt said. "We don't smoke."

"Chew?" Cannon asked.

"No," Hunt said. "We don't do that either."

"How about some coffee?" Cannon said. "You do that, don't you?"

"Yeah," Hunt said. "We drink coffee . . . Wait a minute. I don't like your tone. We don't work for you guys."

Wilson stood up, very quickly, and he had the .45 in his hand. Neither Hunt nor Small had seen him draw the gun. He moved swiftly and swung the .45 out and hit Hunt behind the ear, and Hunt went down on one knee. Small rose to his feet. He half wished he had on his gun, but was half glad he didn't. Had he tried to use it, these men would surely have killed him. He felt a hand on his shoulder. He turned to see the fat man standing behind him, smiling, with potted meat on his teeth.

"Why don't you sit back down there," said Cannon. "Just so's you'll stay comfortable. Know what I'm sayin'?"

Small sat down. Wilson was removing the .45 from Hunt's side, and he wasn't in any hurry about it. The blow had stunned Hunt tremendously. Hunt was bent forward now with his head on the ground. Blood was running out from his hair and onto the side of his face.

Gromvitch walked over to the bearers who had looked to run at the first sign of commotion. He pointed a rifle at them and spoke in their language. They sat back down in a circle.

Gromvitch came back. He said, "They see it our way, those fellas do. They like that I offered 'em some big money too. 'Course, they ain't gonna get it. Or nothin'. But I think it was real big of me to make the gesture, and it's good to see they got about as much loyalty as a duck."

"Our kind of people, no doubt," Wilson said. Then to Small: "Maybe you could put a compress on your buddy's head there. Naw, never mind. It'll stop bleeding pretty quick, way he's fallen over there in the dirt. Dirt plugs stuff good. Now, what were we sayin'? Oh, yeah, your buddy was sayin' how you boys don't work for us. But you know what? We're beginning to visualize you in the role. It could be the beginning of a beautiful relationship. Least from our end of the stick. And about that scientific expedition you're on. I think maybe it's gonna have to wait some. What was it anyway? Catching some kind of rare butterfly or something? Cataloguing grub worms?"

Small shook his head, but offered no explanation.

Hunt, slightly recovered, thought: I get out of this. I get back to civilization. I'm going to hunt up my old Sunday school teacher, and tell her sometimes you *can* judge by appearance, then I'm going to punch her right in the nose.

Wilson reached out and picked up the map Small had folded and placed on the camp table. He opened it. He said, "Well now, and who says there's no such thing as coincidence?"

"How's that?" Gromvitch said.

"Our lost boys here," Wilson said. "They've got a map to this Ur."

"Get out of town," Cannon said.

"We are out of town," Wilson said. "And, it is a map to Ur. Or so it claims."

Wilson studied dark lines that had been drawn on the map, showing Hunt and Small's planned method of approach. He could see immediately that they had missed their destination.

"These fools have been right on top of the city all this time and didn't know it. I figure they've been walkin' all around it."

"It's near?" Cannon said.

"I'll have to study this, get my bearings," Wilson said. "We not only got us a safari now, but we got a map to the place we want to go. That just leaves the wild man to take care of."

"He's nothing to me," Gromvitch said.

"You keep sayin' that," Wilson said. "But don't say it again. Way I look at it, we know the wild man and that man and his daughter are ahead of us. They won't expect us to come on after them, them being armed and all. But now we got guns and we got equipment. I got a hunch them folks is who these jackasses were tryin' to meet up with. That right?"

The question had been directed at Small. Small considered for a moment. Cannon stuck the tip of his .45 in Small's ear. "Let me put a bug in your ear, Mr. Expedition. A man and a woman — a good-lookin' woman. They who you're tryin' to meet?"

Small didn't answer and Cannon slapped him lightly across the side of the head with the .45, but it was heavy enough to draw blood. A trickle ran from the side of Small's head, down his cheek.

"Maybe I should rephrase the question," Cannon said. "You want I should do that?"

Small hung his head. "That sounds like them . . . I suppose it is."

"And now that wild man's with them," Wilson said. "A package that nice ought to have a bow on it."

Hunt and Small were forced to carry supplies, walk in the forefront of the bearers. Wilson, who had been somewhat relaxed in his handling of his own bearers, and those of Hanson, had lost his good will, and he was rough with his newly acquired safari. All Wilson could think about was the wild man. It was bad enough to get whipped, but to have it happen in front of Cannon and Gromvitch, that was unforgivable. So late afternoon, when they hit upon sign of the Hanson party, Wilson stopped his safari.

"Way we're gonna do," Wilson said, "is I'm gonna take these two city boys with me, and Cannon. Gromvitch. You stay here, guard the bearers, the stuff. Have them make camp. No more Mr. Nice Guy. You get crap from one of these fellas, open him up a little. Shoot him in the legs, you got to. Make it slow, you want. That way, rest of these fellas will know we mean business."

Wilson knew Gromvitch would not do any such thing. It wasn't in him. Cannon would have done it in a heartbeat, but not Gromvitch. He might shoot one of them if he had to, but he didn't have the guts for that kind of thing. But he wanted Gromvitch to know he meant business. He didn't want any waffling, any whining.

Wilson had Hunt and Small loaded up with a few supplies, then he and Cannon pushed them onto the trail, in pursuit of Hanson's safari.

It was mid-afternoon, and Wilson concluded from the sign they found, they were less than fifteen minutes from catching up with Hanson. Wilson's plan was to push into the jungle, make a wide circle, and surprise them from ambush. He was going to shoot the wild man, first, as he had decided fighting with him one on one, no matter how much he thought he might like to, could have negative results. He had decided, too, that he would kill Hanson and give the woman to Cannon and Gromvitch. It was not his preferred choice, but if he wanted to keep these two clowns happy, he had to know what bait to feed them, and the woman was just the thing.

Wilson was thinking on all this, when, abruptly, some distance down from them, an antelope leaped across the trail. They paused in surprise, heard the sound of leaves crackling. Tarzan, preoccupied, Nkima clinging to his shoulder, the scent spoor of his enemies blowing away from him, did not smell them as he leaped out of the jungle and onto the trail, bow and arrow in hand, in swift pursuit of the antelope that was to be dinner for the Hanson party. He had left them waiting ten minutes up the trail, and had gone after food, and now it was close at hand.

He jerked to a stop in the middle of the trail and quickly strung an arrow to his bow. But at the moment he was about to let it go, to send it flying toward the antelope, which within seconds would be out of sight in the brush, the wind changed.

The scent of Wilson and his party filled his nostrils, and Tarzan wheeled. But just before Tarzan sensed them, Wilson had raised his rifle, took bead on the ape-man's head, and fired.

And it was in that moment, that Tarzan turned.

The shot caught Tarzan a glancing blow across the forehead and dropped him, but not before his reflexes picked up the glint of the rifle and he let an arrow fly. Nkima, true to his nature, leaped away from Tarzan and went chattering with fright into the jungle.

Wilson saw the wild man go down, and when he lowered his rifle, buried to the feathers in the barrel was the ape-man's arrow. In the instant he had picked up their scent, Tarzan had found the glint of the barrel and released an arrow at the target he had sighted. Wilson felt a cold chill go through him. It was a wonder that bullet and arrow had not collided. Had the man picked up his true target sooner, or had he been off his aim — the glint of the rifle — Wilson knew the arrow would have been driven into his face.

Even Cannon was in awe. "This guy," he said, "sure ain't no regular guy."

"Sure he is," Wilson said, tugging the arrow from the barrel of his rifle. "Now."

Hunt and Small, witness to this sorry spectacle, were pushed forward to where Tarzan lay. Cannon put the barrel of his rifle to Tarzan's forehead. "I'll just scatter his brains some."

"No, that's too easy," Wilson said. He pointed his rifle at Hunt and Small. "You two. Take those weapons off of him, toss them in the brush there. Then . . . whatever your names are, get hold of him."

Hunt and Small, straining under the weight of the ape-man, carried him after Wilson. Cannon brought up the rear, poking them with a rifle. They went through the brush a ways, came to an opening in the foliage. It led them to a beautiful green veldt that extended a great distance. There was a large tree growing nearby. It was dead, split, as if struck by lightning, but it was still solid. Wilson had them carry Tarzan to the foot of the tree and drop him. Wilson opened his

pack and got out a leather ammunition belt. He removed the ammunition, took his knife, cut strips of leather from it. He instructed Small
and Hunt to hold Tarzan up with his back against the tree.

Wilson used the strips of leather to tie Tarzan's hands behind
him, and to the tree. He used strips to tie his feet, then strips to pull
the ankles tight against the trunk. He used a long strip around
Tarzan's neck, pulled it around the tree, made it secure.

"What's the idea?" Cannon said. "Why not just shoot him?"

"You'll like this," Wilson said. "I want him to suffer."

"Now you're talkin' like a grown-up," Cannon said.

Wilson opened his canteen, poured water on the leather straps
at the ape-man's feet, then those fastened to his hands and neck.

"This water will soak in good, start to tighten as it dries, then
it'll tighten some more. You with me, Cannon?"

"Yeah," Cannon said, "I get you."

"It'll cut off his circulation, choke him to death," Wilson said.
"Kinda cheers me to think about it. I tell you, Cannon, way things
been goin', I was kinda gettin' discouraged, but this has been my lucky
day, that's what I'm tryin' to tell you. We got us a safari, a map, and
this wild man, he come right to me. Who says there ain't no coincidence? There ain't no justice?"

Wilson stood in front of the ape-man, threw a hard right at the
unconscious Tarzan. It was a good right, and hit Tarzan's jaw and
snapped his head as much as the wet leather would allow. Anyone else
had taken that blow, it would have broken his jaw. For Tarzan, it
served as a wake-up call.

The first thing Tarzan saw was Wilson, grinning.

"Howdy," Wilson said. "Remember me?"

Tarzan didn't answer. He took in everything. Cannon. Hunt
and Small, who from their manner and lack of weapons, he immediately knew to be captives.

"I just want to wish you a fond farewell," Wilson said. Tarzan's
expression didn't change, and that irritated Wilson some. But only for
a moment. Then his good humor returned. Smiling, Wilson picked
up his pack and headed back through the brush toward the trail.

"Too bad you don't have your big kitty with you," Cannon said
to Tarzan, then poked Hunt and Small with his rifle. "You two
morons, move on."

Hunt and Small flashed Tarzan helpless looks, then with
hung heads they were prodded through the brush by the tip of

Cannon's rifle.

Late afternoon in Africa is not yet a time of coolness. It grows hotter until near sundown, and as the day heated, Tarzan felt the tension in his ankles, wrists, and neck. The bonds were tight to begin with, but slowly they began to dry. In another two hours, before it became dark, they would shrink to half their size. They would literally cut through his flesh.

Tarzan was angry with himself. He had grown complacent. Perhaps he had been away from the jungle too long. He had been so preoccupied with the antelope, he had not been as alert as he might have been. It looked as if now he would not get the chance to rehone his abilities. And that was the way of the jungle. A mistake was unforgiven.

An hour passed, and Tarzan continued to strain at his bonds. He had been successful in thrusting his heels against the tree and pushing at the leather bonds at his ankles enough to break them, but he could not get leverage for the ones that bound his wrists. Wilson had Hunt and Small pull his arms too high and fasten them too tight. Struggling against the bond about his neck was useless. The slightest movement choked him.

Tarzan looked out across the veldt, watched a herd of buffalo slowly grazing toward him. He hoped they would eventually pass him. The water buffalo, Gorgo, was probably the most dangerous animal in all of Africa. The most unpredictable, and the one who hated man the most.

Tarzan watched as a great bull strayed away from the others in his direction and went suddenly alert, sniffing the air. Tarzan knew that Usha the wind had carried his scent to the bull's nostrils.

Gorgo snorted, pawed the ground. His eyes had not yet located Tarzan, but the ape-man knew the animal's great sense of smell would lead Gorgo to him.

Tarzan could see the bull was a veteran of many wars. There were great marks on its sides from the claws of lions, the horns of other bulls. Tarzan could not help but admire Gorgo's strength and power. The bull was a magnificent animal.

Gorgo trotted forward, filling its nostrils. It turned sideways, ran to the right, turned, ran to the left. It tossed its head from side to side. It was zeroing in on Tarzan's scent, for its sense of smell was far better than its eyes.

Suddenly, the bull stopped. It had spied Tarzan. Tarzan thought: at least death will be quick.

Gorgo lowered its great head. It pawed the earth. Sunlight caught the tips of its horns and threw shining rays at the sky.

Then, with a bellow, the great bull charged.

TARZAN
The Lost Adventure

VII

The moment Tarzan had been taken by surprise and Nkima had escaped, the little monkey raced through the trees searching for aid. He had thought of Hanson and Jean, but Nkima had no faith in the tarmangani who were so stupid they could not even understand him. He looked for another, and at last he found him — a great lion lying asleep beneath a tree at the edge of a clearing. Jad-bal-ja.

Screaming, Nkima dropped to the ground beside the great head, where, chattering loudly, he hopped up and down. Jad-bal-ja opened an eye and looked at Nkima, tried to decide why a meal had come to him voluntarily, then realized that this particular monkey was not a meal at all, but someone he knew. Not someone he liked particularly, but someone he knew. Someone who loved the one he loved, Tarzan. Except for that, he would have eaten him, and quickly. Monkey flesh was good.

Nkima continued to chatter and wave his arms and thrash his tail, then the lion understood, and sprang to his feet with a low growl. Nkima leaped to Jad-bal-ja's back and clung to the black mane, screaming directions as the lion trotted off. Jad-bal-ja did not run.

Instinct told him that he could not maintain high speed except for short distances. Instinct and experience.

But all of this was too late. While Nkima and Jad-bal-ja attempted to come to the rescue, out on the veldt, the water buffalo, head bent, horns projected, was charging down on Tarzan.

The ape-man viewed his situation with the cold eye of the realist. The spittle flying from Gorgo's mouth, the dirt and grass spraying from beneath his hooves, every move of the great buffalo's body, Tarzan noted. He had but seconds before Gorgo was on him, and to struggle against his bonds was useless. He would choke himself to death, or break his own neck.

Even if the buffalo's horns missed his flesh, the sheer impact of its hard head would sandwich him against the tree to which he was tied with such force it would crush his insides. There was only one chance, and a slim one.

When Gorgo was less than a few feet away, Tarzan breathed deep, pressed his back tight against the tree, and pushed off with the balls of his feet. Tarzan threw his legs higher than Gorgo's lowered head. As he did, the leather thong about his neck tightened and cut into Tarzan's flesh. Blood ran down his neck and shoulders and chest, and in that same instant, as Tarzan's legs were airborne, Gorgo struck the tree with his hard head and the tree shook. The bull staggered back, dazed. Tarzan's legs came down on the top of Gorgo's horns and hooked and latched there.

Tarzan, groaning as loud as the buffalo bellowed, twisted his legs with all the power he could muster. Tarzan's great muscles strained and tightened. Tarzan felt as if his body would tear in half.

Tarzan called on every ounce of energy he could muster. He used his leverage to wrench Gorgo's head in such a manner that it forced the buffalo's legs to fly out from beneath it. Gorgo crashed to the ground on its side.

But its head did not drop. Tarzan had it locked in his vice-like legs. Tarzan squeezed with all his might. The muscles in his brown legs coiled and twisted like ropes. The sound of Gorgo's neck cracking echoed across the veldt and made a number of hyenas lurking in the high grass dash for cover, thinking it was a bolt of lightning and that soon the dry grasses would blaze with that which they feared most. Fire.

Gorgo tried to bellow again, but the only sound the bull gave up was a cough. Tarzan continued to twist. He twisted until there was another snapping sound and the buffalo lay vibrating in its death throes at his feet.

Tarzan coughed, his mouth snapped at the air, trying to pull oxygen into his chest. The action he had taken had saved his life, but it had nearly caused him to choke to death. And now, with Gorgo dead, he was no better off. Maybe worse. The leather thong was tighter than before, and as the sun rose it would become tighter yet, as did the thong securing his arms behind his back. It might have been better to let Gorgo do his work, end it quickly, but it was not in Tarzan's nature. He would never quit, no matter what the circumstances. Not while he lived.

Moments later, Tarzan saw a comical and welcome sight. Coming out of the jungle, entering onto the veldt, was the great Jad-bal-ja with Nkima clinging to his mane. The monkey was chattering and riding the great lion like a jockey.

The great lion charged when it saw Tarzan, leaped on the dead buffalo and swatted it so hard the blow almost swung its head all the way around on its damaged neck.

So fast had Jad-bal-ja struck, Nkima lost his balance and was hurled from the back of the lion. Nkima went tumbling along the ground, chattering all the while.

"It's all right," said Tarzan in the language of the jungle, his voice weak and raspy. "It's the leather that holds me now, Jad-bal-ja. Loosen me. I can hardly breathe."

The lion stood on its hind legs, a paw on either side of Tarzan's head. Jad-bal-ja nuzzled Tarzan, licked his face, then used his teeth delicately, biting through the leather thong around Tarzan's neck.

When the thong broke, Tarzan fell forward with a gasp. Even as Jad-bal-ja moved to bite through the leather that held Tarzan's arms to the tree, Tarzan, no longer restricted by the throat strap, regained his strength, pushed the flats of his feet against the tree, expanded his chest, and with an angry jerk snapped his bonds.

As Tarzan peeled the remains of the leather from his wrists, Nkima, leaping up and down and gesturing wildly, was relaying a series of unpleasant things about Jad-bal-ja and his ancestry. Jad-bal-ja roared at the little monkey, and Nkima fled up the tree like a shot and continued scolding from behind a thick branch.

Tarzan stretched his neck slowly. He looked up at the angry Nkima and laughed. "Brave monkey," he said.

The lion growled. Tarzan looked at Jad-bal-ja. "I understand, old friend. I am hungry too. Eat."

Jad-bal-ja turned to the corpse of the buffalo. He grabbed it by the head with his great jaws and began to feed on the soft and sweet parts of its muzzle, turning soon to the soft underbelly, which he tore open and eviscerated with his sharp fangs.

Just before the sun fell into the jungle and night rose up like a demon, Tarzan sniffed the air. It smelled damp and forbidding. Tarzan turned his attention to the trees. The tops swayed and there were no animals visible. There was not even a bird.

A storm was coming. A bad one.

Tarzan decided to feed. He knelt beside Jad-bal-jal, scooped a handful of warm innards from the buffalo's open gut, and began to chew, savoring the warm blood. When he had eaten his fill, he put his foot on the corpse of Gorgo, grasped one of its legs, and started to pull and twist. It took some time, but eventually, the bone cracked and the sinew tore, and Tarzan jerked a leg of the beast loose. It was a crude, bloody weapon, but it would serve until he could do better. And there was always an added benefit. It was meat.

Tarzan sniffed the air again. The wet smell permeated the jungle, covering up much of the scent of Wilson and the others, but enough of it remained for Tarzan to deduce they were heading in the direction of the Hanson party.

"Come," Tarzan called to Nkima and Jad-bal-ja, and without confirming their response, Tarzan started off at a trot.

Jad-bal-ja tore a last morsel from the buffalo, then, snout red with blood, tongue flashing over his whiskers, followed. A moment later, Nkima came yammering after them, protesting that there was nothing for him to eat.

Wilson paused and pulled a flashlight from his pack. He shined it down the trail. "I don't like it," he said to Cannon. "It's too dark. Stormy. I think we've gotten off the path."

"Ain't no think about it," Cannon said. "We're lost as gooses."

"Geese," Wilson said.

"What?"

"Never mind."

Hunt and Small stood close to one another in the darkness, watching Wilson shine the flashlight around. Hunt thought now

might be the time to jump Wilson and Cannon. If he could get Small
to understand, maybe that's what they should do.

He thought back to earlier, to how easily Wilson had knocked
him about with the .45. Even a surprise attack wasn't enough when
the most difficult battle he had ever fought was on the tennis court.
And he'd lost. As for Small, well, he wasn't much better, if he was better at all.

Perhaps fighting these brutes wasn't such a good plan after all.

Heavens, thought Hunt, life is hell when you live it as a weak-
ling and a coward. What would Jean think of him?

Most likely she would be the one to jump them, win or lose.
She was that way. Hardheaded. Overconfident. Beautiful.

And she thought he was an idiot.

He was glad she couldn't see him. He hung his head, resigned.

"If we're caught by the storm, so will they be," Cannon said. "I
think we ought to go back to camp, batten down the hatches, and ride
it out. We can visit with them clowns when we want. Besides, I ain't in
the mood for that woman right now and I want to see her when I am.
I'm hungry and tired and I don't like it wet, and it's gonna get wet. I
ain't in no mood when I'm hungry and wet."

"You talk like you're goin' on a date," Wilson said.

"You got to have some romantic notions," Cannon said.

Listening to them talk, Hunt felt a fire go through him. They
were discussing Jean like she was a piece of meat they were going to
buy. The bastards!

Wilson considered for a moment, then said to Cannon, "All
right, but which way is back?"

Cannon turned and studied the jungle. It was so dark he
couldn't see his hand in front of his face. He got out his flashlight and
moved the light around. That didn't help much. Trees. No trail.

"I knew we was goin' wrong," Cannon said.

"You didn't know nothing," Wilson said.

"Yeah, I did. I knew we was wrong."

"Shut up," Wilson said. "Shut up and let me think."

Rain began to blow through the trees. A crack of lightning
rode through the sky and made everything bright, hit the top of a
great tree and split it asunder. In that instant, spurred by his anger at
what they had said about Jean, Hunt grabbed Small and pushed him
toward the jungle, yelled, "Run."

Hunt took off hard and fast and Small raced after him and

fell, stumbled to his feet and kept going. Wilson whipped the light around and spotted the two as they ran, but when he lowered the light to aim his rifle, he lost sight of them and fired blind. The shot tore through the collar of Small's shirt, but he was unaware. He only knew that the bullet came close. It buzzed by his head like a hornet with an agenda.

Small tripped, rolled, found himself tumbling downhill. He wanted to call out for Hunt, but knew that was suicide. He had some advantage here in the dark.

The air was cut by two more shots, fired wild, then the flashlight roamed the shadows and the trees, and Small pushed himself close to the ground and lay tight.

Off in the distance he could hear a crashing noise, and he knew it was Hunt. He could hear him grunting, cussing, as limbs struck him, tripped him, poked him. If Wilson and Cannon had a mind to, they could follow him by his trail of profanity.

As Small lay face down, the smell of rotting leaves in his nostrils, he felt something move across the back of his legs. Instinctively, he knew it was a very large snake. A python most likely. Probably it had not taken shelter when it should have, or had been out hunting. Perhaps its belly was full of mice or monkey, and therefore it was moving slow.

And maybe the snake was so hungry it was shopping for its meal in the rain. Perhaps a stupid explorer would be just the thing for Mr. Python. That perfect hit-the-spot meal.

Small bit his hand to keep from screaming. He thought if he jerked his leg up quickly and wheeled away from the direction the snake was going, he might be able to proceed downhill and find a new place to hide. He didn't want to do that, not with Wilson and Cannon nearby, but the waiting, the weight of that heavy snake crawling across his legs, was too much to bear.

As he was about to bolt, the beam of a flashlight danced above him. Small rolled his head to the side and looked up. Behind the light was a shape. Wilson. He was standing on the edge of the incline where Small had fallen, flashing the light out at the jungle.

God, don't look down, thought Small. Don't look down.

The light bobbed down, then up. Small heard a crackling of brush, then Cannon's voice: "Anything?"

Small buried his face in the dirt.

"Hold the light," Wilson said.

They have me, thought, Small. They've seen me.

"Look there," Wilson said.

"Oh, yeah," Cannon said. "Go on and shoot."

Wilson awaited the shot he would never hear. But he did hear it. The rifle cracked, he jerked slightly. Lay still. How in hell could they have missed from that distance?

"Biggest python I've seen in ages," Cannon said.

"Yeah, but I got him."

"What about them idiots?"

"What about them?" Wilson said.

"I can hear one of 'em crashing along out there. He ain't so far."

"Yeah, well, he ain't so close neither. We might could find him easy, and might not. We could get hurt out there, dark as it is, storm coming. Jungle will take care of both of them, especially tonight. I got the main thing I wanted, that wild-man fella."

"And us?" Cannon asked. "What are we gonna do?"

"We're gonna find that trail and start back. That's what we're gonna do. Later, we'll get what we want from that safari."

"Like the girl," Cannon said.

"Yeah, I reckon," Wilson said. "You want her that bad, you and Gromvitch can divvy her up."

Small listened to them move away. He began to breathe again. They had missed seeing him by inches, had spotted the snake crawling away, and had focused on that.

Miracles did happen.

Small waited a while longer. Just as it began to rain big hard drops, he rose from his position and moved deeper into the jungle, trying to travel in the direction where he had last heard Hunt pushing his way through the foliage.

TARZAN
The Lost Adventure

VIII

Tarzan, Nkima, and Jad-bal-ja had not traveled far when the storm hit. It hit with tremendous fury. Rain, high winds. Even Tarzan could not maintain the trail in weather like this, and he knew they would have to seek shelter and ride it out. His only consolation was knowing the big black man and his partners would have to find shelter too, and that would keep them away from Hanson and Jean and their safari.

Suddenly, the brush crackled and there was movement, and Tarzan, without really thinking about it, spun in response to the sound and swung the leg he had ripped off Gorgo, struck a moving body with it, and knocked it backwards.

Tarzan leaped on the form and pinned it to the ground, a savage growl emitting from his throat. Realizing his prey was a man, Tarzan dropped the buffalo leg and his powerful hands found the man's throat.

"Don't kill me," Hunt said, but his voice was strained by the pressure of Tarzan's fingers around his neck.

It was too dark for Tarzan to recognize the man's features, and the voice was not familiar.

"Who are you?" Tarzan said, releasing his grip.

"You knocked out my wind," Hunt said. "My ribs . . . they're killing me."

"Who are you?" Tarzan said again, and this time there was no room in his voice for delay.

"Hunt. You're the one they called the wild man."

Tarzan grunted, realizing who the man was now. He said, "You were with the ones who tied me to the tree. You and the young black man."

"Small," Hunt said. "But we didn't have anything to do with that. We didn't want it that way."

"I know," Tarzan said. "You are supposed to meet up with Hanson and Jean. They told me about you."

"That's right. Small and I. Listen, I didn't have anything to do with what happened back there. I didn't want it to happen."

"You said that."

"I just didn't know what to do. And if I had known, I don't know if I could have done anything to stop it. From listening to Wilson and the other two, I learned they'd had a run-in with you earlier. With Hanson and Jean. Oh, goodness. That's where they were going. To take the safari from Hanson. To kill him and the others and take Jean."

"I know," Tarzan said. "But I doubt they will go far in this. We must find shelter. And quick."

"We have to help Jean. And Small. Small and I got separated in the storm. I don't know if he's alive or not. Wilson and Cannon were trying to kill us."

"Shelter first. We are no good to anyone if we get ourselves killed."

"It's dark and it's rainy," Hunt said, "but that's no reason to give up on finding Jean."

"Suddenly you're brave."

"Just a little brave."

"It's not the rain," Tarzan said. "Though that will be bad enough. It will be a bad storm. A tornado. No one can withstand the force of Usha when he has gone berserk."

"Who did you say?"

"Usha."

"Who's he?"

"The wind," Tarzan said, as if speaking to one of great ignorance.

"They have tornadoes in Africa?" Hunt asked. "I thought that was in Texas."

"Surprise," Tarzan said.

Tarzan located the buffalo leg, grabbed Hunt, and yanked him to his feet. You'll have to hold on to me, or you'll be lost."

"How did you get loose?" Hunt asked. "I figured you'd be dead by now. Choked to death by that drying leather."

"How does not matter. It only matters that I escaped." Tarzan turned to the lion, said, "Jad-bal-ja."

The lion roared back a response. Hunt said, "My God, there's a beast out there." He strained his eyes, just making out the great lion's form in the darkness.

"Have no fear," Tarzan said. "He will only eat you if I say so. And if you keep talking, I will say so."

"Mum's the word," Hunt said, gingerly feeling of his ribs to see if anything was broken.

Tarzan began to speak in the language of the jungle. He said to the lion: "Do you know a place?"

The lion growled softly and began to trot. Tarzan strained his nostrils for the lion's smell, perked his ears to hear the great beast's movement. He said to Hunt, "Put a hand on my shoulder and keep it there."

Hunt did that. Nkima, who had been cowering in a nearby tree, came down and leaped onto Tarzan's other shoulder and chattered.

"Hush, monkey," Tarzan said in the language of the apes.

Nkima went quiet. Hunt said. "You speak to lions and monkeys?"

"Yes," Tarzan said. "I find they have to be spoken to. Neither can read notes."

Tarzan began to trot, sniffing the air for the great lion. Hunt kept his hand tight on the ape-man's shoulder. Tarzan moved swiftly, yet Hunt knew the jungle man was traveling slower than normal so he could maintain his grip on the wild man's shoulder. Still it was difficult to keep up. The man never seemed to tire, and even in the dark, he was moving with self-assurance.

"Are we following the lion?" Hunt asked.

"Be quiet," Tarzan said. "I must hear."

Hunt listened. All he could hear was the confounded wind and rain. And the wild man had been right. The rain was coming faster and harder. The drops actually hurt when they struck him.

"We must move faster," Tarzan said.

"I can't keep up," Hunt said.

Tarzan stopped running and wheeled so fast Nkima went flying. Tarzan popped Hunt a solid one on the chin, knocking him cold. Before Hunt could fall, Tarzan scooped him up, flung him over one broad shoulder, and began to run. Nkima scurried angrily behind them, complaining loudly about the loss of his seat.

Then, as if a faucet had been turned off, the rain stopped. The wind stopped. It was deathly still. Even Nkima, who had finally caught up with the ape-man and perched himself on Tarzan's free shoulder, no longer fussed and scolded. One arm was around Tarzan's neck and he used the other to cover his eyes.

Presently, the silence was broken by a dismal soughing. The trees bent as though pushed down by a giant hand. Then, quite suddenly, all hell broke loose. Lightning flashed, thunder roared, and the wind howled like a wounded panther. Limbs of great trees tore loose and spun through the air, crashing into trees or smashing to the ground with terrific impact. Trees were uprooted, sucked upward, and hurled about.

A moment later, the jungle sloped down, the terrain became rough and rocky, and the trees were smaller and scragglier. Tarzan followed the scent of Jad-bal-ja until they came to a rocky, brush-covered hillock. At the summit of the hill was an outcropping of rock and there was a great slab of flint jutting out from the hill, and beneath the slab was the slanted opening to a cave.

Tarzan pulled Hunt off his shoulder and lowered him to the ground. Nkima clung silent and wet to Tarzan's neck as the ape-man knelt and looked inside. Jad-bal-ja's scent was strong in the cave, so Tarzan knew there was no danger, or already they would hear the commotion of the lion in combat. Tarzan growled into the opening. Jad-bal-ja growled back.

Tarzan tossed the filthy hunk of buffalo leg in ahead of him, grabbed Hunt by the pant leg, and pulled him into the cave.

The cave was large and glowed with a greenish light. A little stream trickled through the center of it, and Tarzan could see a worn path next to the stream that led deeper into the cavern and around a series of strange rock formations that were filled with what looked like black glass and marbled stones. Apparently, eons of water seepage through limestone had left deposits of calcite, and the flint above the limestone had been broken off by erosion and had worked its way into the formations along with the black glass, which Tarzan deduced was most likely obsidian. All of this was coated with a sort of phosphorescent goo. Possibly crystals of calcium. Tarzan had never seen anything like this in Africa, and he had seen much.

Jad-bal-ja was lying against the cave wall beside the buffalo leg, eyeing it with a hungry intensity.

"Leave it be," Tarzan said. Jad-bal-ja let out a disgruntled rumble, moved away from the meat, and lay on the other side of the cavern wall. Nkima offered a squeak, went silent, and hung tightly to Tarzan. Outside, the wind screamed and moaned and tore at the jungle. Rain pounded the earth as if it were being whipped by the Gods with a cat-of-nine-tails.

Hunt groaned and rolled over. He sat up slowly and felt his chin. "You hit me," he said.

"If you want to complain, I can do it again."

"No. No complaints. But why?"

"You talk too much."

"Where is this place?"

"A cave. An old lion's den. I assumed Jad-bal-ja would know a place."

Hunt noted the lion and became nervous. "You're sure that lion's safe."

"Safe enough."

"That's not the answer I was looking for."

"Life is full of disappointments, my young friend. Stay in the jungle awhile and there will be many more. What is, is."

"Man," Hunt said. "Listen to that wind. Usha. He is one hacked-off rascal . . . Hey, I'm cold. I can't believe it. I'm in Africa, and I'm cold."

"Like I said, you talk too much. Stay where you are. Jad-bal-ja will protect you."

"The lion?"

"Yes."

"Are you certain he won't think you're leaving him a warm dinner? He could misunderstand, you know? You're gone, he thinks, oh, this fella's mine. Maybe I should go with you. Or you take the lion and leave me the monkey."

Tarzan did not answer. He spoke a word to the lion, picked up the buffalo leg, and with the unusually silent Nkima still clinging to his neck, followed the path by the creek.

Hunt squatted in his spot and looked at Jad-bal-ja. Jad-bal-ja put his head between his paws and looked at Hunt. Hunt thought he saw a sparkle in the lion's eyes. Or perhaps it was a glint of hunger.

"Easy, kitty," Hunt said.

The lion continued to stare, never taking its eyes off Hunt. Hunt decided not to look at the lion. He studied the cavern walls and the odd formations and wondered about Small. He felt guilty for running off and leaving Small like that, but it hadn't been intentional. He was merely running and had not meant for them to become separated. He hoped those two gorillas, Wilson and Cannon, had not caught Small. He had heard shots, but liked to think, like the shots that were fired at him, they had missed.

Then again, if the shots hadn't killed Small, the storm might be doing the job right now. The wild man had been right to flee before it, find shelter. Hunt rubbed his jaw where Tarzan had struck him. The wild man had been right to slug him. He had been close to panic.

Who was this wild man? He seemed to know the jungle as well as the animals, and he spoke to the animals. Was that possible? It certainly seemed to be.

Hunt eased a glance at Jad-bal-ja. He hoped, if the wild man truly spoke to the animals, his words carried some weight. What if the lion decided to disobey the wild man and eat him anyway?

Heavens, thought Hunt. Don't think that way. Don't think about that at all.

Exhaustion came over Hunt suddenly. He stretched out on the ground as far away from the lion as possible, and with the sound of the storm screaming outside, the soft breathing of the lion filling the cavern, Hunt fell asleep.

TARZAN
The Lost Adventure

IX

Tarzan had not gone far behind the strange and glittery formations when he came to a huge glowing chamber. Nearly transparent stalactites of gleaming calcium dripped from its roof. The floor of the cave sloped downward, and below Tarzan could see stacks of skulls on either side of the cavern wall, arranged neatly from floor to ceiling. In fact, the walls themselves appeared to be made of skulls. The skulls, like the cavern walls, glowed with green phosphorescence, and there were splatters of red ocher and lines of charcoal on them.

As Tarzan came closer and the glow became brighter, he saw designs had been drawn on many of the skulls with the ocher and charcoal. No, on closer examination, they were not designs, but stick-like drawings of what appeared to be some kind of insect. A praying mantis perhaps. On each of the skulls the insect appeared in some different position. Something about the arrangements struck a chord with Tarzan, but he couldn't quite place it. All of the skulls had holes at the top of the cranium. It looked as if something small and sharp had poked through the bone.

Beyond the skulls, arranged neatly, were stacks of leg and arm bones, and in yet another pile were collapsed rib bones. Tarzan touched one of the bones. It was petrified and permeated with the sparkly calcium. Near the bones were stacks of pottery and chipped fragments of flint.

The path wound deeper into the cavern, and for some distance beyond, the ape-man could see the stacks of glowing skulls and bones. Lying amongst the bones were stacked weapons. Spearheads. Knives. Tarzan bent to examine the weapons and was surprised to see that the knives were made of metal, not flint. The metal was bronze. The blades were huge, almost like bowie knives. The wood or bone sheathing on the hilts had long since rotted away. Tarzan picked up two of the knives, rubbed the nervous Nkima's head, and started back to join Hunt and Jad-bal-ja.

He found Hunt asleep. Tarzan bent and scooped water from the stream and washed his face, removed the dried blood from his neck and chest. He lay against the great lion and cradled Nkima in his arms. In spite of all that had happened, it felt good to be back in the jungle. Here every moment was charged with excitement and danger. It made him feel alive. Civilization had its moments, but in the end it was numbing and repetitious.

He knew time was changing everything, however. Soon the jungle would disappear. Eaten away by human termites in search of lumber. Industry. In some areas, game was already scarce. Even the most distant of jungle trails were now being traveled. Soon, there would be no more adventuring. There was nothing left to do but return to Pellucidar. The lost world at the center of the earth. There, beneath the eternal noonday sun, as long as there was little to no contact with the outside world, changes were gradual. It was a world he knew and understood.

In the end, Tarzan knew he would go there with Jane, his woman. And he just might stay.

Tarzan decided to sleep, store his strength. His instincts told him he would need it. He wondered about Jean and Hanson before he nodded off, but with his usual realistic resignation, decided there was nothing he could do, but rest, store his energy, and wait. He dreamed of his earlier encounter with the lion. Then Wilson's men, and the buffalo. In those moments, he had never felt so alive.

While Tarzan and Hunt slept in the cavern, small dramas were taking place. Small was holed up under a stack of fallen trees that had grouped and entwined in such a way as to make a kind of cubbyhole. He had found his shelter by accident. In fact, he had seen part of the shelter made. The wind had tossed a tree in front of him, the limb striking him across the face, cutting his cheek, and when the great tree crashed into another and brought it down, the limbs twisting together into a kind of wooden maze, Small had scampered to it and found a place where he could crawl under the limbs and hide.

He was not free of the wind and the rain here, but he was better off than out in the open. He squatted in his little den and listened to the wind blow and the rain lash. The rain came through the boughs of the fallen trees and struck him and made him cold. The wind shook him. He feared some wild animal would also choose this spot to hide from the storm. He had read once that during a storm like this, animals, sometimes predators and prey, conducted a sort of unspoken (ungrowled?) truce. Cowering together, at least until the storm passed. It sounded like a lie, but for the moment, Small thought it was a lie he would like to believe and cling to with all his might. Of course, there was another consideration. When exactly did a truce like that end? Was there a free-zone time? Ten minutes after the storm and all bets were off?

Five minutes?

Two?

Or was it when the wind quit blowing it was everyone for themselves?

Small decided it was best not to follow this line of inquiry. He stretched out on the wet ground beneath the thick limbs and tried to sleep.

The night howled like a demon.

When the storm struck, Wilson and Cannon had struggled to find the trail and managed just that. But the storm was furious. They fought their way through the wind and rain for some distance, then it became too intense and trees began to leap up and away, twist into splinters. One of the splinters caught Cannon in the arm, and the impact was like a .45 slug. The only advantage was that it shot completely through the flesh of his tricep and the sleeve of his shirt and kept traveling.

Wilson and Cannon found a low spot behind an uprooted

tree, pushed their backs against the dirt and roots, and listened to the storm twist and throb above and about them. They were hit by the rain; hit so hard welts were raised on their skin. Water ran in the low spot where they crouched and soaked their feet. They crossed their arms and held themselves and shivered.

"It's gonna be one long night," Wilson said.

"Yeah, and me without whiskey," Cannon said.

Cannon opened his shirt and looked at the wound. He clutched a handful of mud and leaf mold from the earth and pushed the cold compact against his wound and closed up his shirt. He grinned at Wilson. "Hey," he said. "Think maybe I got a few splinters in my arm here. Want to pick them out?"

"Go to hell," Wilson said.

Back at Hunt and Small's camp, Gromvitch panicked when the storm struck. Before he realized it, half the bearers had melted into the jungle. Gromvitch went after a couple of them with a stick, but the bearers were too scared of the storm to fear a beating.

A couple of them broke for the jungle in panic, and Gromvitch tossed aside the stick and picked up his rifle. He shot one of the deserters in the back and killed him instantly. Before he could put the bead on the other, the campfire was guttered out by the wind and drowned by the rain.

As Gromvitch stood there in total darkness, the remaining bearers burst in all directions, exploded like seeds from an overripe pomegranate. Gromvitch fired a random shot at the sound of their movements, then the storm came down like a demon and sat on the camp. Gromvitch, scared and foolish, immediately took shelter in Hunt and Small's tent. The storm grabbed the tent and wadded it up and carried it above the trees, high into the sky, leaving Gromvitch squatting on the ground. The storm fed Gromvitch a camp table, knocking out half of his teeth. Then it took him up in a swirl of wind and water and debris and a couple of slow bearers. It whipped them through the foliage so hard and fast they were shredded like cheese through a grater.

The time the storm hit, to the time Gromvitch and the two bearers became nothing more than wet, leathery decorations for the trees, took less than thirty seconds.

Back at Hanson's camp, right before the arrival of the storm, Jean had voiced concern for Tarzan. He had gone out to hunt meat and had not come back. They had resorted to camp fare, hardtack and dried meat, and now the sky was black and the stars and the moon were tucked away like dead game in a croaker sack.

Hanson, Jean, and their head askari, Billy, were standing outside of Hanson's tent, looking at the sky. The kerosene lantern that hung from the front tent pole flickered in the wind, threatening total darkness.

"I don't like the looks of this," Hanson said. "We better peg and tie these tents better."

"Begging Bwana's pardon and excuse, please," Billy said. "But you better do more than tie better knots. What comes is the wind whip."

"The wind whip?" Jean said.

"Whip you up and out of here, put you over in the Congo. Put you over in the Sahara. Drop you out in the big water. Take you faster than a lion takes a mouse."

"You mean a tornado?" Hanson said.

"Have it your way, Bwana," Billy said. "But I tell you this. Lots of wind. Lots of rain. Whip you to pieces. Twist you like rope, tie you in a knot. Throws stuff, the wind whip does. Throws straw through trees. Makes elephant and hippo cower in fear. Not make Billy feel all so good neither."

"Poor Tarzan," Jean said.

"He's no worse off than we," Billy said. "Maybe better. He knows it's coming. He'll find shelter. He's the man of the woods, is what he is. He lives in the jungle. He's part of the jungle."

"The tents won't protect us?" Jean said.

"Tents?" Billy said. "You got to be joking, missy. Wind wrap you up in tents like sausage in pancakes, feed you to the storm."

"That's not good," Jean said.

"Not good," Billy said. "Seriously bad on everybody, is what it be."

The wind picked up, moaned. The lantern went out. The air was damp.

"Suggestions?" Hanson said, relighting the lantern.

"Hook 'em up," Billy said.

"That an old African term?" Hanson asked.

"No," Billy said. "American. Have man say that to me on safari once. He wanted to hunt lion. Lion came after him. He fired shot. Lion didn't fall. Hunter threw down gun, yelled to me, 'Hook 'em up!' and ran. Billy was fast. Hooked up real good. Hunter wasn't. Lion ate him. Or most of him. I say we hook 'em up quick before ole wind-lion get here and feed on us. What we do, is we take tents down speedy, peg them over supplies, close to ground. Then we run like hyenas with brush fire on tails."

"Just run?" Jean said.

The lantern blew out.

"We run that way," Billy said, carefully relighting the lantern. "Land goes down over there. We got to be lower than storm. Only chance."

The lantern blew out again. Billy unclipped his flashlight from his pants and turned it on. "We got just enough time," Billy said. "Talk another couple minutes, better leave tents and all the business. Talk another minute, can kiss ourselves good-bye. Too late to hook 'em up."

"All right, Billy," Hanson said. "Give the orders for it to happen. Let's move!"

Hanson and Jean set about taking down their tent, but as they worked, the sky grew darker and they could hardly see to complete the task. They had just finished pegging it, when Billy came running up, flashlight bobbing in the dark. "Get flashlights and let's hop. None of this stuff make difference if we too dead to use it."

"All right," Hanson said, unclipping his flashlight from his belt. "Let's, as the unfortunate hunter said, 'hook 'em up!'"

TARZAN
The Lost Adventure

X

Hanson's safari began to run. They ran after Billy with his flashlight bouncing ahead, but there was little to see but the light. Hanson hoped Billy knew where he was going. Behind them came the bearers, carrying only a few basic supplies.

Billy's light dipped down and the safari dipped with it. The land sloped dramatically. Hanson's feet went out from under him, and Jean tugged his arm and helped him up. And away they went again, charging downhill.

The storm was at their back and it came over them and howled, and Billy yelled, "Hit dirt!" then gave the same command in his own language to the bearers.

Hanson and his group dove face down and the wind screamed above them, beat their backs with rain. Hanson could actually feel the wind sucking at him, lifting him off the ground, trying to pull him up. He locked a leg over Jean's leg to hold her down and pushed a hand behind her head, forcing her face close to the earth. He pushed his own face into the damp soil, and prayed.

The storm pummeled them and pulled at them and seemed to

last forever, but it finally moved on — or at least the worst of it. Behind it came a fury of rain.

Eventually, Hanson and his party stood up and spat out the dirt and checked the results by flashlights. Two of the bearers were missing. They had been the last in the group, perhaps being at the summit of the rise when the storm struck. It was concluded that the twister had snatched them.

The rain battered them and exhausted them as they made their way back to camp. In the glow of the flashlights, they could see the twister had ripped a swath through the jungle thirty feet wide and no telling how deep. The trees had been clipped so close to the ground, it looked as if loggers had been working there.

When they arrived at camp, the wind was still high, so it was decided to leave the tents pegged, except for making enough room to crawl under them, out of the rain. Hanson and Jean squirmed beneath his tent, arranged themselves as best they could on the ground, and tried to sleep.

The night seemed interminable, an eternity of suffering and terror. Hanson and Jean cowered beneath the tent in dumb misery. Hanson thought about the lost bearers, torn away by the storm and taken who knows where. Hanson realized he did not even know their names. He realized too, had it not been for his persistence in finding the lost city, those men would still be alive. He wondered about Tarzan, but worried about him least of all. If there was someone who could take care of himself, it was Tarzan.

An hour before dawn, the storm ended as suddenly as it had begun. The clouds rolled away and the moon shone. Hanson pulled himself out from under the tent and Jean crawled out after him.

When Jean rose to her feet, she said, "My legs have gone stiff as wire."

"Shake them out," Hanson said. "Get the circulation going. Then let's put up the tent, get to our dry clothes."

Jean flexed her knees a few times and stamped her feet. "Wow, that hurts. It helps, but it hurts."

"My God," Hanson said. "Will you look at the moon?"

The moon stood full and gold and bright. Easy to see because the twister had torn down the trees that might have blocked it from easy view.

"After that horrible storm," Jean said, "there's something that beautiful."

"We'll take it as a good omen," Hanson said. "There's been enough bad, we need some good."

Hanson shook out his legs, then shouted for Billy. Billy scuttled out from under his tent and trotted over to Hanson.

"One hell of a wind whip, Bwana," Billy said to Hanson.

"I'll say," Hanson said. "The men who were lost. I'll provide something for their families, of course."

"That's good, Bwana. But they knew their job. They knew it was risky. It's not your fault."

"Get the men to put up the tents. We'll dry out a bit."

"That good, Bwana, but I say we move on."

"Shouldn't we wait for Tarzan?" Jean said.

"I think he find us easy," Billy said. "I think we move on. I don't like staying here. Makes me itchy."

"Itchy?" Jean said.

"Think them bad ones might come back," Billy said.

"I believe Tarzan took care of them," Hanson said. "If those scoundrels headed for the coast as Tarzan ordered, we haven't anything to worry about."

"If," Billy said. "I give you an if. If Tarzan had cut their guts out and fed them to lions, then they be taken care of. I think Tarzan been away from jungle little much. Lion attacks you, you don't slap him. You kill him, or you get way away. I say we get way away."

"Certainly, without weapons, those men are of little consequence," Jean said.

"Weapons, or no weapons," Billy said. "A bad man is a bad man. We do not want to be around when they decide to be bad. Don't have a gun to shoot you, they put your eye out with a pointed stick. Bad is bad."

"All right," Hanson said. "We'll eat, pack up, start moving when it's light."

"Thanks, Bwana," Billy said.

"Dad," Jean said, "we can't just go off and leave Tarzan."

"Billy said Tarzan could catch up with us," Hanson said.

"Catch up or get ahead," Billy said, "it's all the same to him."

Hanson considered for a long moment, said, "Billy's right. I really must move on. We are running low on supplies, and a bit of hunting for game wouldn't be a bad idea. I'm sick of hardtack and jerky. I came here to find a lost city, and that's what I'm going to do. Tarzan can certainly take care of himself."

"I don't like it, Dad."

"It'll be okay, baby. Really."

"Worry about Tarzan is no good," Billy said. "Worry about us. We need some worry."

"Get the men together," Hanson said. "We're moving out."

By the time breakfast was prepared, Jean and Hanson had changed into dry clothes. Vapor rose from the steaming verdure, birds sang, and monkeys chattered. All was well with the world. When the gear was packed, Hanson gave orders to Billy, and Billy shouted to the carriers, and the column was on the move again. The path they were following was an easy one, as a large swath had been cut through the jungle by the storm.

As they proceeded, Billy walked next to Hanson and Jean. "Feel a lot better moving on. Every time we stop, bad things seem to happen. Tarzan here, would not be so worried. He knock a knot on a hippo's head, it needs it. But without him, we move on."

"It's all right, Billy," Hanson said. "I'm convinced."

"You, missy?" Billy asked Jean.

"I don't like it," Jean said. "But I'm walking . . . Dad, I keep thinking about Tarzan and those apes. Could he actually have been raised by them?"

"Unless you think he's a liar," Hanson said.

"No," Jean said. "But it's so fantastic."

"First of all," Hanson said, "they are not truly apes. That's merely a convenient handle. They are considerably more hominoid than gorilla. Closer to Australopithecus. I presume they have rudimentary language. If not, Tarzan would never have learned to speak. If after a certain point in a child's development he or she does not learn to speak, the child never will."

"I know all that," Jean said. "You know I do. It's just so hard to accept."

"What I think," Hanson said, smiling, "is you are very interested in this Tarzan, and not just his background."

"Dad!"

Shortly after dawn, the sun shone bright and the jungle steamed as the heat increased and the rain evaporated. Birds began to chirp in the trees and monkeys fussed and made noise in the branches. Billy suggested shooting one of the monkeys for a meal, but neither Jean nor Hanson would have it. They thought they were too cute.

"They cute, all right," said Billy, "but they cook up nice you put a stick through them. That Tarzan's monkey. He sure look good. Nice and fat. I would like to put him on a stick."

"I don't think Tarzan would like that idea," Jean said.

"You right," Billy said. "We will not say I said that. But I tell you, you get hungry enough, monkey starts to look less cute and more plump."

Soon the carriers, who had been silent all night, commenced to joke and laugh. They told stories of the two dead men. Stories of their lives and exploits. They told all they could tell that would honor them, and in their honor, they tried not to be sad. The dead men had lived their lives as best they could, and now they were gone to the other side, where all men eventually go.

Midday they came upon a wild hog and Billy shot it. They made camp shortly thereafter and roasted the pig on a spit over a large fire. The meat was good and sweet, and soon they began to feel rested and refreshed.

Hanson, a belly full of roasted pork, felt the worse had been done, and that it was smooth sailing from here on out.

Of course, he was wrong.

In the camp of the renegades, all was not so well. In fact, there wasn't a camp anymore, and as Wilson and Cannon approached it, they found Gromvitch.

Part of him anyway. The head actually. It was lodged between low tree branches at about their head-height. The rest of him was nowhere in sight.

Cannon grunted. "Gromvitch seems to have lost his head."

"Your sentimentality overwhelms me," Wilson said.

"Lookee here," Cannon said, removing his knife from its sheath and poking it into Gromvitch's mouth. "He ain't got but a couple teeth left here, and they got gold in them."

Cannon used the point of his knife to pop the teeth loose. He put them in his pocket.

"Sure you don't want to boil his head down," Wilson said, "save it for a souvenir?"

"I knew how and had the time," Cannon said, "I would."

"You're somethin', Cannon. And ain't none of that somethin' any good."

"What I'm worried about is practical stuff," Cannon said. "Like is there still supplies enough for us? Ammunition. Guns. Look at it this way, Wilson. Gromvitch dead has its good side. Now we just got to divide what we get two ways."

Cannon ducked under the limbs that held Cannon's head, proceeded toward the campsite.

"Hey," Wilson said. "It was Gromvitch, our heads were hanging up there, he'd bury us. Don't you think?"

Cannon turned and looked at Wilson. "Yeah. He'd slit a throat for a dollar, but he was like that. Way I see it though, what Gromvitch would do is one thing. What I'll do is another. You dig a hole, you're feeling Christian. My point of view is he don't deserve nothing no more than Talent got, and Talent didn't get nothing, and you didn't want to give him nothing. You're gettin' dewy-eyed all of a sudden, ain't you?"

"Just sayin' what Gromvitch would do is all."

"Bury his noggin', you want. Me, I say let the bugs take care of him."

With that, Cannon proceeded into what was left of the camp.

Wilson took a long hard look at Gromvitch's head. There was a look of surprise on Gromvitch's face. Not horror. Just surprise. His nearly toothless mouth hung open as if in idiotic satisfaction. It was as if he had just opened a present and found it to be exactly what he wanted.

Wilson ducked under the limbs and followed Cannon toward the campsite. He realized he was losing his control over Cannon. Cannon was gradually starting to see himself as the big dog of the pair, and Wilson felt certain he would have to eliminate Cannon at some point, or at least teach him some manners. He needed him right now, at least until he found the city, found the treasure that was there. Then, when Cannon helped him carry it out, he'd kill him. Quick and painless. A shot in the back of the head.

Might as well. He knew for a fact, if he didn't kill Cannon, Cannon would kill him.

TARZAN

The Lost Adventure

XI

When Hunt awoke the sun was shining brightly through the slit of an opening that led into the cave. The air smelled cool and sweet. He saw Tarzan asleep and apparently relaxed on the rough stony ground with Nkima snuggled in his arms. The great lion was nowhere in sight.

Tarzan opened his eyes and looked at Hunt. "Do not stare if you are watching someone. I can feel you. Always glance, take in what you see, but do not hold the look. If a person is sensitive enough, he can feel the gaze of others."

"Sorry . . . Where'd you get those knives?"

"I found them. Around the corner of the cave there are burials and weapons."

Hunt's heart beat faster. His love for anthropology and archaeology flared up. "Really, can I see?"

"Take a look. But don't go far."

"The lion isn't around there, is he?"

"He went off to hunt. There is no way to know when he will return."

"Yeah, well, that breaks my heart," Hunt said. "Least he isn't viewing me as food. And I guess that's a plus."

"You can be certain it is," Tarzan said.

Hunt followed the trail by the stream, went around to look at what Tarzan had discovered. He was overwhelmed. Many of the skulls appeared to be quite primitive, fossilized by the dripping of calcium through the rocks. But as Hunt proceeded along the cavern wall, he was amazed to discover some of the skulls were not that old. In fact, they could have been as recent as last week. Hunt experienced a burning excitement. He wished he could tell his mentor, Professor Hanson.

Here was an incredible discovery. At a glance, it appeared this cavern was a sacred burial place for a primitive race here in the jungle. Perhaps there was some connection with this and the lost city they sought. And even if there was no connection, it meant this ill-fated journey to Africa might have a happy ending after all.

That led Hunt to thinking again of Small and Jean. He hurried back to Tarzan. Neither Tarzan or Nkima were in sight. Hunt had a sudden sinking feeling, then Tarzan crawled into the cave opening and pulled a pile of brush in after him. He went out again, brought more brush back.

"Where is the monkey?" Hunt asked.

"Off to find fruit," Tarzan said. "He has a short attention span. He likes my company best when he is frightened. Now that the storm is over, he is brave again."

"I know how he feels," Hunt said, "though I'm not that brave."

Tarzan began snapping the brush into kindling.

"You're building a fire," Hunt said.

"Nothing escapes you, does it?" Tarzan said.

"You don't have to be snide," Hunt said. "Isn't the brush too wet to burn?"

"Some of it is damp, but most of it I pulled from the lower quarters, so it is drier. Besides, this kind of brush dries quickly, and it burns well."

"How long have we slept?" Hunt asked.

"Most of the day."

"Shouldn't we help Jean and find Small?"

Tarzan grunted. "Rest and food are our greatest allies. We have had one, now we must have the other."

Tarzan opened a small bag fastened to his breechcloth, took

out a piece of flint and steel. He used them to make a spark, got the brush going.

"Good," Hunt said. "I'm freezing."

"It is the wet clothes," Tarzan said. "Take them off."

"What?"

"Suit yourself."

Hunt thought this over for a while. It was hard for a civilized man to travel about naked, but finally he removed everything but his undershorts, shoes, and socks.

"Use some of these limbs to make a prop for your clothes," Tarzan said. "Let them dry by the fire. After you eat, go outside and stand in the sun till you dry. But, with your white skin, you will have to put your clothes on before too long, or you will burn like an ant under a magnifying glass."

When the fire was going, Tarzan blew on it and added more brush. He used one of the knives to cut meat off the filthy buffalo leg. He tossed the meat into the fire.

Hunt used a couple of limbs to make a rack for his clothes by the fire.

When he saw the meat sizzling, he said, "You don't by any chance expect me to eat that, do you?"

"I do not expect anything of you," Tarzan said. "You may eat, or you may not eat. That is your choice."

"But that meat is . . . rancid."

"Another day and your stomach would not tolerate it at all," Tarzan said. "It would poison you. It may now. I cannot say for certain. Two more days and mine would not tolerate the meat. Only the animals could eat it then. But for now, it is food."

"Couldn't we kill something fresh?"

"I have not the time."

When the meat was charred black, Tarzan used the knife to remove it from the fire. He cut it in two, offered half to Hunt. "Eat or do not. It is your choice."

Hunt grimaced, but he reached out and took the meat. He sniffed it. It smelled burned, nothing more. He bit into it. It was not the best meat he had tasted. In fact, it was pretty awful, but he was starved, and in a matter of minutes, he had devoured it and was licking the grease off his fingers.

Tarzan finished eating as well. He wiped his greasy hands on his thighs, bent, and drank from the creek water.

When he was satiated, Tarzan said, "And now, I must go."

"Go?"

"To find Hanson and Jean, and perhaps this man that was with you, Small."

"But, I'm not ready."

"Nor will you be. Not for the way I travel. I am going to follow in their last direction until I pick up their spoor. You stay here and wait for me. When I'm sure Wilson and his companions have not harmed them, I will come back for you. You are safer than they are. I was wrong not to have killed those men when I had the chance. Civilization is like a disease. It infects you with stupid sentiments. If I see them again, I will kill them."

Although Hunt was aware of Tarzan's jungle savvy, he was still unaware of the extent of Tarzan's uncanny sense of vision, smell, and hearing. To him, Tarzan was just another human being, with a better knowledge of jungle life than he had. He did not realize that this man, contending from childhood with the beasts of the jungle, had been forced to acquire the senses and the cunning of all of them to survive.

"Listen here, whatever your name is," Hunt said.

"Tarzan."

"Well, Tarzan, you may go around without your pants and run faster than I do, but don't feel so high and mighty. I can keep up. I can do my part."

"No. You stay here. I do not want to hunt for you later. Watch out for the big cats. Make a blind for the cavern mouth here to keep animals out, or find a tree and make a platform."

"You can save your advice," Hunt said. "I'm coming, and that's that."

"Very well," Tarzan said. "I have warned you to stay here. But I think a man should do what he wants, even if it is stupid. You tell a child, do not put your hand in the fire or it will burn you, and the child will believe this and not do it, or he will not and will put his hand in the fire and burn it, and not do it again. You are like the child who has to put his hand in the fire. I am not even sure you are smart enough to withdraw it if it catches ablaze. Come out into the sun and put on your clothes, and follow if you can. Here. Take this."

Tarzan gave Hunt one of the knives. Hunt put on his partially dry clothes and stuck the knife in his belt, then the two of them went outside and stood in the hot sun.

"Will you look for Small, too?" Hunt asked.

"Jean and Hanson are my first concern," Tarzan said. "I promised to lead them on their expedition, and I foolishly allowed myself to be captured, putting them at the possible mercy of Wilson and his comrade. I feel their safety is my responsibility. When I find them, then I can find Small."

"He's all by himself," Hunt said.

"And soon," Tarzan said, "so shall you be."

"I might surprise you, Tarzan," Hunt said. "I'm hardheaded, and I've got more endurance than you think."

"Good. You will need both. Now listen. If you refuse to stay here as I have suggested, when we become separated — "

"If we become separated," Hunt said.

"When we become separated, if you feel you must find Hanson and Jean, I can tell you only this. Head north. Watch the sun. Judge by that. It falls in the west, rises in the east, and you want to go north. At night, find a tree and climb it. Better yet, do as I first suggested and stay here."

Tarzan walked over to a low bush and picked a red berry from it. "These are edible. They grow in abundance. They are not very filling, but they are plentiful. Bird eggs are good too, if you are willing to crack them and drink them raw. Look above you in the trees and you will see the nests. But be careful climbing or you will break your neck. And do not fight a snake, or even a monkey, for an egg. You will lose."

"You're trying to scare me."

"I'm trying to prepare you. You will not be able to keep up with me, Hunt. I will travel by the trees."

"The trees?"

"It takes a great deal of practice. I was raised by an ape. Kala. She adopted me when my parents were killed. She taught me to move through the trees when I was still a baby. I clung to branches, climbed around in trees even before I could walk."

"Get out of town," Hunt said. "Raised by apes? Yeah, and a pack of dogs reared me under the porch of the White House."

"Have it your way," Tarzan said, and with that, he leaped into the trees and began to climb. By the time Hunt realized what was happening, the ape-man had found a thick vine and was swinging across a vast expanse of jungle.

Hunt leaped up, grabbed a limb, tugged himself into the tree Tarzan had first climbed, clambered upward, hand over hand, limb to limb. When he had reached a fair height, he began looking for a suitable limb by which to swing to a nearby tree, but saw none. He decided he would have to leap to a limb some distance away. He coiled his legs and jumped. His shoes slipped on the limb, and he missed his target.

He fell a short distance before a small broken branch struck him, poked through his belt, and left him dangling upside down like a Christmas tree ornament.

As Hunt struggled, he decided this traveling by tree looked considerably easier than it really was. He felt very silly hanging like an oversized fruit, and sought out a handhold. He labored for some time, and while he labored, a horde of curious monkeys showed up to eat fruit and watch him strain.

After a time, the monkeys began to chatter and leap up and down, obviously delighted by his predicament. The whole episode was making Hunt angry, even embarrassed. It didn't get much worse than having a band of monkeys ridicule you.

Or maybe it did.

The monkeys, bored with his antics, began to throw fruit at him, and finally more monkeys came into play, and some of them were carrying heavy nuts to throw. They bounced them off Hunt's head and body. They were very good shots and had strong arms.

Hunt became so infuriated that he began to struggle wildly. He was amazed at how fast he could cuss the monkeys. The words rolled out of his mouth and came together in unique combinations.

The monkeys, however, were not impressed. They did some cussing of their own, and had Hunt understood the language of the apes, he would have found them as inventive as himself.

The limb attached to Hunt's belt cracked and broke, and down he went to the chorus of screaming, delighted monkeys.

He smacked the ground hard, but fortunately, the sward was padded with rotted foliage and Hunt managed only scratches. When he scrambled to his feet and looked about for sign of Tarzan, there was none. The ape-man was long gone.

"How does he do that?" Hunt said aloud.

There was only the sounds of the birds and the screeching monkeys, whom, Hunt decided, he hated. He wondered if that monkey of Tarzan's was among them. Maybe he had even instigated the fruit-tossing business.

Then he thought about the lion. What if the lion came back and Tarzan was not around? Were all bets off, then?

If it wasn't one thing, it was two. Or three.

Exasperated, Hunt decided to finish drying his damp clothes. He removed them, stretched them out on a rock, and was once again dressed only in his shorts, socks, and shoes. He began to pluck and eat the berries Tarzan had pointed out.

The warm sun felt good, and while he ate, Hunt tried to determine his next course of action. One thing was certain. The trees were out.

Damn monkeys.

When the storm was over and the rain had stopped, Small was far too exhausted to move. He lay until the sun was high, dozing off and on, then awoke miserable in his wet clothes.

Small crawled out of his hideaway and looked about. No one tried to shoot him. Nothing tried to eat him. He decided he was off to a good start.

The jungle was thick, so the sunlight gave little warmth. Small removed his clothes and wrung the water from them, draped them over a limb and stood about in his wet underwear and shoes.

He walked a short distance until he found a gap in the foliage overhead and stood there trying to take in the sun, looking up through the limbs at the bright light of midday. Then, out on a limb he saw something that made his stomach fall.

A panther was moving slowly and stealthily down from the height of a tree.

"Oh, God," thought Small. "It's seen me!"

Small broke into a wild run through the jungle, leaving his clothes behind. He would not realize he was nearly naked until he had fought and clawed his way through the jungle for a distance of a half-mile. By then he would be scratched and poked and dotted with bruises and blood.

But in the meantime, the panther, totally unaware of Small, sprang on the real target of its stealth. A large, colorful bird setting on a nest of eggs. The bird was dispatched in a rush of squawks and a wild rustle of red and yellow feathers.

The panther stretched out on a limb to enjoy the bird, feathers and all. It ate slowly, contemplating the second course. The bright bird's shell-covered children, were snug in their nest, oblivious to their fate.

As Hanson's party followed the path the great tornado had cut through the foliage, the jungle was alive with movement. Birds and monkeys were especially notable. But one movement was not noted by the travelers. The most dangerous movement of all went undetected. The very jungle itself was moving. Bushes and small trees. They crept like alien creatures, so subtly that the limbs did not knock and the leaves did not rustle. When the party looked in their direction, they did not move. When the party looked away, they slipped through the jungle, blending with the true foliage.

Once, Billy, trained in the ways of the jungle, turned his head quickly but saw only that which he should see.

Solid vegetation.

Had he looked closer. Much closer. Or had he possessed the considerable abilities of a wild animal, or Tarzan, he might have seen that many of the plants had eyes. Or seemed to have. For disguised within the bushes and trees were living beings with dark faces ritualistically scarred by the placement of hot blades on their flesh. Foreheads marked by white bands of paint made from white clay and the whites of bird eggs completed the savage decorations.

When the disguised warriors had followed Hanson's party for a quarter of a mile, suddenly a signal was passed among them, and the false plants and trees broke loose from the forest and rushed down on the unsuspecting safari.

Billy was the first to respond. He wheeled, jerked his rifle to position and shot one of the living bushes, knocking it back. Then the bushes swarmed them and Billy was struck with the shaft of a spear in the side of the head. He went down, tried to get up, but a spear was slammed through the pack on his back. The impact was incredible. So intense, it jarred Billy's spine and sent him flat against the ground with a moan.

This was followed by a blow from a club to the side of his head.

Billy could hardly move. He managed to open his eyes and see the safari overwhelmed by the warriors in their leafy disguises. He heard shots fired by Hanson and the bearers. He saw Hanson struggle valiantly with a warrior, then he saw a bronze sword flash and Hanson doubled up and went down.

Billy tried to rise. Couldn't.

He saw Jean fire her pistol into a bush, pointblank, saw the bush fall, then he saw her overwhelmed by a horde of similarly attired warriors.

Billy closed his eyes. He felt warm, strangely comfortable.

The sounds of shots and screams caused him to force his eyes open again. And it wasn't worth it. The stealthy warriors had attacked and overwhelmed the safari completely. All this had been accomplished in but a few minutes.

Billy watched Jean as she was led away with the captured bearers. Her head was hung and her hands were bound behind her back, a leash of leather was firmly fastened around her neck, and a native, now devoid of his bushy costume, tall and regal, much scarred, his face decorated with stripes of white paint, was leading her off the trail and out of sight.

"Sonofabitch," Billy said.

Then a shadow fell over him and a tall native stuck a spear into Billy's shoulder. Billy didn't feel the pain at all. He felt nothing now. He thought of Hanson, Jean, his friends. He wished there was something he could do. He wished he'd stayed home. He closed his eyes again, felt the world swing away from him as if on a string.

"And here it ends," he thought, then he thought nothing at all.

TARZAN
The Lost Adventure

XII

When his clothes were dry, Hunt dressed and tried to concoct a plan. He eventually decided his best bet was to wait here, as Tarzan had suggested, but found he could not muster the patience to do that. He could not stop thinking about Jean and those two terrible men. He considered trying the trees again, in spite of all that had happened, but this was a consideration that rapidly passed.

Hunt was not a man who loved weapons, but right now he wished he had a rifle. It would make him feel a bit more secure, and he could perhaps provide himself with meat instead of berries, a food he had quickly tired of. And with a rifle, the idea of going to Jean's rescue would be more realistic. What could he hope to accomplish with a knife?

Hunt worked a heavy branch off a tree by swinging on it until it cracked, then he used his knife to sharpen one end so that it might serve as a spear. With his new weapon and knife, he located what passed for a trail and, trying to maintain a northerly direction, set out.

As he went, he did not forget Tarzan's advice entirely. He kept his eyes open for landmarks and trees that he could climb, for he knew that after feeding, the lions would be lying up somewhere in the neighborhood. Even with full bellies, they might make an exception in his case, and decide to gorge on some fresh tenderfoot.

By noon, however, having seen no signs of lions, Hunt experienced a feeling of relief and security. The feeling of security was tempered, however, by his lack of a rifle. His sharpened stick had given him a bit of courage, but now, traveling about, hearing the movements of animals in the bush, he felt less brave. Ultimately, a stick, sharp or not, was just a stick. Also, he was hungry and was not sufficiently familiar with the fruits of the jungle to risk eating anything other than the berries Tarzan had shown him, and they were no longer available.

Late in the afternoon, Hunt noticed a change in the nature of the forest. His quick apprehension of this change was the result of his having spent the day walking and visually searching out trees he could climb. He discovered there weren't any trees in sight that would serve this purpose. The boles of the nearby trees were very large, no limbs grew near the ground, and no lianas dropped within his reach.

He accelerated his speed a little, hoping soon to find more gracious and hospitable foliage. And then, at the far end of a straight stretch of trail, he saw a lion, and worse yet, the lion saw him. It was coming slowly in his direction. Now it stopped. So did Hunt.

The lion lashed its tail and growled. Hunt slowly cocked his spear, then thought better of it and drew his knife. He decided he would rely on neither weapon totally, so he seized the blade between his teeth, and held the spear at ready. He was determined to sell his life dearly. It was either that or lie down and let the beast have a free lunch.

The lion growled softly, arched its body, but Hunt stood his ground. In spite of his willingness to fight, Hunt knew he had about as much chance as a June bug in a hen house. Even if he ran, in a few seconds the lion would overtake him and he would go down without ever defending himself. If he fought, his spear might not even pierce the lion's thick hide. If he used the knife, well, the odds weren't much better.

The lion was not hurrying. He moved steadily forward. When the beast was about twenty feet from Hunt, it dropped on its belly and swished its tail spasmodically, gathering its hind legs beneath its body.

This is it! thought Hunt. Then a large, round fruit struck the lion in the side of the head and blew apart in a red meaty spray. The lion jerked its head, insulted. Another fruit struck him. Then another.

From above, the fruit fell like rain. Heavy rain. It slammed the lion from head to tail. Finally, hurt, humiliated, the great beast turned and darted into the cover of the jungle.

Hunt removed the knife from his mouth, looked up, and laughed. The trees were full of monkeys. One of the little males seemed to be the leader. He leaped up and down on a limb and shook his arms as if they were nothing more than huge, hairy strips of spaghetti.

The monkey slowly descended the tree, and came chattering toward Hunt. Hunt realized it must be Tarzan's monkey, Nkima. He realized too, that this beast had been the instigator of the attack on him, and now, using the same tactics, Nkima and his friends had saved him from a lion.

Hunt laughed. "Thank you, Nkima."

He doubted the monkey could understand what he was saying, but he hoped his attitude revealed his sincere thanks. Surely, Tarzan had left the monkey behind to keep an eye on him. That had to be it. Tarzan had not abandoned him entirely after all.

Nkima made a chuckling noise, barred his teeth in what might have been a monkey smile, then suddenly leaped into a tree and disappeared into the flora.

When Hunt looked up, trying to spy Nkima, none of the monkeys were in sight. Hunt lowered his head and laughed.

A large, ripe piece of fruit hit him solidly in the back of the head.

"Hey!" Hunt yelled, but his yell was concealed beneath the humorous chattering of a hundred monkeys hiding amongst the African greenery.

Hunt wiped the fruit from his neck, licked his fingers. The juice of the fruit was sweet. He decided it was edible and tried a piece. It was delightful. He shopped for chunks of the fruit that had exploded against the lion's body, and fed himself. When he was full, he sat down on the ground and thought over his situation.

He was going from bad to worse. He had not only failed to follow Tarzan's orders about staying put, he could not even find trees to climb, and he had been rescued from a ferocious lion by a pack of fruit-throwing monkeys.

Additionally, had he not been hit in the back of the head and tasted the juice of the fruit, he might well have gone hungry. He was about as nimble in the jungle as a sumo wrestler performing ballet.

Hunt did not like the idea of abandoning Jean, but he faced the fact that Tarzan was far more suitable as a rescuer than he. Actually, Hunt couldn't quite determine what he was suitable for. He made a great bull's eye for the monkeys. Maybe that was worth something. He got home, perhaps he could find a job at the zoo as a target for irate monkeys. Kind of a Saturday afternoon kid show thing. There might even be some money it.

Sighing, using his spear to climb to his feet, Hunt started back in the direction he had come, trying to relocate the cavern of skulls before night set in.

Hunt was only a bit confused. When he left the cavern, he had taken in certain landmarks, peculiar trees, an almost head-high anthill, odd rises and drops in the terrain, and by relocating these he was able to return to his original shelter.

He found an antelope lying dead at the mouth of the cavern. Its head was badly chewed, and there were chunks out of its flank. Hunt determined the meat had been left for him purposely by Tarzan's lion. The lion had helped himself first, but at least he had left a healthy portion.

Hunt was grateful for that, but the idea of eating raw antelope was not appealing. He pulled the carcass into the cavern, left it lying by the stream, and went in search of some stone that he could use against the edge of his knife to strike a spark.

He soon found himself in the cavern of skulls. He followed along the piles of bones farther than he had gone before, and presently came to the end of both skeletal remains and illumination. The rocks beyond were bleached of their phosphorescence, and the cavern was swallowed by absolute darkness.

Stuck between two skulls stacked against the wall with others, Hunt discovered an old torch. He pulled it down, but it crumbled useless in his hands. Even though it was rotten, Hunt realized it had to be relatively recent. Nothing made of wood could have survived since prehistoric times.

For the moment, however, he let that mystery pass. He continued his search for something with which he could strike a spark, and in the mouth of one of the skulls, he found two small pieces of flint, and realized suddenly that here was a primitive light switch. You used the stones to strike the torch to life. Of course, the torch was now nothing more than wood dust.

Hunt returned to the mouth of the cave, went outside and gathered fire tinder and wood, and returned to the comfortable interior of the cave. He struck the pieces of flint together, and after several false starts threw a spark into the tinder and gently blew on it, bringing it to life.

He added wood gradually, until a healthy fire was going, then he cut a portion of antelope meat off the carcass, and began roasting it on a stick he held into the fire. When the meat was somewhere between raw and burned to charcoal, he ate it.

Finished, he felt renewed strength and a stronger sense of purpose. His only problem was he wasn't sure of his purpose. He wanted it to be rescuing Jean, or possibly finding Small, but so far he had discovered that his woodcraft was somewhere on the level of a stone, and therefore, like a stone, it was best he stayed in one area.

But Hunt finally became bored with sitting and waiting. His archaeological curiosity got the better of him, and he felt it better to occupy his time with that than to think about Jean, Hanson, Small, and their predicaments. He drank deeply from the stream, and using strips of wet hide from the antelope's carcass, he bound his knife blade to a long, stout piece of firewood. He then used a couple of sticks to fashion torches by wrapping them with moss and dried vines he had pulled in for the purpose of fire tinder.

Hunt lit one of the torches, put out his cook fire by spreading it apart with a stick, and, taking up his spear and handmade torches, went exploring. He soon reached the end of the illumination and decided to proceed by torchlight. He had not gone far when the torchlight revealed drawings and paintings on the wall. The drawings were done with charcoal, the paintings with some sort of red and yellow ocher. Hunt held his torch close to the cave wall and examined them.

They were of great beasts: lions, buffalo, and creatures he could not identify. The unidentifiable creatures looked more insect than animal. The scenes depicted prehistoric humans battling them with spears. Hunt tried to decide what the creatures reminded him of, and finally came to the conclusion that if a praying mantis could grow to be six to seven feet tall and had heavier body construction, that would be what they most resembled.

What was even more curious was that in some of the drawings, the mantises were in strange and extravagant postures. There was something about the postures that rang a distant bell, but Hunt couldn't quite place them.

Hunt wondered if he had discovered a prehistoric documentation of an afore unknown creature, or if the drawings represented exaggerations. Storytelling. Made-up monsters. Perhaps the drawings were symbolic. The insects could be locusts, they could portray a plague to crops, and the warriors with their spears were representative of mankind battling the horrid plague.

Plague to what?

Crops?

No. These prehistoric humans were hunters and gatherers, not farmers, and they had little time for silly symbolism. Leave that stuff to the professors who taught Hawthorne's *The Scarlet Letter* by using symbolism charts in the backs of their teacher's editions.

Hunt proceeded into darkness, the torch flickering before him. He decided to advance only a few more feet and then return to the sanctuary of the brightly lit cavern behind him, but the drawings and paintings became more frequent, and he was entranced by them. This was an even greater archaeological find than he had first expected. It was phenomenal, in fact. Once he reported this to Hanson, the cave might even be named after him.

Wouldn't that be something? A prehistoric site named after him.

Hunt's Cavern.

Yeah. Hunt's Cavern. It had a ring to it. He liked it.

Following the cavern wall with his torch, trying to discern the content of the drawings, seeing more and more representations of the stick-like insects, Hunt continued to explore, and did not realize how long he had been walking until his torch began to sputter and smoke.

Pausing to light his spare torch, Hunt was amazed to find he was surrounded by darkness. The torch gave him immediate light, but when he turned to look behind him, extended the torch in that direction, he could no longer see the illuminated walls. He determined that, preoccupied with the paintings, he had most likely turned a corner and had gone off track.

He attempted to start back and was horrified when he came up against solid rock. He turned right and went along the cavern wall, using his torch to examine the paintings, hoping to spot a familiar one, but all of the paintings looked different. Some of them looked to have been painted quite recently.

Hunt tried several directions, but the results were always the same.

He was lost.

How had it happened?

He had been on course one moment, and the next he was utterly and completely confused. He decided to try and backtrack his steps again. He studied his situation, became confident of the problem, certain where he had made his wrong turn, and set out to correct it.

No sooner had he made his first assured step, then the floor went out from under him and he dropped down into empty and total darkness, the torch hurtling ahead of him like a burning meteor.

TARZAN
The Lost Adventure

XIII

Tarzan traveled quickly through the trees, and soon he came across the camp of the renegades, formerly the camp of Hunt and Small.

The storm had torn it apart. Supplies had been tossed in all directions, filling the brush and trees. Tarzan walked about the camp, sniffed an odor. His nostrils led him to the decaying head of Gromvitch lodged in a tree. It stunk and was covered with flies. Soon it would be the home of thousands of squirming maggots.

From the smell of rotting flesh, the amount of flies on the head, Tarzan determined how much time had elapsed since Gromvitch died. That was an easy one, since it was obvious he had died in the storm. No beast had done this. The man had been torn apart by the tempest, like an angry child ripping up a paper doll. Afterwards, the wet head had boiled in the heat of the day and the flies had come. They were so thick, Gromvitch's head looked like an idol for flies; an insect mecca where they came to prostrate themselves and pray.

Tarzan noticed that the sides of Gromvitch's mouth were damaged. He used his knife to probe inside the mouth. Flies rose up in a blue-black tornado, twisted about Tarzan's hand and head. He ignored them. He looked inside Gromvitch's mouth, saw where teeth had been popped free. This had not been the workings of the storm. This was man at his worst. Most likely gold fillings or gold teeth had been removed.

Tarzan returned his knife to the loop on his loincloth, and the flies settled back to their prayer.

Tarzan considered the head and missing teeth, and this consideration gave him a fuller picture of the events. At least one of the renegades had survived the storm after being caught outside of camp. He returned, found the head here, and had taken the teeth.

Tarzan determined that would not be the black man, but the remaining white man. That was only a guess, but from the manner of the white man it seemed to fit. It would not be the sort of reasoning that would suit a court of law, but out here Tarzan was the law, and he trusted his instincts.

Tarzan examined the ground around the head carefully. All right. Two of the renegades had survived. The footprints of their boots were clear, especially after the storm had dampened the ground and the sun had begun to dry the impressions of their steps in the mud and leaf mold. The bearers did not wear boots. They either went barefoot or wore sandals, usually the former, so these were the prints of the renegades.

Also, one set of tracks was deeper than the other, and Tarzan knew that would be Cannon, the white man. Cannon's boot marks stopped right in front of the head, and Tarzan could tell at a glance that Cannon's feet had shifted from side to side. This was due to Cannon using his knife to work the teeth out of Gromvitch's mouth. The deed had required a bit of body English, so therefore the peculiar markings.

Tarzan returned to the camp proper, looked about, determined many of the bearers had escaped the storm and were probably now well on their way home, provided they hadn't run into trouble from animals. However, some of the bearers had not escaped. He found their remains.

The fresh tracks in camp told Tarzan another story. The two renegades had come back here, supplied themselves with what they could find in the way of guns, ammunition, and food, and moved on. It was clear to Tarzan they would pursue Hanson's safari, for it was a source not only for supplies, but bearers to carry them. This would be the way these men would think. They would want someone else to provide for them, someone else to carry their load.

Tarzan found a tin of rations that had rolled under a bush, and using his knife he opened it and ate, scooping it out with his fingers. It was a mushy potted meat and tasted like the leaf mold at his feet. He would have preferred to make a kill, drink the blood of an animal for energy, but for the time being, this was the easiest and quickest way to gain vitality and return to the chase. There was a great possibility that the renegades had already reached the Hanson party, and if not, traveling light as they were, they were closing fast.

Tarzan finished eating and took silently to the trees.

When Small had been startled by the panther and had gone off at a run in his shoes and underwear, he ran until his sides hurt. Finally, he sat down on a log to rest and was startled by a small black snake crawling out from under it and between his legs.

Small leaped to his feet, started to run again and went headlong into a tree. It was not a tremendous impact, but it was enough to spin him around and cause him to slide to a sitting position with the bark burning his naked back.

From there, exhausted, he watched the small snake, its middle swollen, slither away. There was a bird's nest lying there beneath the log. In the nest was one cracked egg. There had most likely been others, and that was why the snake had been plump. It had taken advantage of this meal dropped into its path by last night's storm.

Small eyed the egg carefully. He was ferociously hungry. He scooted over to the nest and picked up the cracked egg, held it over his mouth and separated it with his fingers, dripping the yoke into his mouth. It tasted pretty good.

Small eyed the log on which he had been sitting on. It was rotten and filled with plump, white, insect grubs. Small watched the grubs quiver in the wood for a moment, then, plucked one of the grubs between his thumb and finger, tossed it into his mouth, and began to chew.

It was a gritty meal, but not as bad as he expected. Not as good as one could hope, but still, serviceable if you were nearly naked and lost in the jungle and tired and filthy and had just run away from a panther after spending the night under fallen trees in a storm. Not to mention that prior to the storm you had been chased and shot at, and had a huge python crawl over your legs. All those events considered, a meal of a bird's egg and grubs was, time and place considered, fairly cosmopolitan.

Small began to eat the grubs like popcorn. He ate them until the log was absent of them. Then he found a low-limbed tree, climbed as high as he dared, located a cluster of criss-crossing limbs and vines, and stretched out on them. Glad for the hot golden sunlight that was leaking through a gap in the foliage, Small slept.

As Small slept, the wind picked up, and the tree rattled as if it were a dry skeleton. Small sat up. He felt strange. He climbed down from the tree. He began to walk, and as he walked the jungle opened up before him. On either side of him he saw great black walls, and in the black walls, as if they were trapped beneath tar, figures moved. Small observed them with an odd detachment. But even beneath the thick black tar, the shapes were recognizable. Jean. Hanson. Hunt. The wild man he had seen tied to a tree. Cannon and Wilson and Gromvitch were there. The tar-covered figures writhed and wadded together, and twisted into a great black knot, and from the knot, oozing out of the squirming black wall there dripped pops of blood so red a prize-winning rose would have paled beside it. Small looked at the blood, and as it rolled toward the ground it came to rest on a piece of ancient stone wall, and on top of the wall the blood gathered and swelled and took the shape of a heart, steaming and pulsing.

Small felt a tinge of horror, but no more than that. And he considered that most strange, for he knew the heart was his own. He touched his chest. There was no wound, but he knew the heart was his.

And then as he watched, the heart went soft, became a red puddle, and the puddle leaped off the stone and onto the wall and fled upwards until it reached the great black knot of humanity. It entered the knot. The knot went flat against the wall, and Small stirred in his sleep. He opened his eyes, blinked, and found that he was still in the tree. It had been a dream. A moment of trepidation swelled inside his chest. His mother had once dreamed of her own death. She told him she saw her own heart lying on a table, steaming and beating. Then it ceased to beat, and she awoke.

She told him this, and then she died a week later. She said she knew she would die. It was an inherited ability. Her grandfather had envisioned his death in a similar manner. Their ancestors, long ago traded to whites by other Africans, had been descendants of a power-ful shaman who could foretell the future. It was his mother's belief that the trait had been passed on to later generations — at least in one way. The ability to sense one's own demise.

Small disregarded the vision. The dream. It was nothing more than his natural fears swelling inside him. He would be okay. He would be all right.

Maybe.

His anxiety could not fight away his exhaustion. He slept in spite of the dream, and he slept deep, and sound, and good.

Jean felt empty. She no longer cared what happened to her. The warriors had abandoned their tree camouflage, and were push-ing her quickly along a rough trail. They were silent as they walked, and she noticed the warriors were both men and women. Due to their size, she had at first assumed they were men, but now, devoid of their tree camouflage, she saw at least a third of them were women.

Many of the warriors were quite young. All were very tall with classic Negroid features and skin black as wet ebony. They were well built and muscular and wore white paint on their foreheads and cheeks to complement the scars burned into their flesh. A few of them wore plumes of feathers. Those without plumes wore their hair long and well oiled. Some carried short, thick spears while others carried long, almost floppy spears. Several had bows and quivers of long arrows strapped to their backs. All wore huge knives — swords actual-ly — in loops at their waists, or in scabbards slung over their shoul-ders. Under other circumstances, Jean might have found them fasci-nating. But now all she could think of was her father who had fallen before their attack. She was happy to see the body of the warrior she had killed being carried on a litter. She never thought the death of a human being would please her, but she was glad she had killed this man. It did not bring her father back, but it was something and she was glad.

The man who led her was not happy with her progress. He tugged and the leash tightened, causing her to stumble. When Jean regained her footing, a bolt of anger shot through her. In that moment, she felt the best thing to do was fight. Fight until her captors became so angry they killed her. That way she would not have to think about her father, about poor Billy and the others who had been slain or captured.

But no, that would not be the way. That would not be her father's way. That was not a Hanson's way. You stuck with it to the end. That's what life was about, hadn't her father told her that?

You lived life no matter how hard. And if she was going to die at the hands of these people, then so be it. She would die in time anyway, so she determined that she would sell herself dearly with a good and noble death.

That would be the way to go. For now, she would push her fear, anger, and pain deep inside. Wait and watch. And when the moment came, she would try and escape, and if escape seemed impossible . . . well, she was uncertain. But she would do something. She would not lie about like a turnip in the ground waiting to be plucked.

She would do something, even if it was wrong, but her first course of action was, if at all possible, to do something right. To be calm, and observe.

They trekked for some distance, then to Jean's amazement they came upon a road. An actual road! It was built of dark, dried blocks set in concrete and was twelve feet wide. Jean assumed it had been constructed in a fashion similar to that used by the Romans to build roads. Layer after layer of material. Whatever, it was an incredible feat of engineering.

The road went for a great distance, then twisted out of sight behind a great rise of trees. The road was well kept and along its sides the jungle had been cut back so that limbs did not overlap it. A row of carts and chariots stood parked beside the road.

Nearby, a handful of men and women, none of them dressed in warrior garb, came forward leading zebras. The zebras wore bridles and reins and appeared very tame. The stock workers fastened the zebras to the chariots.

The big warrior pulled at Jean's leash, forced her to step into one of the chariots. A woman of powerful proportions stepped up beside them, took the reins, and the chariot moved forward.

Glancing back, Jean saw other chariots following, and behind those the remaining warriors and stock handlers walked. It was a colorful procession.

The equatorial sun was burning hot and high when the winding road broke from the jungle into a vast clearing where Jean saw a large number of sweaty workers in the distance struggling with huge blocks of cut stone. They were pulling the stones from a quarry with thick ropes. Whips flashed in the sunlight, cracked on the backs of the struggling slaves.

An hour beyond the quarry, she was surprised to see the walls of a great city. They were high and thick. There was the wink of sunlight against spear tips at their summit. Jean could make out numerous sentries patrolling the wall.

When the chariot came closer, she observed that the walls were made of clay, thatch, and stone. The blending of wood, clay, and stone was odd, but artful. The tribe had pragmatically used the materials at hand, but their use of these substances revealed they were more than a village of crude savages. Quite the contrary.

The city of Ur. She had found it.

Or rather, it had found her.

For a fleeting moment, Jean forgot her anger and hatred and marveled; here was what her father had come to find, and he had not lived to see it. Ironically, the very people he wished to investigate had slain him.

The gate that led into the city was huge, made of seasoned, black wood, and like a medieval drawbridge, was designed to lower on chains over a moat that was easily thirty feet wide.

A sentry sounded a horn and the drawbridge lowered. As they drove over it, Jean glanced at the dark water of the moat, saw bobbing garbage, as well as rare, white crocodiles. The moat obviously served as both dump, sewer, and feeding trough for the crocodiles, who provided further protection against invaders.

Inside the city were beehive huts thatched with grasses, and in the center of the city an open space. Behind all this rose sophisticated structures of clay and stone. The walls were decorated with elaborate murals representing everyday activities, as well as depictions of warriors battling one another or animals.

One design confused and fascinated Jean. It was of a man with a spear fighting what looked to be some sort of a insect. The insect was taller than the man and stood in an odd posture, on one hind leg, raising the other as if to kick; both forelegs were lifted to guard its upper body from attack. The creature looked similar to a praying mantis, though it seemed more muscular and humanoid. Jean instantly decided these decorated buildings were the dwelling place of royalty.

Women, children, and old men crowded around the prisoners as they were led into the open compound. The children showed special curiosity, being so bold as to dart forth, reach over the top of the chariot, and touch Jean. Jean could not decide if their actions were a kind of coup-counting exercise, or if her white skin intrigued them. They did not laugh as they performed this feat, and were in fact, for children, strangely silent and serious in manner.

They drove straight toward the praying mantis design, and when it seemed as if they would come up against it, a horn sounded above, and what first appeared to be a seamless wall, parted allowing them entry.

As they rode through, Jean observed the wall had been parted by a great chain-and-pulley apparatus on either side of the entryway, and that it was operated by a horde of ragged-looking men wearing ankle chains. The men were obviously of a tribe different from that of the warriors. Some were pygmies.

Jean began to realize the purpose of the attack on her safari. Slaves.

A short distance beyond the opening, thick rods projected from the wall, and dangling from them six feet off the ground by chains were metal cages, and in the cages were skeletons and rotting corpses, as well as living humans. Some of the corpses were riddled with arrows.

One old, naked, black woman with hair white as fresh-plucked cotton, barely alive, almost a skeleton from starvation, reached out and spoke pitifully to Jean's chariot driver. The driver ignored her. The man who held Jean's leash turned and slapped at the extended hand, causing the woman to scream in pain and the cage to swing violently back and forth.

Jean pivoted on the balls of her feet, brought her arm around in a short loop, and struck her captor on the side of the head. It was a clean, sharp blow, a left hook like her father had taught her, and it clipped the warrior so cleanly he was knocked from the chariot, but the leash, fastened around Jean's throat and his wrist, caused her to be jerked to the ground with him.

He grabbed her immediately, wrestled her, straddled her. His sword flashed in his hand. Before he could bring it down, the chariot driver barked at him and he hesitated. He looked at the woman, she scowled and spoke rapidly.

With a snort he returned the sword to its place and jerked

Jean to her feet. He grinned at her, but there was no humor in the gesture. Behind him the entire procession, which had stopped when the struggle began, was watching. Jean knew she had made a mistake. She had caused the warrior to lose face. A mere captive had knocked him on his butt.

The warrior jerked the leash and yanked Jean back into the chariot, and a moment later they were rolling again.

Jean looked back at the old woman. She was clutching the bars of the still swaying cage. She nodded at Jean, and Jean nodded back. Jean knew the woman had little time left to live. And all things considered, maybe that was good.

They came to an archway overlaid with gold, rode through that into a massive courtyard. Here was a palace built of bright red clay, gold, jewels, driftwood, and the skulls of humans and animals. Moorish architectural features blended with a sort of rococo style Jean had never before witnessed. The design was one of twisted genius. It was beautiful, but it made Jean's skin crawl.

In time, the chariot circled the palace, and out back was an empty field, and in the distance Jean could see the rear wall of the city. She reasoned that beyond the wall would be villages that paid homage to this great city, providing warriors, food, and goods. This was an empire.

To the left and the right of the field were long barracks, and the chariots and warriors split left and right and went into these. Jean's driver went right, and when the zebras were brought to a halt in a shotgun-style stall, the driver took the leash from the man and roughly led Jean away.

Jean decided not to make a play. Not now. She would wait for the right moment, when the woman least expected it. Better yet, she would wait until she could concoct a complete plan of escape.

She looked about to see how the other captives were faring, but as far as she could tell, they were all housed inside the barracks. She alone was being brought across the back courtyard toward the palace.

The back door to the palace was a large gate and it was open, and she was led through it. Once inside, Jean let out her breath.

There was a row of naked natives, not the bearers who had worked for the Hanson safari, but tribesman she had not seen before. There were eleven of them lined up between a horde of armed warriors. The eleven were crying and wailing, flaying their arms, falling to their knees and pleading.

At the fore of the line was a huge block of wood, and even as Jean watched, a woman was jerked forward by the hair, forced to place her head on the block. Out of the crowd of warriors, a tall muscular man with an large sword appeared. He was ritualistically scarred and wore a thin mask of white paint around his eyes.

The woman caterwauled, and in mid-cry the sword whistled and her head bounced up with a bright spray of blood. The head rolled in the dust, came to rest looking at the burning sky. The captives screamed and the warriors rejoiced with a shout.

The woman leading Jean turned and smiled. Jean felt a snake of ice run up her spine. The woman, still smiling, yanked Jean toward the line of captives. The woman yelled to the executioner, dragged Jean along the line to the forefront. Jean looked down at the bloody block of wood, then at the decapitated head of the woman. Jean thought, or perhaps imagined, she saw the woman's eyelids flicker, then cease movement.

The woman with the leash spoke to the executioner and he smiled. He came forward, took hold of the leash and jerked it hard. Jean went to her knees gagging, her forehead banging against the bloody block of wood. The woman stepped on one of Jean's bent legs and pressed. Jean let out a moan of pain.

Oh, hell, Jean thought. I should have made my move. I should have taken my chance. It's too late now. So much for a brave and noble death.

The executioner spoke to the crowd of warriors, and one of the men leaped forward and took Jean's leash from the executioner's hand. He pulled it tight so that Jean's neck was stretched out over the block, like a Thanksgiving turkey.

Jean rolled her head slightly, saw the smiling executioner lift the sword. She thought of the flicking of the dead woman's eyelids. She had once read that the brain lived shortly after decapitation, that the eyes and senses were momentarily alive, that in theory, the eyes of a decapitated head could gaze upon its blood-spurting body, could realize what had happened.

Jean hoped this was an old wives' tale.

Jean closed her eyes, heard the whistling of the falling sword, hoped the strike would be quick and clean and true.

TARZAN
The Lost Adventure

XIV

When Hunt fell, the torch fell before him, a bright star speeding into dark infinity. Hunt, seeing the torch go fast and away, knew he was lost. Then he struck something solid and the breath exploded out of him.

As he lay there aching, he could still see the torch falling, and for a moment he was confused, then realized what had happened.

He had stepped into a chasm and had landed on a ledge, his head hanging off of it, and he could see the torch falling. Falling. Falling. And then it vanished. Either it had gone out or struck bottom. Hunt suspected the first.

Hunt lay where he had fallen for a time, trying to regain his breath and decide what to do. He was in total darkness, and he feared any move he might make would send him after his torch, yet he could not remain here.

Carefully, Hunt eased to his knees. His ribs ached, but nothing seemed broken. He backed along the ledge until he came up against a rock wall. In backing, he touched his spear and recovered it.

Hunt put the spear across his knee and applied pressure with his hands until the shaft cracked. With this done, he removed his shirt and wrapped it carefully around the broken stick. He used the knife-end of his broken spear to hack at the wadded shirt, fraying it. He recovered the flint from his pocket, set about creating a spark. Since he did all of this in the darkness by feel, it took a long time, but eventually a spark jumped onto the shirt and caught. Hunt blew on the spark and it went out. He tried again, was finally rewarded with a blaze. Hunt realized his torch would not last long, so he lifted it high so he could see how far he had fallen.

Twelve feet!

He had been lucky. It was a miracle the impact had not broken his ribs, though they certainly felt deeply bruised.

Hunt tried to find a way to climb up, but the wall was straight and slick as glass. Checking to his left he saw that his ledge wound into an opening in the rock. He proceeded in that direction. As he did, the flame on the torch rippled. There was a strong current of air coming from the shaft.

Stepping into the tunnel, Hunt paused for a moment, considering. The torch had little life left. He could either go back to the ledge and try and scale that slick wall, or he could see where this led. The latter seemed the only logical decision.

He had gone only a few steps when the torchlight revealed open clay gutters running along the sides of the tunnel wall — man-made gutters. He held the torch over one of the gutters. It was full of some kind of black liquid. Stagnant water perhaps. It was clogged with thousands of insects. Hunt stuck a finger into the blackness, rubbed it between thumb and forefinger, sniffed it.

Oil. The gutters were filled with oil. Suddenly, he understood their purpose. Hunt took a deep breath, plunged his torch into the gutter. Flames vaulted up and the corridor turned the color of a jack-o'-lantern. His shadow writhed against the opposite wall.

Hunt lit the gutter on the other side. His path was now well illuminated. He tossed the torch away, took a solid grip on his short spear, and proceeded forward.

When Small opened his eyes he was looking into a man's face. It startled him and he rolled violently to his left and fell from the tree.

Or would have, but a strong hand grabbed him and pulled him back.

Tarzan said, "Take it easy. I will not eat you."

"You," Small said. "Thank, heaven. I thought you were dead . . . hey, wasn't me did that to you. I wasn't in on that. Me and the other guy, Hunt, we didn't have anything to do with it. We were captives ourselves."

"I know," Tarzan said. "I have much to do, so shut up, and let me tell you all that has happened."

When Tarzan finished, Small said, "What about Hunt?"

"I needed to move fast, so I left him."

"What about me?"

"You're a problem," Tarzan said. "I had a good place to leave Hunt. Nkima and Jad-bal-ja can provide him assistance, if he does not decide to be stupid. And I fear he might."

"Hey," Small said, "I've got to tell you, I'm beginning to think Hunt and I don't do anything that isn't stupid."

"I hope you are not proud of it."

"Hardly. But you were saying about me. That's something that concerns me. Me, I mean."

"I have no place to leave you that I feel is safe. I suppose I will have to take you along. The only advantage is that I believe we are not far from the Hansons. Their sign and spoor is strong."

"How did you find me?"

"I smelled you. You stink."

"Yeah, and you're a rose. I'm out here in the jungle, man. You outrun a panther, hide in a tree, and eat grub worms, you get a little ripe."

"What I mean is your natural body odor is a stench. All men smell strong to me. I was raised with the animals. I do not have their highly developed sense of smell, but there is not more than an ounce of difference between me and them."

"How do you manage to be around humans, then? Uh, other humans? I mean, we're so ripe to you, looks like you'd be over-whelmed all the time."

"If I live in civilization, I become accustomed to it in time. But now, back in the jungle, I find my senses are more acute. And there-fore, you stink."

"Might I ask about the aroma of animals? Is their smell like perfume?"

"No," said Tarzan, "but it is not nauseating."

Tarzan helped Small down from the tree. Small tried to brush his underwear free of dirt and bark, but it was an insurmountable task.

Tarzan grinned. "You look very silly."

"This from a man in a G-string."

Tarzan laughed.

"Maybe we could find my pants and shirt?" Small said.

"No time," Tarzan said. "Come. We must cover territory. Not only is the spoor of the Hanson safari strong, there is an overlapping spoor. That of your former captors."

"Hey," Small said, "let me tell you about those two, they're meaner than snakes."

"I have been subject to their hospitality," Tarzan said.

"Oh, yeah, that's right. But trust me, they don't mellow out at all. They stay tense. What they did to you, they could do that hourly. Maybe worse."

"You are afraid?" Tarzan asked.

"Yeah," Small said. "I'm afraid. I won't try to snow you. I'm scared to death. Of the jungle. Of them. Even you make me a little nervous."

"Are you coming?"

"Of course. I didn't say I wouldn't. What am I going to do by myself out here? And I want to stop those guys anyway. They're going after the Hansons, and it isn't to share coffee."

"Yes, I know."

"And this other guy that was with them," Small said. "You say he's dead?"

"He could not be any deader," Tarzan said.

"And our safari is gone?"

"Either dead from the storm or they have run off. Now, come."

With that, the ape-man started off at a trot and Small did his best to follow.

Billy awoke and was surprised by the sun. The great storm had cleared such a path that the sky was easily visible. Growing up in the jungle, it was seldom Billy had seen such a vast expanse of sky. Sometimes on the veldt he would look up at it in awe, but his natural habitat was the jungle, and of course he had seen the sun before, but now, here it was, big as a flaming ostrich egg, and all about it was a radiant blue sky.

At first Billy thought he might be dead. That this was the beauty of the other side. Then he felt pain from his wounds and knew, in fact, he was alive. Billy sat up slowly, looked around, saw the bodies of two bearers, friends of his. Hanson's body lay nearby.

Billy eventually made it to his feet, checked the bearers. Quite dead. Hanson, on the other hand, groaned when he touched him.

"Bwana," Billy said. "I thought you dead."

"Help me, Billy."

Billy rolled Hanson on his back. Hanson was bloody, but breathing well enough. There was no gory spittle on his lips, so Billy concluded that no major internal organs had been punctured.

"Sit me up," Hanson said.

"I don't know, Bwana."

"It's all right. I'll be okay."

"Talking about me. Not sure I am strong enough to sit you up. Doing good to squat here."

"Of course. Sorry."

"All right. Give me time, then maybe I hop around like frog, wrestle crocodile, and sit you up. Right now, though, not feeling all that hoppy. Think I will lie down beside you."

Billy practically collapsed beside Hanson.

"Billy?" Hanson said.

"Yeah, Bwana."

"We going to make it?"

"Not a soothsayer. Can't tell. I think old men in village who read future in smoking animal guts probably not know. Figure all along they just handling hot guts. Me, I can lie without guts. But I prefer not to. Too tired to make anything up. We live maybe. Die maybe."

Hanson was uncertain how his simple question had led to reading the future in smoking animal entrails, but all he could say was: "Jean?"

"They took her away, Bwana. Alive."

"Thank God!"

"Took everyone else away, except for two dead. Udalo. Ydeni. Friends of mine. Good men. Both dead."

"Yes, good men."

"I don't think tree-people meant to kill anyone."

"Nice to know it was all an accident."

"They not mind killing. But Billy think they prefer to take alive, for whatever reason, and I got feeling we knew reason it would not make us happy much. They would take us, they thought we were alive. Try and kill us only because we give them serious trouble."

"They leave the guns?"

"No."

"At least Jean's alive. I have to go after her, Billy."

"I know that."

"God, I'm so sleepy."

"Loss of blood. Both of us leak like rotten boat."

"I'm not still bleeding, though, am I?"

"No. You have not so good wounds, but not so bad either . . . Bwana, got to tell you, don't know when or if I'm gonna feel froggy."

"Got to . . . they've got Jean and your friends."

"Right now, Bwana . . . right now, think maybe I got to nap little bit."

Hanson did not respond.

"Bwana?" Billy said.

Then Billy heard Hanson's deep breathing. Pain and loss of blood had caused him to pass out.

Rest a little, thought Billy. That's all we need. Rest a little, then we'll be okay. Go after Jean and friends. We'll get them back.

But just as Billy was about to close his eyes, he realized things had gone from bad to worse. A man stepped into view and stood over him. Billy recognized the face.

Wilson.

"Dangit," Billy said.

When the great sword fell Jean closed her eyes and hoped there would be no pain.

And there wasn't.

The sword struck with a thunk.

Jean opened her eyes. She could still see. Oh, no, she thought. The head does live for a time after decapitation. But at least she did not feel pain.

Laughter.

Jean tried to move. Her neck turned.

It was connected to her head.

She lifted her chin. The laughter was coming from the warriors, the executioner, and the woman who had led her to the block. They were having a merry time.

The sword that would have taken her head was buried close to her neck in the block. It had all been a joke.

The executioner worked the sword back and forth, managed to remove it from the block. When this was done, the woman jerked the leash, pulling Jean into the dirt. She yanked again and Jean struggled to her feet.

So, thought Jean, all that business before, this woman making the male warrior leave her alone, that had apparently been to expedite matters, and had nothing to do with feelings of humanity.

Jean studied the woman's face carefully. She did not want to forget it. Her time would come, and when it did, this woman would die. And there would be no joke about it.

As Jean was led away, one of the male captives was forced to his knees, his head pushed down on the block.

Jean turned away, heard the sword whistle and thunk soundly into the chopping block. Afterward came the wailing of the condemned and the cheers of the captors.

TARZAN
The Lost Adventure

XV

Hunt moved along the tunnel by the light of the flaming gutters and he could feel the draft was growing stronger. It was a long tunnel and many tunnels branched off of it, but they led into darkness. Hunt decided to stay with the light. Could be the other tunnels were also provided with gutters of oil, but he decided to stick with this one, see where it led. Judging by the way the fire was burning — the fact that there was still plenty of air to breathe and the flames seemed to be whipping in a direction that indicated an oxygen feed — Hunt was optimistic.

This optimism was soon tempered. Now and then, Hunt would turn as if expecting something to leap on him from behind. He sensed the presence of someone, or something, following him. He thought perhaps it was his imagination, but he also believed his senses were becoming more sensitive. Perhaps, like Tarzan — though on a much lower level — he was gradually losing some of his civilized veneer and the more primitive aspects of his reptilian brain were at work, allowing him to use his faculties to a greater degree than ever before.

And possibly he was illogically frightened and the only thing following him was his shadow. Still, he could not shake the feeling that something was stalking him. Hunt clutched the short spear tightly, and continued to cast an occasional glance over his shoulder.

Then something happened that made the hair stand up on the back of his neck. There was a sound down one of the long, dark tunnels. It was a kind of rustling sound, a crawling sound, a clacking sound; it reached inside his brain and sharply prodded buried racial memories. It was a nameless dread that rattled and banged and slithered.

Hunt paused, took a deep breath, and listened.

This was a different sensation than the earlier one. Before he had felt he was being followed, and that was nerve-racking, but this . . . this was worse. Something was waiting.

The horrid sounds stopped. The feeling of dread lessened, but now Hunt was aware of his original concern — that of being tracked. This was compounded by the fact that he could hear his pursuer's soft tread. In a moment it would come around the bend in the passageway and become visible.

Hunt clutched the short spear with all his might.

And waited.

Jad-bal-ja, after a long nap, had awakened and raced to the cavern where the man was supposed to be waiting — the man Tarzan told him to protect.

Jad-bal-ja sniffed at the opening of the cavern, but the spoor of the man was weak. Jad-bal-ja entered the cavern and confirmed what his nose had suggested. The man was gone. But his scent, though weak, was still present; it led into the depths of the cavern. The lion followed after it.

Jad-bal-ja soon determined that the man was as dumb as Nkima. Perhaps dumber. He could not even climb a tree or find his own food. At least the little monkey could do that. And now the dumb man had wandered off into the darkness of the grotto.

Jad-bal-ja followed the winding path of the man and eventually came to where Hunt had fallen. Jad-bal-ja leaped lightly onto the ledge below, saw the flames inside the cavern, and went in there. The fire was warm, and down here in the cool of the cavern that was good. Jad-bal-ja did not care for the cold. When it rained it was too cold for him. When the wind blew on a wet night it was too cold. And it was too cold in the cavern. Except for here. This felt good. Warm as the veldt in the middle of summer.

Jad-bal-ja followed the man's scent.

Before long, he caught the scent of another, and Jad-bal-ja felt something he had never felt before. Terror. Bone-deep terror. There was something down here besides the man, and it moved unlike any man or animal moved.

Jad-bal-ja growled softly, forced himself to proceed. The spoor of the thing was strong now, and it was overlapping the scent of the man he was supposed to protect. He had been given the duty to protect the man, and protect him he would; he would die if necessary to uphold his duty to Tarzan.

As Jad-bal-ja neared where the man was, the scent of the other faded. The jungle cat's ears picked up the thing's movement in one of the distant tunnels of the cavern. It was moving away from him. Jad-bal-ja sensed that whatever it was it knew he and the man were here, and that its departure had nothing to do with either of them. It did not fear them. It feared nothing.

As Jad-bal-ja rounded a corner he saw the man in the firelight. The man's shadow jumped across the tunnel and danced on the wall. The man was trembling, yet he held his ground, a sharp thing in his hand. Jad-bal-ja growled and the man trembled more, but still he held his ground.

The man had courage. He was stupid, but he had courage.

As Hunt waited for sudden and certain death, he recognized the beast. It was Tarzan's lion. It had tracked him. But what was its purpose? To protect or destroy? Perhaps the lion had tired of the game, no longer felt Tarzan's orders were valid, and was more interested in a meal. Certainly, Hunt knew he would be easier to catch and softer to eat then most any other animal in the jungle.

The beast swished its tail, strolled toward Hunt. But the great lion's countenance had changed. It came on slow and soft, and the set of its head indicated an almost lackadaisical attitude. When the lion was six feet away, it sat down and turned its head to one side, examining Hunt. It's tongue came out and the lion panted like a dog.

"Nice lion," Hunt said, and hoped his tone was not too condescending. Could lions sense that sort of thing? Patronization?

Hunt lowered the spear to his side, screwed up his courage, and extended his free hand to the lion.

Jad-bal-ja sniffed. It was a noble sniff, as if he were sucking in the reek of something rotten and liking it not at all.

"Easy, boy," Hunt said.

Hunt stretched his hand toward the lion's face. Jad-bal-ja growled softly. Hunt pulled back his hand. Okay, thought Hunt. Enough was enough. No use trying to make a pet of the beast. It's enough he isn't going to eat me.

At least not at the moment.

Jad-bal-ja turned his royal head toward one of the dark corridors. It was the tunnel where Hunt had heard the noise; the one from whence came the strange sensations that had chilled his inner being with numbing, inexplicable dread.

Hunt noticed the mane on Jad-bal-ja's neck was standing out as if it was made of black porcupine quills, and Hunt perceived the reason. The lion sensed the thing in the cavern as well. The fact that the king of beasts was worried about what lurked there in the darkness re-ignited the fear in Hunt. He looked toward the murk, and now that his eyes had had time to adjust, he saw that the opening to the tunnel was a false one. There was a great chasm between this tunnel and the next; a rift in the rock perhaps forty feet wide, and beyond that, a narrow walkway. Hunt decided the thing must have been on that walkway, watching them. And since it could not make the leap, it had moved on.

Jad-bal-ja strolled over to Hunt, looked at him, swished his tail, and moved past. Hunt watched the lion for a moment, then the cat turned and looked at him with what Hunt knew was a look of perplexity. Jad-bal-ja growled, swished his tail, moved down the tunnel a few feet, stopped, turned, looked at Hunt.

"I get it," Hunt said. He started after the lion and the lion picked up its pace, and soon Hunt had to trot to keep up. But he did not mind. He could not help but feel that something inhuman and horrible was at his back.

Hunt shivered, wondered if this tunnel was a dead end or a way out. He wondered as well if the oil in the gutters would burn a long time. The idea of being trapped in darkness with that thing was not something he enjoyed pondering.

Both Jad-bal-ja and Hunt increased their pace.

Inside the great city of Ur was a smaller city and inside that city was the palace. Jean was led through the palace, and she could not understand why. It was as if her captor were giving her a tour of the opulence that was Ur's.

Inside there were great rooms lined with gold and silver and bright tapestries. She was led into a great chamber. The floor was covered in purple carpet, the vast windows with yellow curtains, and the stone throne was inlaid with diamonds and rubies; it sparkled in the light from the numerous candles lit and placed about the throne room. Chained to either side of the throne were two enormous, jet-black lions.

Jean had never seen anything like them. They were even bigger than Tarzan's lion. As they neared the lions, the beasts swished their tails, as if ready to spring. The woman pushed Jean toward the lions, then even as one of the cats shot out a paw full of claws, the woman jerked Jean back with a laugh.

Jean thought: this one, she certainly had a sense of humor. A real funny woman. So funny, I'd like to crack her skull. Jean smiled at the grinning woman, then with a quick movement she kicked at her tormentor's knee.

The woman lifted her leg slightly, turned her foot sideways, and blocked the attack with the sole of her sandal. Then she slid in with blinding speed and slapped Jean with the back of her hand, causing her to stumble.

Jean stood up slowly. Blood ran from her mouth. She wiped it away with the back of her hand. She realized now that taking this woman wasn't going to be as easy as she thought. No matter how mad she was, this one, she knew what she was doing. Jean realized something else as well. The woman had not only protected her from the man earlier because she wanted to expedite matters, it must have been because of his inability to deal with Jean's attack. The woman had been embarrassed for him. And Jean knew deep in her bones there was another reason. This woman was saving her for something dark and special.

Why else would she give her a tour of the palace? She had wanted Jean to see the luxury and know there were people living in comfort, excess. This made what was about to happen to her all the worse, and Jean was certain this was intentional.

But why had the woman chosen her over the others?

What was so special about herself? If special was the right

word. Why was this woman determined to make her life miserable?

Eventually, they went out of the palace proper, along a long cool corridor, down a flight of wide stone steps, and into a dank darkness lit only by foul-smelling torches arranged every eight feet or so in metal sheaths along the walls. There were a number of sweaty-looking men and women wandering about, all of them armed with whips and short swords. They eyed Jean as she came in, amazed at the whiteness of her skin. If this was, as Jean suspected, the city of Ur, it was unlikely many white skins had been seen in this city. But it was also obvious that any natives living nearby were fair game for these marauders.

Jean was led to a stone door, and a huge man in a sweaty loincloth came forward, pulled back a bolt, took hold of a heavy ring, and tugged it open. Foulness sprang from inside the room and landed on Jean. Her stomach twisted, and for a moment, the smell of human excrement, sweat, and misery was so strong she thought she might throw up.

The woman said something Jean couldn't understand, and the next moment the leash was being loosened from her throat, and she was shoved into the dungeon. The door slammed and the light went away and the darkness and stench gathered about her like a foul wool sock being pulled over her head.

Then Jean heard movement in the darkness. Something was scuttling toward her.

Cannon said, "Now, this time, we got to take another finger and palm another coal. How does that set with you?"

Billy was lying on his back, his hands and feet bound, his hands forced open and held wide by leather strips and deeply buried wooden pegs. Blood was running freely from his recently amputated little finger. He reflexively tried to push the smoldering coal out of the palm of his hand, but the way it was pegged and tied down, he could not. He succeeded only in flexing the muscles in his hand enough to roll the coal a little to the left where it found fresh flesh to burn.

Billy bit his lip to keep from giving them the pleasure of a scream.

When Wilson and Cannon had found Hanson and Billy, they had immediately set about quizzing them in their own inimitable style. They wanted to know where the rest of the safari had gone.

Hanson, knowing that once that information was revealed

they had about as much chance as a tick in a tar bucket, had said: "They went to find the treasure of the lost city of Ur."

At those words, the eyes of Wilson and Cannon had lit up, and Hanson knew he had a bargaining chip. Wilson and Cannon were decent trackers, but they weren't at the level of the Urs, and shortly after Hanson and Billy were captured, the renegades had bound them and set about trying to find the path the warriors had taken on their own, but could not. The Urs, through superior woodsmanship, had successfully concealed their trail. Had Hanson merely held back the direction the safari had taken, the two men might have bored with them, killed them, and gone about their business, guessing as to the whereabouts of the city. But now, thinking they were close on the trail of gold, they were adamant in their desire for directions. Specific directions.

So now Hanson and Billy were in the midst of being interrogated. Renegade-style. It wasn't an easy way to exist, but Hanson felt it would steal them some time.

"Look here," Wilson said, as he leaned over Billy. "This guy here, Cannon, he don't mind doing this all day. I don't care for it none. Ain't my way. Just tell us where they went."

Billy had caught on to Hanson's ploy and was doing his best to maintain. Already Hanson had lost a finger and had his hands burned, but he had not given up the information they wanted. The pain had been so intense, Hanson had passed out twice. Billy wished he could pass out, but something seemed to be holding him awake. He hurt something awful, why didn't he just pass out?

"I can make it quick," Wilson said. "Cut your throat. A bullet. It's all over, know what I mean? You don't tell us nothing, it's gonna turn out that way anyway, but after some time. Eight fingers and two thumbs later. Enough hot coals to burn to the bone. And there's other places we can cut and burn. I can make you a list."

"Thanks," Billy said. "But I do not need a list."

Wilson smiled. "You're a tough little monkey, aren't you?"

"Cannot say I feel all that tough," Billy said.

"Yeah, well, let me tell you this," Cannon said, slapping the dying coal from Billy's hand. "I got another coal here, and we're gonna put that in your other hand. Maybe against a bare foot, down your pants. You like that idea?"

"It does not appeal," Billy said. "No, sir."

"Listen here," Wilson said, "you and your boss, you ought to talk. We got some idea where we're going anyway, we just want to make the trip easier. We ain't got so much supplies that we need to be running off in all directions, see. For all we know they went up."

"No," Billy said, "they did not go up. That much I can help you with."

"I'll get another coal," Cannon said.

Cannon came back from the fire balancing a coal on the flat of his knife. He smiled at Billy, said, "Where's this one gonna go, my man?"

"We get what we want from you," Wilson said, "we find this place easier, we end all this business quick. You just die. You don't suffer and die, you just die."

"I don't think so," Hanson said.

"Hey, look who's stirrin'," Cannon said. "Maybe I ought to give him the coal."

"You spare us," Hanson said, "and we'll not only lead you in the direction they went, we'll take you to the city. I know where it is. Exactly."

"Yeah," Cannon said. "Then you tell us, and we'll go on without you."

"You go on without us," Hanson said, "you might find it, you might not. You do, it might be after you've used all your supplies. Run out of ammunition. I'm going to tell you how to get there, you're going to have to take me and Billy with you."

"I don't know," Cannon said. "I hate to waste a hot coal."

"All right," Wilson said. "We'll take them with us."

Cannon grinned. "We don't need to take them with us. They'll give us what we want, provided you let me do all the askin'."

"Time's a wastin'," Wilson said. "Besides, I don't have the stomach for this."

"You had enough stomach to tie that wild man to a tree."

Tarzan, thought Hanson. They're talking about Tarzan. Hanson had been hoping the ape-man would show up. Now he had to let go of that hope. Had to think of other alternatives.

"I didn't stick around to see it happen, though," Wilson said.

"So go off in the woods there," Cannon said. "I'll take care of this part."

"The wild man," Wilson said. "That was personal. That's why it was different, it was personal. This here is business. Let 'em go. We'll keep an eye on them. This way's easier."

"So you say," Cannon said. Disappointed, he let the hot coal roll off his knife and into the dirt.

Wilson stood up. "Cut them loose."

Cannon looked up at him. Wilson liked it like that. Him standing over Cannon, Cannon looking up. Making Wilson do his bidding was a step in the right direction. A step toward recovering control.

"Take us with you, Bwanas," Billy said. "You no need to carry your packs. We do it."

Cannon thought about that, smiled at Wilson. "All right, Wilson. I'm tired of totin' supplies. This time we do it your way."

Cannon used his knife to cut Billy's hands free. He said to Billy, "Think maybe you'd want that little finger I cut off? As a kind of souvenir?"

"No thanks," Billy said. "I would kind of like to keep the other fingers though. I have grown much attached to them."

"Hey, that's funny," Cannon said, cutting Billy's feet loose. "I like it when guys are funny. Gals don't do much for me when they're funny, but I like a funny guy."

Fifteen minutes later, their injured hands bound with rags, Hanson and Billy were forced to carry Wilson and Cannon's packs. It was a painful ordeal, considering their wounds, loss of blood, and exhaustion. But they had little choice. They gritted their teeth and proceeded. The two renegades walked behind them with their rifles, side by side, neither letting the other fall too far behind.

TARZAN
The Lost Adventure
XVI

Just before nightfall, Usha the wind gave Tarzan a gift.

Small did not notice it, of course, and it is unlikely that any man alive would have smelled what Tarzan smelled. The scent of many humans, some of them Hanson's bearers, and most important to Tarzan, the scent of the woman, Jean.

She had been taken far away from where he expected the safari to be, and there was no scent of Hanson or Billy. The scent of those she was with was different, tinged by smells unlike those of the bearers. Tarzan instantly concluded Jean had been taken from the safari by force.

Tarzan stopped and sniffed.

Small said, "What is it?"

Small sniffed too, but smelled nothing other than what he had been smelling. His own body odor.

"Come on," Small said. "What is it?"

"Jean."

"You've found them?"

"No. I have found her. And she's not nearby. The wind has

carried her smell to me, and it's an old scent. The wind is carrying her passing to me."

"Moved on. Passed on. You don't mean . . . dead . . . do you?"

"She was alive when the wind stole her smell, but it is a fading smell. She was in this area, two, three hours ago."

"Are you sure?"

"I am sure."

"How far away then?"

"A few miles to where the scent is originating."

"What about the others?"

"I do not know, but if Jean is no longer with him, it is possible they are dead."

Tarzan started to run through the jungle, and Small tried to keep up. Tarzan kept having to pause so as not to lose him. Exasperated, Tarzan stopped, waited for Small to catch up.

"Listen," Tarzan said. "I must hurry. I am going to leave you here, in this tree." Tarzan pointed to a large tree with many low branches. "You stay here and I will come back for you. If I am not here by nightfall, do not come down. I will come for you in the morning. If I do not come back, you are on your own. That is the way it is."

"I'd rather come along."

"I cannot wait. Do as you choose, but I have warned you."

With that, Tarzan raced off. Small followed him for a while, but the ape-man outdistanced him within moments. Small felt miserable, once again he was left alone in the jungle. He didn't know if he ought to be mad at Tarzan or grateful he was willing to help Jean.

He supposed he should be grateful. She was in more immediate danger than himself, but he had wanted to be there to help. Boy, wouldn't that be nice. He could show up in his socks, shoes, and underwear, bare-hand any problems, then fight his way out of the jungle, eating birds' eggs and grub worms all the way to the coast.

Small found a tree similar to the one Tarzan had pointed out, climbed high as he could, and looked out over the jungle.

Tarzan would realize later, when it was over, that Usha the wind had given him a gift, but it had betrayed him as well. The wind carried the scent of Jean, Hanson's bearers, and their captors' to Tarzan, but there were warriors from Ur behind him and their scent was being pushed away, not carried to him by the wind.

They were part of a small party ordered to roam the game trails. If fate was good to the Urs, the trails were traversed not only by game searching for the next meal or water hole, but by humans who could provide the city with slaves, gladiators, and sacrifices.

There were four of the warriors, and they had rambled the trails all day, taking in a wild pig and an antelope. They were excited as they returned to Ur. They had been part of the group of warriors who had helped capture Jean and Hanson's bearers. They knew that in the next day or two there would be great sport in the arena. Sacrifices to The Stick That Walks.

Just thinking of The Stick That Walks gave the men cold chills. They had seen it from time to time, when there was an appropriate sacrifice, but no matter how many times they saw it, the next time was as fascinating as the first.

The Stick That Walks was the Undying God of Ur.

The warriors were discussing this as they went along. They talked about the number of times they had seen the god, about how it moved, its strange postures. The warriors paused to demonstrate certain postures to one another. They put aside their kills, and playfully, imitating The Stick That Walks, clashed and hooked each other with their arms and wrists, kicked short snap kicks at one another's knees.

After a bit, they quit laughing and gathered up the animal carcasses and started walking faster. It was almost dark. They came to the edge of the jungle and into the clearing where the great road lay. They had a cart parked there, zebras hobbled out, eating grass. And as fate would have it, with the way the wind was blowing, the fact that they had grown silent and Tarzan was preoccupied with following the spoor of Jean and the warriors, he did not notice them at first.

Tarzan was by what remained of an old shed. The shed had been built as a shade for the warriors of Ur. A place where they might rest before returning to the city after a raid, or a hunting party, but the thatched covering to the shed had long since worn away, and now there were only the posts. Out in a natural meadow of wild grasses, Tarzan observed hobbled zebras eating grass. He could tell immediately by the way they ignored him that they were domesticated. He knew too, that this area must not attract many wild animals. Man's spoor was too strong here, even if animals like the zebras were easy pickings. That meant this road was well traveled by humans, and therefore Tarzan concluded there must be a large gathering of humans nearby. It stood to reason that would be the city the Hansons sought. Ur.

Tarzan saw something sticking out of the tall grass near where the zebras gazed. It was a stone fragment, and he went to examine it. It was part of what had once been a wall. At one point, perhaps the city of Ur extended all the way to this point. Or perhaps the city had been moved to a more convenient locale. Perhaps when a watering source dried up.

On the stone were strange hieroglyphics. At first glance Tarzan thought they represented men, but on closer examination he saw they showed some sort of stick-like creature in various postures. The postures were familiar to Tarzan. He had seen poses like them when he studied the Chinese fighting arts on the outskirts of Peking under the tutelage of a former Shaolin priest. They were not the exact moves Tarzan had learned, but the hieroglyphics certainly had more than a passing resemblance to the Seven Star Praying Mantis system. Tarzan found this baffling. There were a number of African fighting systems, so why would people in Africa adopt a Chinese system? Could the Chinese have brought their methods here to Africa in ancient times? Possible, but . . .

Well, now that he studied the stone closer, he realized the system was not quite Chinese. The moves were reminiscent of Chinese movements, but many of the stances did not appear possible for a human being to perform; the human anatomy did not function in that manner.

Tarzan marked the stone up as a mystery that perhaps he could investigate later. Just as he turned from the stone, one of the four warriors took Tarzan into his sights and fired an arrow. The arrow shot straight and true, traveling so fast it was inevitable that it would find its mark.

Or such would have been the case had Tarzan been any ordinary man, but in the moment the arrow was flung from its bow, the wind shifted, and on it rode the snap of the bowstring, and the scent of the warriors. Tarzan, his ears stuffed with the sound, his nostrils full of the smell of the warriors, turned. Even as the arrow sped to its mark, the ape-man, as if snatching a horsefly, seized the arrow in flight, whipped it about in his hand, and flung it with all his might back at the warrior who had fired it.

The warrior was not as quick as Tarzan. The arrow struck him in the right eye and came out the back of his head with such ferocity it sent a jagged chunk of skull flying before a stream of blood and grey matter.

The remaining warriors let out yells of surprise, fear, and anger. Clutching their spears, they charged Tarzan.

Tarzan turned sideways, went into a shallow crouch. As the first of his assailants reached him, the warrior leaped high into the air and tossed the spear. Tarzan dodged. The spear slammed deep into the earth beside the ape-man, and as the warrior landed on his feet and tried to draw his sword, Tarzan sprang forward, grabbed the back of the warrior's head with one hand, and slammed his other into the warrior's chin. The motion of jerking and striking broke the man's neck. The bone snapped like a pottery shard beneath a jackboot.

The two remaining warriors attacked simultaneously. They were fast, trained, and very good. But they were not as good as Tarzan. He moved to the outside, letting them run past him. He stuck out his foot and tripped one. The other raced past, perplexed. Where had the man gone? How could he move that fast? Nothing moved that fast.

Tarzan was suddenly behind the confused warrior. His arms locked around the man's throat, and by dropping to one knee, jerking, he snapped the man's neck and back as easily as an ordinary man might snap a pencil.

The warrior he had tripped was on his feet now, and even though he had not lost his spear, he broke off running. He ran toward the old shed. Tarzan picked up one of the warrior's spears, took a deep breath, and tossed the weapon.

It was a good toss, but Tarzan's target stumbled slightly, and was saved by luck. The spear soared just over his head and smote the ground in front of him. The warrior regained his footing, reached one of the upright shed posts just as Tarzan took hold of another spear.

The warrior peeked out from behind the post. Nearby, the zebras grazed. He thought if he could reach one of them he might escape bareback, using his heels to guide the animal.

He paused to consider his plan a moment more, and that was his undoing. Tarzan launched the spear. The warrior, looking around the post, saw the launch, and ducked back out of sight.

The spear struck the post with such impact it shook and split, and the blade passed through the post and the warrior. This was done as neat and clean as if the spear were a hot knife cutting through butter. The man's knees folded and he hung there against the post, supported by the blade of the spear.

Tarzan dragged the bodies out of sight, chose one of the warrior's spears, recovered the bow and arrows from his first assailant, and set about nabbing one of the zebras.

In short time this was done. Using his knees to guide the beast, clutching the mane which he had plaited for a makeshift bridle, Tarzan started off down the road toward Ur, and Jean.

From his perch in the tree, Small could see much of the countryside by the dying red light of the afternoon sun, but he could not see Tarzan. He heard something down below, but he doubted it was Tarzan. Too much noise. It sounded like a hippo coming through the jungle. Birds took to the sky in a flurry, and in the distance monkeys fled through the trees.

Small climbed higher and looked out. Now and then he glimpsed the author of the noise, but couldn't quite make it out. It was moving through the bush and he could see it now and then, but never quite clearly. Whatever it was, it was moving in his direction.

Moments later, he realized what it was. Men. Four of them. The two in front were side by side, the two in back were side by side. He watched carefully. Soon he recognized one of the men. His boss, Hanson. A moment later, he recognized the other two.

"Uh-oh," Small said softly.

Small watched with amazement as the four men came directly toward his tree. It was obvious that Hanson and the black man — probably one of Hanson's bearers — were captive.

Wilson and Cannon had rifles and they were walking with that overbearing manner he had noticed the moment they first stepped into his and Hunt's camp. Self-righteous anger surged through him.

Small concluded that if they kept on the path — and that was likely as everywhere else the jungle was thick with undergrowth — within a few minutes they would pass beneath his tree. He could remain calm, let them go, wait on Tarzan for aid, or he could do something now.

What if Tarzan didn't come back? And there was another thing. If he let these four pass on, and something happened to Tarzan, he wouldn't have any chance, not out here by himself without a gun and supplies. He would be better off to stop Wilson and Cannon, kill them even, toss his lot with Hanson and the other.

And maybe, Small thought, I can borrow some pants. There might be some clean clothes in one of the packs, and if not, well, one of the renegades could do without his.

But how could he take two armed men?

Small observed that neither Hanson nor the bearer were tied. Wilson and Cannon obviously felt their rifles were all that were needed to keep Hanson and the other in line.

But what if he surprised Wilson and Cannon? They wouldn't expect an attack from above. What if, for a moment, their guns were put out of commission? He felt certain that if this were so, if he could provide enough time, a distraction, Hanson and his partner would turn on Wilson and Cannon and help him dispose of them. That would make it three against two, odds in their favor. Add in the element of surprise . . . well, that was like a whole other person.

Four against one.

Small looked about, found a liana he could cling to. It was perfect. The path it would follow was perfect. All he had to do was swing on it. Wait until they were in the right spot, then swing.

Taking hold of the liana, freeing it from a limb, Small gave a tug. It felt firm, as if it could hold his weight.

He looked down at the four men.

Could he do it?

Sure, he told himself. Sure, I can.

But, man, what a drop that was. The vine didn't hold, he caught a limb . . . bad business.

And the renegades, they've got guns and they don't mind using them in the least.

Yeah, but they won't expect me, Small told himself. Surprise is on my side.

And if you're off just a little bit . . .

Don't think about it, Small told himself. Don't think at all. Just do it.

Small took a deep breath and waited.

One . . .

Two . . .

Three . . .

Three and a half . . .

Oh, goodness, Small thought. This will be something, me swinging out of the trees in my underwear. Why have I got to be in my drawers?

Four . . .

Six ought to do it. I count to six, I'm going.

Five . . .

Got to do this just right.

SIX!

Small clutched the vine, whispered a prayer, pushed off with his legs, and swung.

TARZAN
The Lost Adventure

XVII

Small realized too late that he had timed incorrectly, and that his vine would reach the ground well in front of Wilson and Cannon. In fact, he swung between Hanson and Billy and one of his legs struck Hanson and knocked him down. Small went twisting, causing him to lose his grip on the vine, and he hit the ground and started to roll.

His roll sent him hurtling up against Cannon's legs with enough force to knock him backwards. Cannon hit the ground and lost his grip on the rifle. Small scuttled on top of him and began to use his fist like a hammer, breaking Cannon's nose.

Wilson jumped forward, brought the stock of his rifle down on the back of Small's head, knocking him off of Cannon. Billy leaped on Wilson and knocked him backwards. They scuffled for the rifle.

Hanson scrambled to his feet, got hold of Cannon's rifle, wheeled, and yelled, "Stop it!"

Wilson quit struggling with Billy, but they both held on to the rifle.

"Give him the rifle," Hanson said to Wilson. "Give it to him, and no tricks."

Wilson reluctantly let Billy have the rifle.

"All right," Hanson said. "The worm has turned."

"Not completely," Cannon said.

Hanson wheeled to cover Cannon, and his heart sank. Cannon had scooped up the unconscious Small and was holding him under the chin with one hand, lifting his feet off the ground. With the other he had his knife against Small's throat. Blood ran from Cannon's broken nose and over his lips. His breath rattled out of his chest in locomotive blasts.

"I get any trouble," Cannon said, "I give this one another mouth."

Wilson grinned. "You might as well give up, Hanson," he said. "You two aren't up for it. You're hurt, and you haven't got the guts for it."

"We're not giving up anything," Hanson said. "Let him go, fat man."

"Not likely," Cannon said. "Wilson, you come over here."

Wilson got up confidently, started toward Cannon. Billy brought the stock of the captured rifle around quickly and caught Wilson hard enough in the forehead to knock him down again. Wilson raised up on one elbow and rubbed the goose egg that had already appeared on his forehead.

"You sonofabitch," Wilson said.

"Now, now," Billy said. "No use to talk bad. Lay down now so Billy not have to shoot hole in your head."

Wilson settled back, but his eyes blazed.

Small's eyes blinked open, then went wide when he realized the position he was in.

"Easy," said Cannon to Small, "get nervous, you're likely to get some kind of cut. Hear?"

"I hear," Small said.

"Let him go," Hanson said.

"I let him go, you shoot me," Cannon said.

"You don't, we're going to shoot you," Hanson said. "You let him go, we'll let you live. Tie you up, but let you live."

"I don't think so," Cannon said, and he pressed the knife tight against Small's throat. A necklace of blood appeared on Small's neck, ran onto his bare chest. "I might just cut him anyway. Just for the hell of it. I done had two guys in their underwear give me trouble. The first one, this wild man, Wilson and me, we done him in. This one, he's gonna die too."

"The ape-man is alive," Small said.

"Th' hell he is," Cannon said.

"I was with him earlier today. He is very much alive."

"That cinches it then," Cannon said. "I ain't gonna wait around for him to show up."

With a quick jerk of his wrist, Cannon cut Small's throat, bolted off the trail and into the thickness of the jungle.

Small collapsed as if he were a marionette being gently lowered on strings. He fell to his knees, then backwards, his legs tucked under him as if he were about to be folded and placed in a trunk.

"Small!" Hanson yelled.

Billy fired after Cannon, two quick shots, but the shots were wild and the man darted deeper into the underbrush and out of sight.

Hanson rushed over to Small, dropped the rifle, and tried to hold the cut on Small's throat together with his hands. It was useless. It was too deep. The blood gushed through Hanson's fingers like milk through a sieve.

Small tried to talk, but his voice only gurgled. Hanson lowered his ear to Small's mouth so that he might hear. He thought what he heard Small say was: "Not in my drawers."

Small's body went limp. Hanson lowered him to the ground, gently. Hanson glared at Wilson. He picked up the rifle and pointed it at him. Sweat was popping off Hanson's forehead and his teeth were clenched. He could hardly get the words out. "One word. Just one. And I fertilize the dirt with your brains."

Wilson glared, but held his tongue. He had his eyes on Hanson's trigger finger. It was vibrating.

Billy said, "Watch him, Bwana. I get the other one." Billy went into the jungle after Cannon.

Night dipped down full and complete. The moon rose up like a shiny balloon. Hanson sat beside the body of Small, his rifle pointed at Wilson.

Out in the jungle, in the dark, Billy stalked Cannon.

Earlier, when Jean first heard the movement in the dungeon, without really thinking, she said, "Who's there?"

There was a long moment of silence, then came, "Nyama. I am Nyama and soon I die."

Jean squinted into the darkness. Her eyes were adjusting, and she could see the shape of the speaker. A woman.

"You speak English," Jean said.

"Missionaries," Nyama said. "I can read too. And quote Bible verses. You like to hear them?"

"Not just now," Jean said. "Maybe you can teach them to me later . . . how did you get here? What missionaries? Missionaries to this city?"

"No," Nyama said. "Of course not. I am from the high forest land. One day these people of Ur raided us and I was one of those they stole away. I do not know if any of the others of my people who were brought here are still alive. I think not."

"How long have you been here?"

"I do not know. Long time in the city of Ur. But here, in this place. Not long. Since Kurvandi tired of me."

"Kurvandi?"

"He is the King of Ur. One in a long line of Kurvandis. I was brought here to be one of his wives, and he forced me . . . I made him miserable. Finally, he had me brought here. Soon, I die. But, I had it to do again, I would still make him miserable. I prefer this to his bed chambers. I do not like to be treated like a breeding cow. You are lucky he did not like your looks."

"I don't know if that makes me feel insulted or happy."

"Let me have a look at you," Nyama said.

"That won't be easy in the dark," Jean said.

"I am accustomed to darkness. But here, come."

The woman took Jean by the elbow, led her toward the closed door.

Around the edges of the door a bit of light seeped in, and Jean could feel fresh air from the outside. The air was not sweet, but it certainly smelled better than the air in the cell. The light and air heartened her a little.

"You are quite pretty," said Nyama, her face close to Jean's.

"And so are you," Jean said. It was an honest evaluation. Nyama was indeed quite beautiful.

"I am surprised he did not want you for one of his women," Nyama said. "Perhaps it's because he views pale skin as inferior."

"Why does he want to have me killed?" Jean said. "I didn't come here of my own free will. I've done nothing to the people of Ur. True, I would have come here anyway . . . but why must they kill me?

Kill us?"

"He has his reasons," Nyama said. "But without reasons, he would kill us anyway. He eventually kills everything. He is mad. They are all mad. Full of the glory of their great city and their gods . . . one thing, though. Their god, unlike missionary god, you can see. I have seen it. It is mad like Kurvandi. A horrible god."

"You have seen their god?"

"Yes."

"Is it a statue . . . an oracle?"

Nyama sighed. This was followed by a long silence. Finally, "No. I do not believe any of that. Statues are statues, and oracles are old men and women with their fingers in bird guts. I believe what I see. And I have seen this god."

"A moving, breathing god?"

"Do not patronize me," Nyama said. "That is the word, is it not? Patronize?"

"I'm sorry," Jean said. "I didn't mean to . . . "

"Yes, you did."

"But a moving, breathing god?"

"Missionaries believed in a god I could not see. Wanted me to believe in it. I could not. But Urs, they believe in god you can see. I have seen it. Makes more sense, a god you can see. But still, god or not a god. I do not care for it. It is a god of death and destruction. Very ill-tempered."

"Are you saying it's to this god we will be sacrificed?"

"In one way or another. They kill in honor of the god and his moves, and they give the god offerings that it kills for itself."

"You said in honor of its moves. What does that mean?"

"It moves in all manner of ways," Nyama said. "Every way it moves, the move brings death. It has a dance of death, and when it dances, people die. Very bad deaths. Very bad. Those that are not given to the god, they are sacrificed in his name."

Jean and Nyama moved away from the light and to a stone bench. The smell was not so bad in this corner, and Jean found she needed to sit. She was exhausted. Grief and fear made her exhaustion even more complete.

Jean and Nyama sat beside one another and talked. Nyama's English was very good, and soon Jean had some idea what Ur was all about.

It seemed the Urs were a people descended from a great and

glorious culture. Ur had been a great city before Solomon was king. It was a city of wealth and riches, and once all of Africa had been under its rule.

But the royalty of Ur, unwilling to contaminate their blood with that of outsiders, gradually restricted "foreigners," and in time, to keep the blood pure, royalty married royalty. Over generations, this practice resulted in genetic deficiencies. Insanity.

In the last few years, even though the King was mad, he realized that for the line to continue, for Ur to regain its glory, he must reach outside of his kingdom, bring in slaves, women for his harem. Women who could bear him children. In this way, he hoped to freshen the blood of his line.

And there was another reason — the god Ebopa, The Stick That Walks. Legend said that Ebopa had come up from the center of the earth through catacombs beneath the city and that the Urs trapped him there for all time. It was the Urs' belief that as long as Ebopa could not return to the center of the earth, his powers would bring the city great fortune. Several times a year, for more years than Nyama knew, there had been sacrifices to the god. And for a time, all had been good.

But in the last thirty years, crops had not yielded as well as before. Game was not as plentiful. Many children were born with defects. Great metal birds were seen flying overhead more and more often. The Urs had seen them now and then over the years, buzzing along, supported on their silver wings, but now there were more and more of them. Bigger birds. Flying higher, leaving trails of smoke. Jean decided Nyama meant planes, but the Urs did not understand this. They thought they were winged messengers from the god Ebopa, and Ebopa's message was not a merry one. He was angry.

Therefore, it was decided Ebopa was mad and must have more glory. There were more sacrifices to the god, both direct and indirect. Like the Romans with their bread and circuses, this became standard. And each new Kurvandi had to search more diligently for sacrifices. Jean, Nyama, the safari bearers, the people Jean had seen in the line for beheading, were the most recent.

It was not a question Jean wanted to ask, but she could not help herself. "How are we to die?"

"It could be many ways. One way is beheading, but if they planned to do that, they would have already. That is the common way. Since we have been placed here, I believe we are being saved. We may be prepared for the crocodiles."

"They feed prisoners to crocodiles?"

"Yes. The crocodiles that live in the water around the city. But that is not bad enough. No. They very carefully prepare the sacrifices. They hold them down and take a big war club, and slowly, they break the bones in the arms and legs. Break them up small."

"Oh, God," Jean said. "How horrible."

"That is only the beginning. They are doing that to prepare the meat."

"For the crocodiles!"

"The crocodiles are white, and therefore sacred. They must have prepared meat. Easy to chew. To prepare it, the meat is tenderized by breaking the bones. Then, they bury the sacrifices in a pool of mud and water to the chin. But they do not let the sacrifices die. They leave them until the water softens the flesh. When the sacrifices are near death, they pull them out and tie ropes to their feet, lower them off the drawbridge, just above the water. When the sacred crocodiles come, they drop the sacrifices into the water."

"And they will do this to us?" Jean said.

"Unless Kurvandi is saving us for something special."

"I presume the harem is out at this point?" Jean said.

"To be one of Kurvandi's wives is a fate worse than death," Nyama said.

"I'd prefer to be the judge of that," Jean said. "This harem business is beginning to have an unexpected appeal."

"If it is not the crocodiles," Nyama said, "then it will be the arena, or . . . Ebopa. At least, if it is Ebopa, it is quick."

"Thank Ebopa for small favors," Jean said.

Hunt came to a fork in the tunnel. The tunnel they were traveling ran up against a cavern wall. There were unused torches jutting out of sockets drilled in the rock, and all along the wall were paintings. They were recent paintings of the thing Hunt had seen earlier.

Jad-bal-ja growled softly.

"I know," Hunt said. "I'm nervous too."

Hunt moved toward the tunnel on the left. He stared into the darkness. He went back to the decorated wall and took down a torch and dipped it into one of the blazing gutters and waved it first at the tunnel on the right, then the left.

"Which way?" he said to the lion.

Jad-bal-ja turned his head from side to side.

Hunt said, "Yeah, me too."

Hunt used the torch to poke into the left tunnel. He checked first to see if this tunnel was outfitted with gutters of oil. It was not. The tunnel was wide and Hunt could see that after few afeet there was a drop-off. But there was also some kind of wooden framework lying at the edge of the chasm. Hunt moved forward, and Jad-bal-ja, growling softly, followed.

"Yeah, me too," Hunt said in response to Jad-bal-ja's growl.

Hunt held the torch so that he could examine the wooden framework. He recognized what it was immediately. A pile of narrow sections for a bridge. It was made of a light wood and appeared newly fashioned.

Near the edge of the drop-off there were notches in the dirt. Hunt concluded the supports of the bridge were supposed to fit into it. He held his torch high. The light was not good, but across the way, some forty feet, he could see where the bridge was supposed to fit into two deep grooves.

Examining the bridge closer, Hunt saw the bridge sections were hooked together and that they folded out into one long section with sleeves that fit over the crude hinges and made the bridge solid. He found a place in the rocks to lodge the torch, and working by its light he began to fold out the bridge and slide the sleeves over the pegged hinges. Soon he had a single length of bridge just over forty feet long.

When he was finished, he doubted his ability to pick up the bridge, extend it over the gap, but he soon discovered two long poles. They were over fifty feet long, and if you stuck the tips of these into the far ends of the bridge where leather loops were provided, it was easy to lift the back end of the bridge, and by standing all the way at its front, it could be boosted across and lowered into the slots provided. The slots on this side of the chasm were even easier to fit.

"There," Hunt said. "Damn clever of whoever, don't you think, lion?"

Jad-bal-ja purred. He had watched all of this carefully. He did not know what to make of the ways of men, but of one thing he was certain. Jad-bal-ja did not like where the bridge led.

"I don't know anything to do but cross," Hunt said, talking to the lion as if he were a favored companion. "This doesn't work, we try the other tunnel."

Hunt took a deep breath and stepped onto the thatched flooring of the bridge. It vibrated slightly.

"Don't care for that," Hunt said, but he kept going. When he was halfway across, Jad-bal-ja followed, treading as lightly as a house cat.

When they reached the other side of the bridge, a cool wind drafted through the cavern, and with it came a stench, followed by a sound. The same frightening sound Hunt had heard earlier. Once again, he felt a nameless dread that crawled about in his brain like a clutch of spiders.

Jad-bal-ja growled softly.

"I know," Hunt said. For a moment, Hunt considered traveling back across the bridge, pulling it up so that whatever was down here couldn't cross. Hunt determined that was what this bridge business was all about anyway. There was something trapped down here by design, and that something was most unpleasant.

The sound died away. Perhaps, it — whatever it was — was not yet aware of them. Hunt took some comfort in the possibility. With torch and spear held tight, he chose a direction away from the sound, and he and Jad-bal-ja went that way, ever alert to whatever might lurk at their backs.

Tarzan, astride the zebra, came to the rock quarry shortly after nightfall. The jungle broke open wide, like a rift in the universe, and gave way to the great quarry. The moon rode over the quarry, full and bright, so massive as to look like a bronze shield frozen to the sky.

The quarry was nothing more than building stone, but there in the moonlight the stones had turned a golden color, and in that instant it was as if the earth had given up all its riches by means of an open wound.

Tarzan rode past the quarry, and in time came within sight of the great city of Ur. Tarzan reined in the zebra and marveled at the city. It was like a fairy world, there in the moonlight. Tall and wide and golden. It lay at the end of this great road like the Emerald City of Oz.

There was a time when the African landscape was riddled with such wonders, but now the ways of the ancients, the jungle magic, was slowly dying. Sometimes, Tarzan felt the world he knew was sneaking away, like an old man grown weak, hoping to find a place to lie down and die.

Tarzan decided he was close enough to the city by road. He wanted to make his entry into Ur to find Jean, unobserved and as silently as possible. He dismounted, led the zebra into the jungle, and without hesitation, pulled his knife and cut its throat. The zebra fell, kicked, the blood pumped. Tarzan placed his face over the geyser of blood, let it spurt into his mouth. The warm liquid energy revived him. He cut a chunk of meat off the zebra's haunch and ate it raw. He skinned the zebra in record time, and plaited the wet skin into a serviceable rope about ten feet long. He tied the rope to a tree, took hold of it, and pulled until he had wrung most of the blood out of the plaiting, then he coiled the rope and hung it over the hilt of his knife and began moving through the jungle. He took to the trees, swinging from branch to branch, vine to vine, more by instinct and feel than by sight.

When he reached the edge of the jungle, he paused in the branches of a tree and studied Ur. There was a great moat around the city, and the drawbridge was up. There were sentinels at the summit of the wall. He could see their spears flashing in the moonlight as they went about their rounds.

Tarzan determined that most likely there would be a few warriors hidden somewhere on the outskirts of the city, stationed to report any incoming danger. Tarzan also determined that they would be lax in their duties.

That was human nature. Ur, except for the natives in the general area, was relatively unknown. Or was until Hanson and his safari decided to track it down. Ur was also a mighty power, and they would feel there was little to fear from any enemy that might know of its existence. And they would not expect one man to pass its sentries, its moat, scale its wall, and enter.

Tarzan felt a moment of anger. It was directed at himself. He should never have suggested that it was okay for the Hansons to continue on their hunt for Ur. He knew, deep down, he had allowed it for his own personal reasons.

He wanted adventure. He had wanted a wild baptism to wash the stench of civilization from his heart and soul. He thought briefly of Jane, his wife, back in England. Comfortable there. He thought of things they had said to one another. He thought of the vast, lost world at the earth's core, perhaps his next refuge. But would Jane come? It was not like the old days. Time changes everything. Time changes people. He and Jane had changed, no matter how hard he tried to deny it.

But he would not think of such things. These were the things of civilization. To survive in the jungle one had to put thoughts of yesterday and tomorrow out of one's mind, had to put aside sentimentality. Here, there was no place for that kind of thinking.

Survival. That was the only thought he should think. That and rescuing Jean, helping Hanson's safari. Hunt and Small. It would be like the old days.

Or should be, but Tarzan was less than pleased with his performance. It was not all his fault, he knew, but he did not like things to happen to those he had sworn to help and protect. It made him feel inept. It made him feel like other humans.

He felt other sensations as well. Twin sensations.

Anger.

And revenge.

The two burned in Tarzan's breast like the eyes of the devil. Burned so furiously, it was a full moment before the blood haze passed from his mind and he became collected.

Anger and revenge, he had been taught by civilized humans that they were the two basest of instincts, but for now they were his friends. They were the fire in his heart and soul, the fuel for what he must do.

Tarzan dropped from the tree, then to his belly. He crawled out of the line of the jungle and into the high grass, crawled slowly like a stalking lion, toward the city of Ur.

The sentinel post was a small shack of poles with a mud and reed roof. The walls were mostly open so that the two sentinels who occupied it could see in all directions. One guard was supposed to walk a path from the hut to the moat and back again. Then the other guard would take his place. They would rotate time after time.

There were other sentinel huts along the banks of the moat, built into the tall dry grass that looked white in the moonlight. The huts were three hundred feet apart, stationed all the way around the city. In case of attack, or danger, the sentries were supposed to signal to one another by horn. They were the first line of defense.

No one had signaled anyone in a long time. For that matter, the sentries seldom walked from the hut to the moat. In the daylight, when they might be seen, or the king might hear of it, they walked then. But at night they did not. They sat in the hut and played games of chance. Games with clay dice and flat clay cards with dots painted on them.

Tonight in one hut, Gerooma and his partner Meredonleni were playing a game of chance that involved both cards and small black stones. They had played the game for only a few minutes when Gerooma, who was losing, decided he was bored.

"You are not bored," Meredonleni said. "You are mad that you are losing. You already owe me much."

"I am bored," Gerooma said. "Every night. The same thing. Gambling."

"That is right. I like gambling."

"Well, I do not."

"When you are losing you do not," Meredonleni said, then snorted.

"Do not do that," Gerooma said.

"What?"

"That noise. That snorting. I hate it when you do that."

"What is the matter with a snort?"

"It is a kind of laugh."

"No, it is not."

"Yes, it is. You're being derisive. You are pretending that I'm inferior to you for not playing. That I hate to lose."

"You do hate to lose."

"I do not like being laughed at."

"It is not a laugh. It is a snort."

"I will not discuss it further."

Gerooma picked up his pipe of clay and reed and walked outside the hut and down the trail toward the moat. He stopped after a few feet and put the pipe in his mouth and took a dried herb from his pouch and packed the pipe. He removed his flints from his pouch and squatted and knocked a spark into the dry grass. The grass flamed, Gerooma pulled up a blazing strand, and put the blaze to his pipe.

"You keep doing that, you will set the whole grassland afire."

Gerooma turned and looked at Meredonleni. "I know better than that. I wouldn't let that happen."

"A wind comes up, it matters not what you would not let

happen. The wind will carry the fire and you and I will be beheaded for causing it. I will die because you are stupid and careless and I have done nothing."

"Go gamble with yourself," Gerooma said, puffing on his pipe.

"You are not even carrying your spear," Meredonleni said.

"Since when do you care?"

"I have mine. I have it now."

Gerooma glanced back at Meredonlini, puffed his pipe. The blaze in the bowl of the pipe was as red as a cherry.

"It does not surprise me you have your spear, frightened as you always are," Gerooma said.

"Some of us have a sense of duty."

"How would your sense of duty be if I chose to gamble? Would you carry your spear then?"

"I would not gamble with you at all. Not at all."

Gerooma copied the snorting sound Meredonlini had made earlier, then turned his back.

Meredonleni fumed. He faced the jungle, trying to think of something to say. Gerooma was beginning to tire him. He must talk to the chief of sentries. He must find another man to be in his hut. He must . . .

Meredonleni narrowed his eyes. He thought he had seen something move in the tall grasses. He stepped forward, cocked his spear. A cool wind stirred up and moved the grasses and shook the leaves and limbs of the trees in the jungle.

Meredonleni thought he saw it again.

Something white and sleek, low down to the ground, moving through the waving grass.

A white panther?

There were white crocodiles, so why not white panthers?

He saw it again.

"Gerooma!"

Gerooma turned and looked in Meredonleni's direction. Meredonleni was facing the opposite direction, his spear cocked. Gerooma said, "What?"

"There's something out there."

"Oh, Meredonleni. You cannot stand to be bested. So now you say there is something out there."

"There is."

"Is it an army, crawling through the grass on their bellies?"

Meredonleni did not answer. There was only a hissing sound. Meredonleni took one step backwards, and froze.

In the moonlight, Gerooma saw Meredonleni's bare back give birth to a dark rose shape. Gerooma could not figure it at first, and then Meredonleni swiveled slowly, turned towards him. A long arrow vibrated in his chest. His face had a look of profound disappointment. The moonlight struck his teeth and made the blood on them shine like rich berry juice.

Gerooma's pipe fell from his mouth. He started to run toward Meredonlini, but he had taken but one step when the air whistled again and an arrow caught him in his slightly open mouth and punched out the back of his neck.

He kept running forward, his teeth clenched around the arrow. He ran until he reached the hut. Then he stumbled. He grabbed at a post, held himself upright. He lifted his head, took hold of the arrow in his mouth, tried to pull it loose, but it hurt severely. When he tugged, he felt as if his whole head would come off.

Striding toward him in the moonlight was a giant of a man. The moonlight made his bronze skin look white. He had a bow in one hand, a spear in the other. A quiver of arrows hung on his back. He wore a knife at his waist and a crude rope was draped over its hilt. The man was walking purposely toward him. He was neither slow nor fast. Just determined. Gerooma knew then, this man was what Meredonleni had seen moving through the grass.

Gerooma tried to say something, to plead for his life. But Tarzan did not understand his language, and besides, the arrow made it impossible for Gerooma to speak clearly.

Besides, it wouldn't have mattered.

Gerooma slid down the pole, his mouth filling with blood. He lifted his head as Tarzan took hold of his hair. The ape-man had dropped the spear and drawn his knife. With one quick motion of the blade he cut Gerooma's throat.

Finished with this task, Tarzan saw that the grass was starting to blaze, due to Gerooma's dropped pipe. He put his foot on the pipe and crushed it. The calluses on his bare foot were so hard he did not even feel the heat. He could have walked across broken glass on those feet.

Next he stepped on the blaze the pipe had started, then he

looked in all directions. He sniffed the air. Listened. It was his conclusion that he had killed both men almost soundlessly.

So far, so good.

Tarzan moved at a crouch through the grasses, onward to the moat.

When he reached the moat, he squatted on his haunches in the high grass, parted it with his hands and looked at the water. It was foul water, he could smell that, but in the moonlight it looked like a silver-paved street.

Tarzan studied the width of the moat, examined the city wall. It was made up of all manner of debris, and was actually quite easy to climb. Not for an ordinary man, but Tarzan knew that for him it would be effortless.

He decided to leave his spear, bow, and arrows. He would carry his knife and rope. He coiled the rope around his waist, crawled on his belly to the moat, and slid into the water, silent as a python.

He had not swum far when he felt movement in the water. He turned his head. Gliding toward him, long and white and deadly in the moonlight, was the largest crocodile he had ever seen.

The croc began swimming faster and Tarzan thought at first he might try to outswim it. But he could see yet another white croc in front of him. Like his cousin, he had also noticed Tarzan.

The first crocodile snapped at Tarzan, but the ape-man was no longer there. He dove beneath the water and came up under the crocodile's belly and cut a vicious gash in it with his knife.

The crocodile practically leaped from the water, came down with a tremendous splash. It twisted toward Tarzan, and Tarzan pushed his palm against the side of the raging crocodile's head, got out of the way. Tarzan went beneath the reptile again, and used the knife again on the soft underbelly.

The crocodile's stomach and intestines exploded from the wound. The water went thick with blood. The other croc arrived on the scene. Driven wild by the smell of intestines and blood, the crocodile began attacking its wounded cousin with a blind ferocity.

Tarzan swam down and out toward the city. When he came up, he was against the wall. He could hear shouting above him. He pushed himself tight against the stones. The natives were speaking a tongue he could not understand, but he realized quickly from their tone, they were talking about the crocodiles, not him. He had managed to escape before being noticed. Perhaps they were placing bets on which beast would win.

Tarzan watched the water boil. The two crocodiles were locked in a vicious struggle. The wounded crocodile was rapidly losing ground. They rolled and twisted and splashed. The water foamed with blood.

Tarzan watched as the eyes of other crocodiles bobbed out of the water. Two. Three. A half dozen. The crocodiles were swimming toward the fighters, ready to take their share of the loser.

Tarzan returned his knife to its sheath, very carefully took hold of a stone, and, pulling himself from the water, began scaling the wall.

Tarzan's strong fingers held the stones where there was very little to grab. Even an ape would have had trouble scaling the stones, but Tarzan moved up the wall like a lizard.

When he was near its summit, he listened carefully, then slipped over the top of the wall and landed in a crouch on the sentry walkway. He looked to his right.

A sentry was moving away from him.

To his left, two sentries were talking. The shadows were thick here, and Tarzan went unnoticed.

Tarzan dropped from the walkway to the ground. It was a long drop, but his splendid muscles and great skill would have allowed him to take the fall without injury. But, at that moment, an off-duty sentry had stopped to relieve himself against the city wall, and as he finished and stepped from beneath the concealment of the overhead walkway, Tarzan dropped directly onto him.

When Tarzan struck him, the man yelled. Tarzan growled with anger as he sprang to his feet. The sentry clamored to his feet and began to scream for help. He looked at the bronze giant before him, and screamed even louder. The big man looked more like an animal than a man, his teeth were barred and the sounds coming from his throat did not sound as if they were of human origin.

The sentry's screams were cut short as Tarzan sprang, his knife stealing the sentry's voice.

But it was too late.

Tarzan looked up. Sentries had rushed to the edge of the walkway. They yelled at him and began casting spears and firing arrows. Tarzan slapped one of the spears away, dodged an arrow. Others rattled at his feet.

The courtyard filled with warriors. They charged him. Tarzan struck right and left with his knife. Dying men and women fell back from Tarzan's brutal onslaught.

Close as the warriors were to one another, arrows were out of the question, so they charged the ape-man *en masse*, armed with their blades and spears.

The sounds of Tarzan's knife glancing off spear points and sword blades filled the air. The warriors foamed over him like ants on a carcass. The first to arrive were the first to die. Tarzan's knife wove a web of steel so intricate and fast, that there in the moonlight it looked as if he were a six-armed god wielding a weapon in every hand.

They tried to leap on him all at once, but the entire crowd was pushed back. Tarzan came clear of them snarling like a wild beast, the remains of some unfortunate's throat clutched in his teeth. Tarzan spat out the warrior's flesh, raised his head, and bellowed, "Kreeegah! Tarzan kill!"

The warriors foamed over him again, and once again the ape-man threw them back, flicking them from him the way a dog might shake water from its fur.

But now more warriors were arriving, scores of them, and even Tarzan with all his skill and might could not hold them. They rose over him like a great storm wave, washed him to the ground beneath a rain of fists and feet and weapons.

TARZAN
The Lost Adventure

XVIII

Underground, unaware of Tarzan's plight, or that of his comrades, Hunt and Jad-bal-ja proceeded. Hunt noticed there were large, rotting timbers throughout the cavern. Many of the timbers had crumbled down, and others were in the process. It appeared that at one point, whoever had used these caverns had abandoned them to whatever it was that lived down here. The bridge they had used to cross the chasm showed that the area was still visited periodically, but it appeared repairs were no longer maintained.

The reasons for these repairs seemed to be the gradual weakening of the cavern itself. The centuries had worn it down, and whoever was custodian of these caves had attempted to keep it in shape with the timbers, reinforcing it like a mine shaft. As this mission was abandoned, the timbers had begun to rot. In time, Hunt concluded, this entire cavern would fall in on itself.

The torch was still burning briskly, but Hunt knew that shortly, it would be exhausted. He knew too, as Jad-bal-ja knew long before him, that the thing down here was stalking them now, almost playfully. Hunt could smell it. It had an odor. A strange odor. Like something dry and ancient. From time to time Hunt thought he could hear more than its footsteps, a kind of rattling and rustling of parchment skin, but ultimately it was an unidentifiable noise that reached down into some forgotten part of his brain and fired an alarm. Hell was coming.

Even the great lion that padded beside him had taken to looking over its tawny shoulder, watching for the appearance of something unnamable. Hunt and Jad-bal-ja turned as the tunnel turned, and shortly thereafter, came to a dead end. Hunt felt a tightening in his chest. It was not bad enough that he was being stalked by an unnamable thing, but now there was nowhere to run. He and Jad-bal-ja were trapped.

Going back the way they had come was useless. The thing would be blocking their path. It had known it was driving them into this corner, and now Hunt could hear that rattling and rustling sound louder than before. In fact, the only thing louder than the noise it was creating was the pounding of his heart.

The tunnel filled with the creature's foul smell, and Jad-bal-ja crouched, twitching his tail, not anxious, but ready to do battle when the moment arose.

Hunt moved the torch around the tunnel, lifted it upwards. Above them there was a split in the rocks. It wasn't a great split, but it was enough that if they could manage their way up there, they could slide through.

Hunt stuck the torch between two rocks, put the spear partially through his belt, and tried to find hand- and footholds. This was relatively easy. A large number of rocky slabs jutted out from the tunnel wall. Hunt began to climb. He moved swiftly. When he reached the summit of the tunnel wall, he turned and looked toward the hole, which from this angle he could see led into a narrow tunnel. It was a slightly precarious jump, but it was not a leap of great distance.

Hunt held his breath and jumped, caught hold of the interior of the tunnel, and pulled himself inside. He looked down. Jad-bal-ja had not moved. Hunt was unsure if the lion would understand him, but he knew he had to speak to him, try something. "Come."

The lion lifted his head and looked at Hunt above him. The lion studied Hunt for a moment, then the wall. He bounded up the slabs of rock, and as Hunt moved aside, the lion leaped easily into the open shaft.

A heartbeat later, the torch began to flicker, and something moved into the tunnel below. Its shadow creeped against the cavern wall. Hunt's pounding heart pumped furiously, knocking his temples like bongos. He could not see it clearly, there in the shadow of the dying and flickering torch, but what he saw of it unsettled him to the bone.

Actually, the flickering of the dying torch gave the creature an even odder appearance, as if its image had been painted on cards in various positions, and an unseen hand was flicking the cards, giving the beast the illusion of movement. It had to be an illusion.

Because nothing Hunt had ever seen moved like that.

An instant later, Hunt decided its movements were not like flipping cards after all, but like old film, only faster. The thing clicked and clattered like an electrified poodle on a tile floor, but it gave the appearance of having been constructed of sticks glued to a single, larger shaft. Sticks that substituted for arms and legs. Sticks wrapped in mummified leather, with knots where muscles should have been. A stick thing with great mantis-like hooks on its "hands" and a head that resembled a great rotting pumpkin full of very nasty, twisted teeth constructed not of bone, but some kind of dark chitinous material like an insect's skeletal structure.

There were no doubts in Hunt's mind that this was what he had seen depicted in the cave drawings. But the drawings, which made it appear like a rabid praying mantis, did not do it horrid justice.

This was a thing from the pits. It moved its body as if it were not subject to the natural laws of musculature — animal or insect. It rotated its head completely around. It stalked about the dead-end corridor like a spoiled child that had misplaced a toy.

It looked up and saw Hunt and Jad-bal-ja looking down. And the thing smiled. If a blackened pumpkin full of gnarled, chitinous teeth can be said to smile. The torch flickered over the smile and gave the teeth a reddish glint.

Then the torch went out.

The sun rose pink against a startling blue sky, and the day grew hot early. All night Hanson had sat by the body of Small, his rifle pointed at the bound Wilson. Neither he nor Wilson had spoken or slept. Wilson was not in a position to do much of anything, bound the way Hanson had bound him, and Hanson was in such a black, raging fever it was all he could do not to empty the rifle into the man, even though Wilson lay in a helpless position.

During the night, Hanson had listened for Billy's return, or the stealthy reappearance of Cannon. To prepare for such, he had built a small fire in the middle of the trail and surrounded it with dirt so that it would not spread, then he had dragged Small's body and Wilson into the jungle, and there they had sat. Hanson, hot with revenge, throbbing with pain from his wounds, alert to the return of Small or an assault by Cannon, had positioned himself in such a way he could see the fire, and if Cannon were to return with murderous designs, drawn by the light of the campfire, Hanson hoped to get the man in his sights and kill him. It was all he could think about. Cannon and Wilson were responsible for so much misery, they deserved to die.

Jean was lost, now Billy was out in the jungle searching for Cannon — possibly dead by Cannon's hand — and Cannon had slain Small. Wilson and Cannon, they had initiated all that had gone wrong.

Small. God bless him. Without his intervention, he and Billy would still be hostage. Dead perhaps. Cannon was certainly inclined to murder, and Wilson was only marginally better.

This marginalia was all that kept Hanson from putting a bullet in Wilson's heart and telling God he died.

So the night had crawled on, and out in the darkness, from time to time, Hanson heard movement, a few rifle shots. Even though Billy had the rifle, Hanson feared for him. He watched for Cannon to return, but Cannon did not appear. Once a leopard had come very near them. Hanson could see its yellow eyes glowing in the dark like demon lamps. The eyes had observed them for a long time, and Hanson was so unnerved by their steady gaze, he considered putting a bullet between them, but could not bring himself to kill the animal, not if that was its greatest threat — the demon-yellow stare. He could more easily have killed Cannon and Wilson than an animal he did not intend to eat.

All night Hanson feared sleep would creep up on him and lay him down, but it was a useless worry. He was so charged with fear and hatred and disappointment he did not feel sleepy at all.

He thought of Jean often. He had little hope she was alive. If she had been captured, not killed right away, then her captors had a purpose for her, and Hanson found to his dismay that he could imagine a multitude of purposes, none of them comforting.

He should never have let her come. It was his fault. All of this.

Small's death. Hunt's probable death. The bearers, dead by storm, or captured. Billy out there in the jungle, perhaps dead by Cannon's hand.

And Tarzan. Small said that Tarzan was alive, but perhaps he had said that to unnerve Cannon. To make him think things had not entirely gone his way.

It had been a mistake. Tarzan, dead or alive, was a sore spot with Cannon, and the possibility that he might be alive had driven Cannon to rage. A rage that resulted in Small having his throat cut.

Thinking about it now, Hanson's finger sweated on the trigger of the rifle. He wanted Wilson to pay. He wanted Cannon to pay. And Wilson, well, he was here now. It would be so easy. One small squeeze. One shot. And it was all over. The man was out of the gene pool.

It was tempting.

Hanson looked at poor Small. The early morning light was growing and he could see the savage wound in Small's throat. The wound was covered in flies, each jockeying for position. Ants were crawling on Small's face, onto his open eyes. He remembered Small's last words and suddenly he understood them.

He had not wanted to die, or be left here in the jungle in his underwear. In one sense, it was a silly thing to be concerned about, but in another it was a last desire for dignity.

Hanson stood up and lorded over Wilson, the rifle pointed at his head. Wilson glared at him.

"All right," Wilson said. "Go on. You been wantin' to all night. Go on. Quit thinkin' about it and do it."

Hanson was quiet for a long moment. "That's too easy," he finally said. "It's what I want, but it's too easy. I'm going to cut you loose, and I want you to take off your pants for Small to wear."

Wilson studied Hanson carefully. "Say what?"

"You heard me," Hanson said. "I'm going to cut you loose. Remove your pants. If you try and escape, I will shoot you full of holes. I would enjoy that. Understand?"

"The man's dead. What's he need pants for?"

"Because he didn't want to die like that, and I don't want him to lie like that."

"He's already covered in ants. It ain't a thing to him."

Hanson's voice was as sharp as a razor. "It matters to me. Roll on your belly."

Wilson rolled on his belly. Hanson used the knife he had taken from the pack and cut Wilson's hands and feet loose. He stood back and pointed the rifle. "Take them off, or don't," Hanson said. "One way or another, I'll get them onto Small."

"I got an extra in that pack you was carrying," Wilson said. "Let him have a pair of them. I think maybe they was his or that other fella's, anyway. What was it? Hunt?"

"No," Hanson said. "You take those off. Take off the shirt, too."

Wilson removed his pants and shirt, tossed them to Hanson.

"Good," Hanson said. "Now sit down."

Wilson, wearing only his underwear and shoes, did as he was instructed. Hanson gathered up the cut portions of rope. There was still enough there to retie Wilson. He tossed Wilson a long piece of rope. "Tie up your feet. I'll check to see you did it right. You didn't, I won't be happy."

"Well, if there's one thing I want," Wilson said between clenched teeth, "it's to make you happy. I live for it, the making you happy part."

"Good," Hanson said. "That's real good."

Wilson tied his feet together. Hanson told him to roll on his belly and he did. Hanson carefully tied Wilson's hands behind his back, then lifted Wilson's feet and tied them to his hands.

Hanson brushed the flies and ants off of Small very carefully, pulled the pants on the stiff body, and closed the eyes with considerable effort. He carried the body to a low tree and placed Small in it, having to bend his legs like pipe cleaners so that he would rest there.

Hanson stood back and looked at his work. Flies and ants would still get to Small, but this way it looked as if he were merely resting in a tree. It was kind of silly, but somehow Hanson felt better about it. It was certainly better than leaving Small's body on the ground and undressed. There just wasn't any dignity in that. None at all.

Hanson broke open one of the packs, found some canned meat, opened it, and ate it with his fingers. Wilson smelled it, said, "Am I gonna get any of that?"

"I'll think about it," Hanson said.

Before the day broke and Hanson dressed Small in Wilson's shirt and pants and put him in a tree, a unique scenario had unfolded in the jungle. Billy, weak from his wounds, had begun to wear down. He had followed Cannon at first by sound, then by instinct. But by midnight he had become exhausted. The wounds, lack of food, it was all coming home to roost.

Billy squatted down with his rifle and tried to listen for Cannon bursting wildly through brush and weeds, but Cannon had finally gotten wise and had either started to steal through the foliage or had found a place to hole up. Billy was considering his next plan when he heard something, then realized he had heard it too late.

Cannon leaped from the brush and came down on top of him brandishing the knife, but the impact of the attack was such that it sent them both rolling up against a tree. This hurt Billy, but Cannon took some of the impact, so the stronger man lost his grip, and Billy, scuttling on all fours, minus his rifle, darted into the shadowy brush just as Cannon recovered the rifle and popped a shot at Billy.

The shot singed the air above Billy's head, but Billy stayed low and kept scuttling. He dove into the brush and Cannon, hot for blood, came charging after him.

Lying low, Billy watched through the foliage as Cannon's feet thumped past him. Billy was angry with himself. He had let his wounds distract him, and instead of being the pursuer, he had become the prey. He had fallen into that trap like an idiot. He realized now that Cannon had been making noise all along, leading him into an ambush, and by the time he realized the big man's game plan, it was too late.

No, thought Billy, I am being too generous with myself. I did not know his game plan, or that he had one until after he played it out. I am an idiot. He not only outsmarted me, he has both the rifle and the knife now.

Feeling weak and stupid, rubbing a chicken-egg-sized knot on his head, Billy sat still and waited. The night crawled on, and after a while he heard Cannon pounding back his way. "Come out, you little punk. Come out and get your medicine. You're gonna get it anyhow, so come and get it. I got the cure for what ails you, boy. Come on out."

Carefully, Billy crawled away from the sound of Cannon's voice, and after a time on hands and knees, rose to a standing position and moved silently through the brush. He considered going back to find Hanson, but the idea of returning without the rifle and without Cannon did not appeal to his pride.

He found a tree from which a number of vines dangled, and

suddenly had an idea. He climbed the tree and found a spot where he could perch on a limb and twist the vine and unravel it. It was hard work and made his fingers bleed, but he managed it, then he did the same to another vine, and yet another, and plaited them together. The three vines made a sound lariat. He made a loop in one end, climbed down, and began to yell.

"Come get me, big man. Come get me."

A shot tore through the brush near Billy, and he knew Cannon was firing at the sound of his voice. He yelled again, and ducked low. Another shot tore through the brush. He continued to yell, and finally resorted to name-calling. It seemed to him that Cannon, having slyly outsmarted him earlier, would be aware that he was leading him into a trap; but it also occurred to him that Cannon might not care. He was an angry man who felt he had the edge. He had both the rifle and the knife, and he was larger than Billy.

Billy thought about that, and determined Cannon did have the edge. At least on those grounds. But to gain the edge over a superior opponent, one had to use his head. Billy bent low and tied a small loop in the opposite end of the vine, then, continuing to yell, he invited Cannon to come closer.

When the sound of the big man was almost on him, Billy turned and took to the tree from which he had procured the vines. He climbed out on a large limb and lay there like a great python. Billy had tried to time his retreat into the tree correctly, and had been successful. The shadowy shape of Cannon broke through the brush and advanced beneath the limb where Billy lay.

Billy almost let him pass, then regained heart. It was now or never. He let the loop of his jungle-made lasso drop over Cannon's head just as the man made a step, therefore causing the loop to catch under his chin and tighten. Billy added to this by slipping his foot into the smaller loop, and dropping from the limb, he let his weight jerk the rope taught around Cannon's neck. Cannon let out a grunt and was yanked up. He let go of the rifle and grabbed at the vine rope with both hands. As he swirled, he saw the body of Billy glide down past him on the other end of the rope.

"Hello, big bwana," Billy said.

Cannon thrashed and spun about like a hooked fish. He continued to grab at the rope above his head, but this did nothing. The knot tightened, biting into his flesh.

Billy watched Cannon spin wildly and kick his legs. Billy

remembered how Cannon had cut the throat of the man Hanson called Small. He thought of how Cannon had put the coal in the palm of his hand and laughed about it. He thought about all this as Cannon spun and bucked against the rope. Then Cannon spun less fast and hardly kicked at all.

Billy, his foot still in the loop, watched and waited. Even after Cannon had ceased to spin or kick, after his tongue protruded from his mouth like a black sock stuffed with cotton, he held his place. He listened to the sounds of the animals in the jungle and he looked up to see the moon through a slit in the boughs. The moon was as white as bone.

A full five minutes later, Billy took his foot from the little loop and dropped to the ground, allowing Cannon's corpse to crash into the brush. Billy recovered the dropped rifle and removed the knife from Cannon's body. Just to make sure, he carefully cut the big man's throat.

Billy climbed back into the tree and found a clutch of limbs on which he could rest. He fell into a deep sleep, and when he awoke, sunlight was cutting through the boughs and vines and spraying him with heat.

Climbing down, he checked the corpse of Cannon. It was covered in insects. He left the body, and found plants with succulent roots. He dug them up with the knife, shook the dirt from them, sliced them, and ate. They were pithy, but satisfying. Having eaten, Billy clutched the rifle and started back toward where he had left Hanson and the big black man.

A few hours after daybreak, Hanson's anger began to subside. His disposition was still dark, but he began to feel human again. He allowed Wilson to put on clothes from one of the packs and eat from a tin of meat. He made him sit with his feet tied, however, and he never once ceased to point the rifle at him.

He looked at where the fire had been in the trail. It had died out and there were only little wisps of smoke crawling up from it, coasting on air, climbing into the treetops. He drank from a canteen, poured some of the water into a cup, and offered it to Wilson while he held the rifle to his head. When Wilson took the cup, Hanson returned to his vigil, and this was interrupted by a voice.

"Bwana, it's me."

"Billy?" Hanson called.

Billy broke out of the jungle smiling. "I come up on you sneaky-like," he said. "But I didn't want to be too sneaky, so you shoot my head off."

"I thought I was being sneaky," Hanson said. "Camping off the trail like this."

"Not so sneaky," Billy said.

"Cannon?"

"No problem," Billy said, and drew his finger across his throat.

"Good," Hanson said, then to Wilson: "What do you think about that?"

Wilson sighed. "Well, I reckon that's all right. I didn't like the sonofabitch nohow."

TARZAN
The Lost Adventure

XIX

Kurvandi bathed in preparation of seeing the great prisoner. He had been told of the bronze giant's exploits. He had killed many of Kurvandi's best warriors. He was glad, however, that the big man had not been slain. A man like that, he would be interesting to watch in the arena; a man like that was a perfect sacrifice to Ebopa. Ebopa would want to take the sacrifice himself.

That would be good. Kurvandi had not seen Ebopa take a sacrifice in some time. It would do the people good to see their god, to know it still stalked beneath their feet, and that it was as powerful as ever.

Another good thing. This bronze giant, he would be a sacrifice of great importance to Ebopa. Not like the weaklings of late that had practically died at the sight of the dancing god, The Stick That Walked.

Kurvandi determined that if the man was as strong, determined, and skilled as they said, he would be just the sort of challenge Ebopa would appreciate. The sort of challenge he and his people would enjoy watching in the arena.

Kurvandi considered all this as he lay in his metal tub and soaked in the blood of sacrifices, blood that had been brought to him warm from their veins. It was his belief that if you soaked in the fresh blood of the living, you absorbed their life and lived longer; doing this, you took part of their soul.

It was also Kurvandi's belief that if blood was spilled on the soil of Ur, it was appreciated by their god Ebopa. Some of Kurvandi's wise men, soothsayers, and sorcerers said this was not so, since so much had gone wrong in the last few years. Childbirth deaths. Diseases that ravaged the countryside. Plagues of insects. Even plant diseases that could destroy an entire crop overnight. Some had even suggested the blood sacrifices were the problem.

But Kurvandi did not believe this. How could he when Ebopa so enjoyed tearing the living apart, feasting on their flesh, blood, brains, and innards? Ebopa loved the blood and flesh of the living, so Kurvandi thought it only right he should also love it. This was the proper way to respect Ebopa, to follow in his image.

Another pitcher of warm blood was brought to his bath chamber by a trembling slave girl dressed only in a loincloth. Kurvandi turned and looked upon her. She was young and fresh and fine to look upon. She trembled even more as she approached the great metal tub. The great black lions, fastened on short chains on either side of the tub, growled at her, narrowed their eyes to slits.

"Come, girl," said Kurvandi. "Fear not the lions. They are pets."

The girl trembled so violently the blood sloshed from the golden pitcher. "Careful," said Kurvandi. "You are spilling it. Bring it while it is still warm."

The slave girl knelt and started to tip the pitcher's contents into the already blood-filled tub. "No," said Kurvandi, grabbing her hand, pushing the pitcher to an upright position. "Pour it over me, girl."

The slave girl did as she was commanded. When the blood flowed freely down Kurvandi's face, he smiled at her. The blood was dark on his lips and teeth. He reached out and took hold of her again. "Did you watch the blood being drained into the pitcher?"

The girl nodded.

"Did it excite you?"

"No, my lord."

"Of course it did," Kurvandi said. "How could it have not?

Now tell me again. Did it excite you?"

The girl hesitated only for a moment. This was the first time she had waited on Kurvandi, her king. She had been taken from her parents when she was only thirteen and brought here, raised in the palace as a kitchen maid until her current age, sixteen. And then, Kurvandi, inspecting the great kitchen and the bread-baking, had spied her, asked that she be brought to him with the pitchers of blood.

And if this was not bad enough, she had been forced to stand by the great stone drain in the kitchen, where the sheep, cattle, and chickens were hung up to have their throats cut, their blood drained, and watch human beings die like farm animals. One of those who had died, the very woman whose blood she had just poured from the pitcher, had been a kitchen maid, a friend of hers. The maid had become a donor to Kurvandi's bath for no other reason than she had dropped a loaf of bread in his presence.

Slaves had contributed to Kurvandi's bath for less than that.

Kurvandi pulled the quaking girl to him, roughly kissed her mouth. The blood from his face stained hers. He pulled her into the bath with him. She fought for a moment, but as his grip increased and she felt his fingers digging deep within her flesh, she stopped fighting. She knew to fight would only make it worse.

He kissed her again. She tried her best to kiss back in self-defense, but she could think of nothing but the blood on his face; the blood she was now soaking in; the blood permeating her loincloth.

"Please," she said. "Let me go. The blood . . . It makes me sick."

Kurvandi grabbed her by the hair and pulled her face close to his. "You should be honored, girl. I am Kurvandi. Your king. The blood of all the Kurvandis flows through me."

"And the blood of the innocent flows over you," said the girl.

No sooner had the words come out of her mouth than she knew she was doomed.

But then, Kurvandi smiled. "You are right."

He pulled her to him, kissed her. Bit her lip. She let out a scream. He pushed her head into the tub of blood and held it under. She thrashed for but a moment, but the will to live was not strong within her.

A few seconds after she had ceased thrashing, Kurvandi let her go, watched as she floated face down in the deep tub. A fleeting moment of regret raced through Kurvandi's brain.

He regretted he had killed her so easily. She would have made a good one for the harem. He must try and control himself. At least a little. He needed male heirs, and he had yet to find a woman within which his seed would grow. This one, she had been young and strong and beautiful. She might well have been the field he should have sowed.

Regret passed.

Kurvandi raised up in his bath, reached out of the tub, and took hold of a jewel- encrusted dagger that lay on the floor next to his glass of wine.

There was no use letting good blood go to waste. Not with it being so close by, and still warm.

He took hold of the girl's head and lifted it out of the bath to expose her throat.

He used the knife.

The lions purred with pleasure. They knew later they would be given special morsels.

Tarzan awoke cold and in pain, shackled in irons, deep in the dark.

In an instant, the ape-man was clear-headed. He pushed the pain of his injuries into a single mental knot, then tried by pure willpower to dissolve it. He almost succeeded. Most of the pain was neutralized.

The first thing Tarzan did was sit up from the cold dungeon floor and examine himself. Nothing was broken. A few cuts, muscle rips, but all in all, he had been lucky. And someone had crudely dressed his wounds. There were strips of cloth tied around cuts on his arms and legs.

He sniffed the air. There were two others in the dungeon. He recognized the scent of one.

"Jean?" he said.

"Yes," came her voice, then Tarzan's keen eyes identified her; he could see like a cat in the dark. Jean was wearing a brassiere and pants, but no shirt. Tarzan immediately realized what his bandages were made of. "We were waiting for you to awaken," Jean said.

"Who is the other?" Tarzan asked.

"Nyama," Jean said, and Nyama moved forward in the darkness.

Tarzan laughed. "I came to rescue you, Jean."

"They brought you in last night," Jean said. "You were unconscious. They were afraid of you. They put you in chains. I did the best I could to dress your wounds."

"You did well," Tarzan said. "I presume I was spared for some special purpose."

"Nyama believes it is for the crocodiles, or for Ebopa, their god," Jean said.

"Ebopa would be the stick creature," Tarzan said.

"You know of it, then?" Nyama said.

Tarzan explained what he had seen on the wall fragment outside of the city. "I believe it is some kind of beast from the center of the earth. From Pellucidar."

"I have heard of Pellucidar," said Jean. "I read of it as a girl. A world at the center of the earth with a constant noonday sun. I thought it was a myth. A legend."

"Your father thought I was a legend," Tarzan said. "He was wrong."

"Not entirely," said Jean. "Any ordinary man would have died if they were beat as you were. And when they brought you in, they beat you some more. They were very angry. Nyama understands their language. She said they were angry you had killed friends of theirs. They only let you live because they were ordered to."

"Then they made a mistake," Tarzan said.

"Ebopa," Nyama said. "You say he is not a god?"

"A god is made of whatever you choose," Tarzan said. "But as I said, I believe Ebopa is some sort of creature from the earth's core. There are all manner of beasts there. Beasts that once roamed topside, as well as creatures that have not — or least not until Ebopa somehow came to the surface. Or almost to the surface."

"According to their legend, this thing has been around forever," Jean said. "How can that be?"

"Who's to say how long it lives?" Tarzan said. "And perhaps there is some other answer. Whatever, wherever it is from, it lives. And so do I. Stand back."

Jean and Nyama did as they were instructed. Tarzan stood up. He looped the chains around his palms and clenched them. He took several deep breaths, then tugged at the chains, straining the braces that held them to the floor. The bolts screamed in the stone floor and popped free.

Tarzan knelt, took hold of the metal bands around one of his ankles, and twisted it with his mighty fingers. He struggled for a full three minutes, then there was a popping noise as the restraining bolt in the ankle band snapped free.

Tarzan went to work on the other. After a time, it too snapped. Now, all that remained were the metal bands around his wrists. Tarzan went to work on them, and ten minutes later, the bands lay at his feet. He picked up a length of chain, coiled it around his bloody hand and let it dangle. Now he was free of the chains and they were his weapon.

"What now?" Jean asked.

"We try and escape. If we cannot, when they come, we fight to the death. If we are to die, let us make it on our own terms."

Nkima, after several days' frolicking with his friends, realized he had forgotten about the man Tarzan wanted him to watch over. Actually, he had temporarily forgotten about Tarzan. He had gotten carried away with his bragging to the other monkeys, and now he realized the sun had dipped down and up and down again, and he did not know where either the tarmangani or Tarzan were.

Nkima returned to where he had last seen Tarzan and began to follow his trail. He moved swiftly through the trees, even more nimbly than Tarzan. He covered distance that would have taken days to cover by ground. By midday, the little monkey came to the outskirts of Ur, and here the smell of his master, Tarzan, was strongest.

Nkima came to the moat around the city and saw that the water was filled with white crocodiles. The crocodile loved little monkeys — to eat. Nkima did not like the thought of trying to cross the moat. He could not stand water, and he liked crocodiles even less. He thought perhaps he should just wait back in the jungle for Tarzan's return. He could play and eat fruit, and he would not have to face the crocodiles.

He thought about this for a time, then decided Tarzan might be in trouble. He thought he smelled the aroma of Tarzan from over the wall. It was an aroma unlike that the ape-man normally emitted. It was strong, sharp. It indicated there had been a great rise in physical activity. A surge of adrenaline. Of course, Nkima did not analyze these things in this manner. He merely smelled a different smell, and the scent alerted him that something was different. Tarzan might be in trouble.

Nkima went into the jungle and found a large bird's nest in a tree. He pulled it down and carried it back to the moat. He placed it in the moat. It floated. He climbed inside the nest. Water leaked in, but still it floated. The nest drifted out into the moat. Now and then the little monkey paddled with his hands. He could see tarmangani walking along the wall, but he and the nest were so small the sentries had not taken notice of him.

Unfortunately, the crocodiles had.

When Nkima was over halfway across, he saw a crocodile raise its eyes out of the water, and behind it, all the way to the great wall, was a row of crocodile eyes.

Nkima wished suddenly he was back with the other monkeys, bragging about his imagined feats.

The foremost croc swam rapidly toward him, anxious to eat.

When the croc was almost on him, its jaws open, ready to consume both nest and monkey, Nkima leaped onto the head of the reptile and hurdled from him to the head of another croc. He did this on the heads of four of the reptiles before they were aware of what was happening.

The fifth moved, however, eliminating Nkima's foot path, and Nkima fell with a screech into the water. The little monkey's head bobbed to the surface just as the jaws of the croc opened to receive him.

TARZAN
The Lost Adventure

XX

Billy and Hanson buried poor Small in a shallow grave beside the trail, then, forcing Wilson to the forefront, they drove him through the jungle. They were uncertain of the proper direction to Ur, but Hanson tried his best to pursue his original intent, hoping it was accurate.

After a few hours, Billy spotted spoor that led them to a wide trail in the jungle. It was a well-traveled trail, and obviously not merely by animals; this trail, they could tell, was regularly cleared by tools, not just the pounding feet of trodding animals.

They had gone only a little bit farther when they broke off the trail and onto the road that led to Ur. Here they found the warriors Tarzan had slain. Out in the field they saw three hobbled zebras, and nearby, they found a couple of chariots.

"We could travel into Ur in style," Hanson said, pointing at the chariots.

"And when the Urs see us," Billy said, "they kill us in style. Better to be sneaky-like."

"Good point," Hanson said.

Billy hustled up the three zebras. He used the harness from the chariots to fashion crude bridles, and in minutes, the three of them were mounted, heading down the road toward Ur.

Kurvandi, freshened by his blood bath, rinsed clean by clear water, and was dressed in his finest purple robes and sheepskin sandals. His magnificent headdress was made of soft leather and plumes of brightly colored birds, which nodded majestically as he walked. He was an extraordinary specimen. Nearly seven feet tall, muscular, handsome. He walked with the black lions at his side, a leash in either hand. He looked very regal and noble as he entered the throne room. He took his place on the throne, and the lions lay at his feet.

His servants came forward to fan him with great leaves. Officers of the court stood nearby, ready to respond to his every beck and call. After a moment of basking in his power, Kurvandi said: "The arena. Is it ready?"

A little man with crooked legs wearing bright-colored clothing wobbled forward. "Yes, my king. It is ready."

"Then bring this bronze giant to me for examination," Kurvandi said.

There was a low murmur in the room.

"Well," said Kurvandi. "What is it?"

"He is very dangerous, my lord," said the man with crooked legs. "He might harm you. He is quite the savage. Perhaps, my king, it is best you see him in the arena."

Kurvandi wrinkled his brows. "Hurt me? The king? Me, Kurvandi. Are you suggesting that he is more powerful than your king?"

The little man with the crooked legs swallowed hard. His body trembled. "Oh, no, my king. He is a fly to you. But he is a savage, and if you were to kill him, or maim him, it would spoil the great delight you would have watching him torn limb from limb by Ebopa."

Kurvandi considered this. "Very well."

The little man was visibly relieved. "Thank you, my king."

"Miltoon," Kulvani said to the little man. "Go stand against that wall."

"My king?" said Miltoon.

"Must I, the King of Ur, repeat myself?"

"No," Miltoon said, and wobbled on his crooked legs toward

the wall.

"Good," said Kurvandi. He waved his hand at one of his guards, an archer. "Bring me a bow and arrow."

The guard rushed forward, removing his bow from its place on his back, pulling an arrow from his quiver.

Kurvandi stood up and strung the arrow to the bow. "Do we have a piece of fruit? Something round that will rest on Miltoon's head?"

A large yellow fruit was found and the bearer of the fruit practically galloped the length of the room toward Miltoon and placed it on the frightened little man's head.

"Stand still now," Kurvandi said. "Let us see if you were lying. I want to know if you truly believe I am more deadly than this bronze giant."

"Please, your majesty," said Miltoon. "You are all-powerful. Everyone in Ur knows that."

"Just Ur?" Kurvandi said, pulling the arrow back to his ear, taking aim.

"Everywhere!" Miltoon said. "They know it everywhere."

"Shhhhhhhh," Kurvandi said. "You are shaking the fruit. Now hold your breath. The truth will come out when I fire this arrow. Am I not part god?"

Miltoon held his breath.

Kurvandi let loose of the arrow.

Miltoon took the shaft in the right eye. His head knocked against the wall and the fruit fell forward, and Miltoon slid to a sitting position on the floor. The fruit fell in his lap.

"Lying," Kurvandi said. He tossed the bow back to its owner. "Run and check the fruit."

The archer bolted across the floor and recovered the yellow fruit from Miltoon's lap.

"Is the fruit bruised?" asked Kurvandi.

The archer examined it. "No, my king."

"Is there blood on it?"

"No," said the archer.

Kurvandi was disappointed. "Very well. Bring it here."

The archer once again bolted across the floor, handing the fruit to his king.

Kurvandi took the fruit and the archer bowed and moved away. Kurvandi carefully examined the fruit.

The archer was correct. No blood.

Kurvandi ate it anyway.

As Miltoon's body was dragged from Kurvandi's view, he considered the bronze giant. No use taking chances.

"Let us proceed to the arena," he said. "Miltoon was right about one thing. I would not want to injure our entertainment."

Even as Kurvandi was being carried toward the arena on a litter by slaves, his lions being led by servants, the word was passed that the giant and the captive white woman, as well as others, were to be brought to the arena.

The dungeon where Tarzan, Jean, and Nyama were held received word first, and when the husky jailer opened the door, followed by half a dozen warriors who were to provide escort for the prisoners, they were surprised.

It was a brief surprise, and far from pleasant. Its only positive element was that it was quick. As the jailer entered the dungeon and the light from the hallway flooded inside, the chain Tarzan held whipped out like a snake, and like a snake, it struck. Its fangs were the cold hard links that made up the chain. The impact shattered the jailer's head like an overripe fruit, and the contents of this fruit sprayed the guards and the messenger, and in that instant, a blinking of an eye really, Tarzan swung the chains, one in either hand, fast and rhythmically, taking out heads and knees. In less than an instant, four men lay dead and two were bolting out of the dungeon and down the hall. Before the one in the rear could make it to the stairs and freedom, Tarzan dropped the chains and took up a spear from one of the dead guards, and flung it. The spear struck the man in the back and passed almost completely through him, punching out of the breastplate armor he wore like a darning needle punching through cardboard.

The man fell, hit on the extended spear, did a pirouette, and went down. Tarzan realized one man had escaped. He cursed his reflexes. He felt that the time he had spent away from the jungle had affected him. None of them should have escaped.

The women grabbed spears. Tarzan kept one length of chain, looped it around his waist, found a spear and a short sword, and started up the stairway.

Had little Nkima been human, he might have spent a moment praying, thinking of the fates, whatever, for when the crocodile closed its jaws, it looked as if for Nkima, the world was about to end.

But then, totally by accident, a gift from the gods, his little hand grasped a floating stick and he struck out with it. The strike was no good. Very clumsy. Which was exactly what saved Nkima's life. The stick went into the croc's mouth and lodged its jaws open. The croc, in pain, unable to snap the stick, began to thrash. Finally, the pressure of its powerful jaws did in fact splinter the wood, but by then it was too late for the croc to enjoy its meal. Nkima had thrashed toward the city wall and made it; he scampered halfway up and stopped on an outcropping of stone to look down on the crocodiles.

What Nkima most wanted to do was to yell and curse the crocodiles and tell them what a brave and courageous monkey he was, and what cowards they were, but even Nkima, who was not strong on reason, determined that this was not the thing to do.

It was important for him to be quiet. Be quiet and enter into Ur in search of his master, Tarzan.

He went nimbly up the wall and over and into the city, right between two guards marching away from each other along the wall's walkway. Neither saw him.

Nkima leaped to the ground below, sniffed the air, and proceeded.

The one who escaped Tarzan was the messenger who had carried word for Tarzan and the two women to be brought to the arena. When he raced out of the dungeon, he began to yell for help. By the time Tarzan and the two women made it to the top of the dungeon stairs, the room was filled with warriors.

Tarzan stabbed with the spear, then as quarters closed in, he fought with the sword until it snapped. Then he broke the spear in half and fought with the bladed end in one hand and the remains of the broken shaft in the other. He whacked and poked and the warriors fell. Few got up again.

Jean and Nyama fought bravely as well. Bodies began to pile up, but the ape-man and the women were forced backwards, down the length of the great hall toward an arch. They fought through the arch and down a long row of steps, and discovered to their dismay that they were being pushed backwards into a tunnel made of stone.

No sooner had they been forced past the mouth of the tunnel, than a metal grate was dropped, and they were trapped.

They turned and ran down the length of the tunnel toward the light, but even before they reached the source of illumination, Nyama realized where they were and said: "The arena."

They stepped onto a large field closed off by walls. It was not actually the arena proper, but instead, a waiting station. Above the walls, seated on tiers of seats, was the populace of Ur. They had been waiting, and Tarzan grimaced, knowing he had allowed himself and his companions to be herded exactly where they were meant to go. He tossed aside the broken spear in disgust.

Tarzan, Jean, and Nyama, covered in the blood of their enemies, returned to the cool darkness of the tunnel, and without so much as a word, sat down and rested.

Tarzan said simply. "Do not give up. Remember. It is not over yet. We still live."

Beyond the walls, there soon came sounds. Sounds of cheering from the seats, sounds of men, women, and wild animals engaged in combat. Never had Jean heard such horrid screams. She began to tremble, but then she remembered her vow. She was going to die with as much dignity as such a situation would allow. And if the only dignity she could muster was a brave death, then so be it.

She looked at Nyama. Nyama did not appear frightened at all. She held her head up, chin lifted high, ready to face whatever came. Jean assumed that Nyama had been preparing for this day for some time, and perhaps she saw this not so much as an end to life, but an escape by death to freedom.

After a time, the arena grew quiet.

A door across from the trio opened, and in came a dozen warriors armed with bows and arrows. Their arrows were strung, their bows bent. They dropped to their knees and aimed the arrows at the three, then spoke and gestured.

"They want her," Nyama said, translating, nodding to Jean. "It is her turn."

The woman who had brought Jean to the dungeon and terrified her with the executioner's sword and the lions, broke through the ranks of archers, smiled, and pointed at Jean. She crooked her finger.

"It's as I thought," Jean said. "She was saving me for herself."

"Her name is Jeda. She hates outsiders," Nyama said. "She especially hates white skins. And you she hates because you are a woman and not a warrior. She hates weakness."

"We should rush them," Tarzan said. "Die together. Keep them from their sport."

"No," Jean said, touching her hand to Tarzan's chest. "It is my turn. It will give you more life."

"Now or twenty minutes from now," Tarzan said. "It is all the same."

"I want to fight her," Jean said. "I can't win. I know that. But if I'm to die, let me do it fighting her. She has insulted me. They have killed my father and my friend Billy. It is the last thing you can do for me, Tarzan. The very last."

Tarzan nodded, not wishing to argue, but he had already begun to formulate a plan. It was nothing terribly strategic, but it was a plan.

The Urs were becoming impatient. Beyond the wall came a roar of disapproval from the viewers. They wanted action and blood.

Jeda began to beckon frantically at Jean. Jean, head held high, walked toward her. A moment later, two of the archers grabbed Jean by the arms and pulled her through the doorway. The others followed, and the door was bolted behind them.

"She has no chance," said Nyama. "Jeda is one of the greatest warriors of Ur. When your turn comes, what will you do?"

"I shall fight to the death. I shall kill as many as I am capable of killing."

"Of course you will," Nyama said. "I knew that without asking. I am nervous. You will kill as many as there are stars in the heavens, as there are blades of grass on the veldt. And so shall I."

Tarzan looked at her and smiled. "Will you be disappointed if I kill only half that many?"

Nyama smiled nervously, tried to keep the spirit in her voice when she said: "Only a little bit."

Hunt and Jad-bal-ja hurried along the low and narrow tunnel, Hunt on his hands and knees, Jad-bal-ja slouched so as not to scrape his back on the low ceiling.

Behind them they could hear the thing attempting to scuttle through the hole, which was almost too small for its head. Almost. The dirt and rock around the opening was starting to crumble, and Hunt could hear the creature pushing its way through.

The thought of the thing behind them, coming for them, caused Hunt to push harder. The rocks scuffed and cut his knees and the palms of his hands, but he kept going. He could not see an arm's length in front of him — a hand's length, but still he pushed on, the hot breath of the lion on the back of his neck.

There came a wild and dreadful shriek from the back of the tunnel, and Hunt recognized it as a wail of both triumph and rage. The thing had pushed its way into the tunnel, and now, on its hands and knees — if those hooks could be called hands, those strange hunks of flesh and bone or chitin could be called knees — it rushed forward, bouncing off the sides of the cavern walls as it came, snapping its jaws with a sound akin to a giant paper cutter slamming through wet construction paper. Its smell permeated the air, and as Hunt breathed, he imagined he was pulling that foul odor into his lungs, and that in a way, that appalling thing was becoming a part of him.

It was at this point that Hunt considered pulling loose his spear fragment, turning, and having a go at the monster. At least, that way he would die with the wounds on the front of his body, not in his back like some craven coward.

But then he saw the light.

TARZAN
The Lost Adventure

XXI

From his position in his private viewing box, sitting upon his golden throne, a purple robe tossed over his knees, Kurvandi had watched the day's events with disinterest. He was anxious to see this bronze giant die. He was anxious to see Ebopa perform. His eyes wandered toward where the great gong hung.

The gong was arranged in such a way that when struck with tremendous force, the echo of its chime would travel through a metal pipe and into the caverns beyond. Within twenty minutes Ebopa usually arrived, hungry and angry. They had but to open the gate on the far wall, the one that led down into the caverns below, and there would be Ebopa, and when Ebopa strode out of the darkness it would shake its head and wipe its eyes, but soon it would adjust to the light and begin to stalk its victim.

Occasionally, Ebopa would spring on its prey, kill it immediately, and eat it to the roaring of the crowd. More often, it would play with its intended, pursuing it about the arena, letting the prey take the lead, and then, abruptly, Ebopa would start to run in that curious and hideous fashion it favored, and within moments the quarry would fall beneath its hooking claws.

Rarely was anyone strong enough, or brave enough, to give Ebopa a true fight. Today, if what Kurvandi had heard of this giant were true, matters might be different. A few more minutes of pleasure might be added to the event. He was even more optimistic, having heard that the giant had escaped from the dungeon with two women, and had fought against overwhelming odds before being driven into the arena. This proved the captive was no ordinary man.

Kurvandi glanced down into the arena, at the door through which Ebopa would come. Unconsciously, he licked his lips.

In the tunnel below the arena, Hunt pursued the light. He came to its source, found that it was a manmade shaft that dropped into his tunnel, and that the tunnel itself ended here against a hard rock wall. From the slimy sides of the shaft and from the wet floor of the tunnel, Hunt deduced that this sluice was designed to drain excess water.

Not bothering to look back, Hunt put his hands on either side of the shaft, pushed up, then used his feet in the same manner. It was slippery work, but by maintaining pressure with his hands and feet, it was a serviceable exit. Above him he could see a metal grate. He tried not to think about that and hoped he could move it.

When Hunt was halfway up, he looked down at the lion. It could not climb the shaft. There were no places where its paws might gain a hold. Hunt felt a wave of cowardice. He should die with the lion. The lion would give him time to make the top of the shaft, but he should die with it. The lion looked up at him and barred its teeth, as if to smile. Then Jad-bal-ja turned to face the screeching horror that was rushing down upon it, and Hunt's final decision was made. He continued to climb upward.

When Jean strode into the arena, Kurvandi leaned forward on his throne. This might be of interest, he thought. Not because he felt this pale-skinned woman would be much of a match for Jeda, whom he had seen fight many times, but because he was interested in seeing how an outsider would die.

Kurvandi's seat for this battle was a good one. It was excellent for all exhibitions, but in this case, the portion of the arena where

Jean and Jeda were to fight was just below him. As Jeda entered the arena, she looked up at his roost and smiled. From time to time, they were lovers. Usually after she fought in the arena, especially if she was covered in blood. Jeda felt being a lover to the king might have its political overtones, and she was ambitious.

She decided she would go slow with the girl, let her linger a while. Then she would make sure it was bloody. Kurvandi liked that. He hated it when it happened quick and there was very little blood.

Jeda smiled at Kurvandi, and he smiled back. He thought to himself: Someday, I will have her killed, before she becomes too dangerous, too popular.

The black lions rose up on either side of Kurvandi, and placing their front paws on the top of the viewing box, looked down too. They, like their master, loved the arena. The blood, the sounds of the crowd, the smell of fear excited them. When it was all over, their master would allow them into the arena for a while, to eat. There were always fine tidbits there.

A rider on a zebra entered the arena. He was carrying two long spears and knives in belted scabbards. He tossed one of each in front of Jeda, the others in front of Jean. The rider said something in the Ur language, then departed. Jeda fastened on the knife belt, took hold of her spear, and Jean did the same. Jean was so frightened she thought the flesh in her legs was melting, and that soon she would turn to liquid and flow into the bloody sands of the arena.

Her hand shook as she held the spear, but to keep from letting it show, she jiggled the spear savagely and called out threats. They were silly threats, but since no one amongst the Urs could understand her language anyway, she knew she could make them sound more threatening with the tone of her voice and her facial expressions.

"Your mother wears army boots!" she called. "When's the last time you took a bath? Who does your hair anyway?"

Tough stuff in an upper-class Austin beauty parlor, but out here, a bit slight. Nonetheless, she told herself, even if I am out here in my bra, I'm Texan through and through and I come from stock tough as horseshoes, and I'm going to reach way down inside of myself and pull it out. I'm going to —

Her musings on toughness were interrupted when with a speedy thrust, Jeda used her spear to open a cut on Jean's shoulder.

Jean couldn't believe it. The lunge had been so fast she had hardly seen it. And now, an instant after it was completed, she felt a warmth flow over her shoulder, and then a stinging sensation. The razor-sharp blade of the spear had cut through her flesh and she was bleeding.

Jeda spun and dropped and used the shaft of the spear to catch Jean behind the knees with it and trip her. Jean was tossed into the air and came down hard on her rear end.

The crowd roared.

Jeda turned her back on Jean and raised her spear to the crowd.

Jean found this the most humiliating event of all. Jeda was not taking her serious in the least.

Jean twisted to her knees, lunged with her spear, and poked Jeda sharply in the rear end. Jeda leaped and whirled to the sound of an arena full of laughter.

Jeda glanced out of the corner of her eye, and took in Kurvandi who was laughing so uproariously his headdress shook. Even the black lions looking over the edge of the box, their big paws holding them in place, appeared to wear expressions of humor.

Jeda spoke sharply to Jean, and though Jean could not understand the words, she understood their intent. She knew she was in for it now.

Maybe that was the best thing, Jean thought. Agitate Jeda until she was so infuriated she would kill her swiftly. A swift death would be better than a lingering and humiliating one.

At that moment, with Jean but an instant from death, Hunt reached the top of the sluice, and at the same moment below, Jad-bal-ja sprang into the face of Ebopa. The creature drove Jad-bal-ja back to the end of the tunnel, then with Jad-bal-ja riding its head like a hat, clawing, gnashing, Ebopa stood up in the tight shaft.

Hunt was forced against the grate by the rising of Jad-bal-ja and Ebopa. Fortunately the grate lifted easily and Hunt was pushed into the open. Unfortunately, the grate was right behind the arena throne of Kurvandi, who, hearing the grate clatter to the floor, turned and gazed around the edge of his throne. What he saw astonished him.

A bedraggled white man was scuttling out of a drain shaft on his hands and knees, and a huge lion was rising out of the shaft behind him on the head of —

Kurvandi sprang to his feet in horror.

It was Ebopa. Kurvandi screeched like a rat being crushed beneath an elephant's foot. The lion was riding the head of Ebopa.

Out in the arena, Jeda, confident of her victory, lost interest in Jean and turned to look at Kurvandi, trying to deduce the nature of his scream. It was a mistake on Jeda's part.

Jean tossed her spear. It was a wide toss and went behind Jeda's head. Jeda whirled back to face Jean, but the Texan had drawn her knife, and now she sprang forward. Had Jeda not been so astonished at the tenacity and ferocity of her opponent, she could easily have slain Jean. But by the time she realized Jean was an actual threat, it was too late.

Jean plunged her dagger into Jeda's eye and rode her to the ground, twisting the weapon into the socket as if she were fastening a corkscrew into the cork of a wine bottle.

Jeda, the great warrior, died easily.

Tarzan had not been idle. From the moment Jean left for the arena, he set about scaling the wall. It was a nearly smooth wall, but with the chains wrapped around his waist, Tarzan set to the task. There were some outlines where the stones had been cemented together, and the ape-man used his strong fingers to take hold of these and gain purchase. He made the slow, agonizing climb, and reached the summit of the wall at the very moment Jean sprang forward and slew Jeda.

Tarzan saw this and cheered.

Jean, straddling her enemy, turned toward him, saw him standing on the summit of the connecting wall beneath a fluttering red flag on a long pole. She raised her knife and let out a yell of victory. Tarzan thought it almost animal-like. Above Jean, in Kurvandi's box he saw a sight that both heartened and agonized him. Jad-bal-ja was clinging to a monstrosity's head, ineffectually biting and clawing at it.

Kurvandi had retreated to the far corner of the box, and the two black lions had joined Jad-bal-ja in his quest to bring Ebopa down. But Ebopa would not go down. It flicked one of the black lions away with its leg. The lion went high and fell on its back in the arena.

Even from a distance, Tarzan heard its back snap like the cracking of a whip. The lion shook and thrashed, then lay still.

In the opposite corner of the box from Kurvandi, Tarzan saw Hunt holding a broken spear, looking willing, if not eager, to fight.

Tarzan jerked the long, limber flagpole out of its sheath on the wall, turned, and lowered it to Nyama. Nyama took hold of it and he pulled her up.

Tarzan and Nyama ran along the top of the wall, and meeting them came a line of warriors. Tarzan did not like the odds, but the situation was ideal. No matter how many of them there were, they could only face him one at a time. He used the flagpole to punch them, trip them, gouge them off the wall. The fall was not enough to kill the warriors, but it was high enough to do them injury. Some of them moaned with broken bones and shattered skulls.

Tarzan told Nyama to jump, and jump she did. They leapt into the arena on Jean's side, and raced toward her. Now warriors were coming off the wall, running after them.

Never before had Jad-bal-ja's claws and mighty jaws been useless. Ebopa reached up with a hooked appendage and clutched the lion and tossed him at Kurvandi. Jad-bal-ja, scratching and biting, landed full force on Kurvandi, and down they went. When Jad-bal-ja rose, Kurvandi was dead, his head crushed between the great lion's jaws like a walnut between pliers.

Ebopa, annoyed with the black lion clinging to his leg, extended it and wiped the lion off on the throne, like a bored man scraping something off his shoe.

The black lion rolled across the floor, and quite by accident, he and Jad-bal-ja came together. In a moment, the fight was one. They twirled about as if they were biting, clawing tumbleweeds of fur.

Ebopa turned its black pumpkin-head and looked at Hunt. Hunt had never seen a gaze like that. It was almost hypnotic. Ebopa crouched. Ebopa made one slow step. Ebopa opened its face to show its strange teeth.

Hunt leaped over the edge of the box and dropped into the arena.

Mesmerized by Ebopa, Hunt was unaware of the crowd of

warriors thundering across the arena toward Tarzan and Jean and Nyama. When he saw Jean, momentarily, he was heartened, and then seeing Tarzan, he was even more enthusiastic. He did not know the other woman, but from her manner, he could see she was with Jean and Tarzan.

Then he took in the warriors thundering toward them.

Out of the frying pan, and into the fire, he thought.

But Ebopa, disappointed in losing his main prey, that which was the tastiest to eat — human beings — sprang from the box and landed light as a grasshopper into the arena behind Hunt, Tarzan, Jean, and Nyama.

The warriors, rushing toward Tarzan and the others, let out a shout and turned to flee from their god. They tried desperately to scale the wall they had leaped from, but couldn't do it. They climbed on top of each other, like ants, crushing their own below them. In this manner, some made the wall while others died underfoot, or pressed their bodies against the wall in fear.

Tarzan turned and looked over his shoulder, saw the source of their panic.

Ebopa was creeping up on Hunt.

"Hunt!" Tarzan yelled. "Behind you!"

Hunt wheeled, saw Ebopa.

Ebopa crouched, bent its legs.

And leaped.

TARZAN
The Lost Adventure

XXII

Tarzan used the flagpole like a pole vault. He went high and came down on Ebopa's head even as the beast leaped. The creature floundered forward and landed in the sand of the arena, face first. It rose up with a roar, shedding Tarzan from its back with a whipping movement of its spine.

It moved into a one-legged posture, its hooks held before it. It changed postures. Danced across the sands, twisted, hissed. Tarzan understood much in that moment. The martial-arts moves he had seen on the stone were the moves of this thing. The common mantis — perhaps some cousin to this beast — made similar moves. Martial-arts systems in China had been based on these movements, and this accounted for the way the warriors of Ur fought. They were trying to mimic their god; had developed an entire fighting system based on these strange patterns.

Tarzan had dropped the pole when he made his leap, and now he yelled for the others to stand back.

"You can't take it alone," Hunt said.

"Wait until it is preoccupied with me," Tarzan yelled. "Then strike."

Tarzan mimicked the creature's moves. He tried to focus only on Ebopa. The intentions of Ebopa were hard to read. Its body English was unlike that of human beings. A slight movement that might lead one to realize an attack was coming from one direction in a human being, could be totally misleading against this monster. Its bones, muscles . . . They did not operate in the same manner.

Ebopa began to hop, posture. Tarzan did the same. The creature struck with a hooked hand, and Tarzan blocked the strike and struck back. Striking the mantis was like striking a brick wall.

Tarzan bounced back, casually uncoiled the chain from around his waist, wrapped it around one of his palms and began to swing it over his head.

Ebopa watched this with considerable curiosity. The movement of the chain was mesmerizing to the creature. When Tarzan felt it was preoccupied, he thrust his right leg forward like a fencer, and whipped the chain out and low, caught Ebopa's foreleg, and twisted the length of the chain around it.

Then Tarzan jerked, causing Ebopa to smash onto its back.

Jean and Nyama and Hunt started to rush forward, but Tarzan yelled them back. The chain had come uncoiled from around Ebopa's leg, and with amazing, almost supernatural speed, Ebopa had regained its footing.

The crowd in the arena had panicked at first, but now they and the warriors watched the spectacle below with bloodthirsty interest. Never, never, never, had they seen Ebopa on its back. Never had they seen a man challenge it with its own movements, or with such bravery.

Jad-bal-ja brought his jaws together against the black lion's throat, shook his foe dramatically, then fell over, the black lion falling on top of him. Jad-bal-ja tried to crawl from beneath the dispatched lion, but his wounds were too great. He could smell the man he loved below, could sense he was in trouble, but he could not help him. The lion began to whimper and painfully inch its way from beneath its fallen adversary.

A little figure scuttled up the steps and moved close to the lion. It was Nkima. The little monkey, searching for Tarzan, had picked up the spoor of the lion and had followed the scent to the arena box.

Jad-bal-ja purred softly, and Nkima stroked the lion's head.

"I would like to eat you," growled the lion.

"You cannot," chattered the monkey, "for I am Nkima, and I am much too fast."

Hanson, Billy, and Wilson arrived in sight of the great city of Ur. Even from a distance, they could hear the roar of a massive crowd.

"Sounds like a baseball stadium," Hanson said.

"If you think we're gonna just ride up there, get this daughter of yours out, you're a fool," Wilson said.

"Shut up," Hanson said. "Shut up before I shoot you down."

"Easy, Bwana," Billy said. "Jackass is right. They put holes through us many times with arrows, we come ride up. We best unbridle zebras, let them go."

"You let them go," Wilson said. "They'll head home. To Ur. The city might decide to investigate the loss of its warriors. Maybe they're already looking."

"If they were a hunting party," Hanson said. "Maybe not."

"Jackass right," Billy said. "Best kill zebras."

"But they are innocent animals," Hanson said.

"I am innocent animal too," Billy said. "And live one. Would like to stay that way. Like zebras fine. Like self more."

"We'll hobble them," Hanson said. "They cannot go far hobbled. We'll leave them hobbled until we're finished here. We might need them."

"You're soft, Hanson," said Wilson.

"Good for you," Hanson said. "If I wasn't, you'd be long dead and meat for the worms."

The interior of Ebopa's brain experienced something it had never imagined it possessed. Surprise. This thing! This frail-looking thing was not frail at all! And it was fast. Almost as fast as Ebopa itself. Ebopa could not understand it. Not only was it strong and fast, it hurt him. It struck with a shiny black tail, and when it struck, it hurt.

Tarzan realized what Ebopa realized. It could feel pain. The lion's attack had been against the hard, bony arms and legs of Ebopa, but Tarzan determined the place to attack with his chain was the creature's joints, what passed for its knees, elbows, and neck. There it was weak.

Tarzan let forth with the cry of the bull ape, whipped the chain like a scorpion's tail, and finally Ebopa, relying on its uncanny speed, rushed the ape-man. Tarzan could not move completely out of the way of one of its hooked hands, and the hook tore the flesh on Tarzan's shoulder, yet the ape-man was able to sidestep enough to grab Ebopa's shoulder, pull it back and down, and whip the chain around its neck.

Ebopa stood up, pranced about the arena with Tarzan dangling on its back, the chain tight around its neck. Tarzan dropped all of his weight and yanked back on the chain, striving for a marriage of gravity; if he could plunge all his weight to the center of Ebopa's back, he hoped he might snap its spine.

Ebopa went backwards, but its "knees" bent the opposite way, taking pressure off of Tarzan's attack. Ebopa shook its head and bent forward and sent Tarzan flying. The jungle man landed, rolled, and scuttled to his feet as the thing hopped toward him.

Tarzan fell on his back before Ebopa's onslaught, brought his foot up, caught Ebopa in the center of its bony chest, pushed up and back with all his might. Ebopa went flying, crashed into the arena wall below Kurvandi's box.

Tarzan whirled to his feet, and saw an amazing sight.

Ebopa was fleeing. It went up the smooth arena wall as easily as if it were running across the ground. It gained the box effortlessly, then leaped from the box into the stands of the arena.

Formerly excited patrons now fled before their god. It sprang amongst them, spraying humanity before it like a wild man tossing wet wash. The Urs flopped and flapped and broke and snapped.

Tarzan took the moment to wrap the chain around his waist, then he recovered the flagpole and used it to launch himself into Kurvandi's box. There he found poor Jad-bal-ja and a panicked Nkima. The lion was badly hurt. Tarzan tore strips from Kurvandi's clothes and bound the lion's wounds to the sounds of Ebopa's destruction: yells of terror, the thudding of feet. Ur was in a panic.

Nkima chattered softly.

"So, my friend," Tarzan said. "In spite of your cowardly nature, you came to try and help."

Nkima told a lie about a brave deed he had performed, but his heart wasn't in it. It was just something for him to say. He made a cooing noise, asked about the lion.

"I cannot say, Nkima," Tarzan said. "Jad-bal-ja is badly injured. But he is strong."

Hanson, Billy, and Wilson were making their way through the woods, and had just reached the grasslands in front of the city moat, when they heard a yell quite unlike that of any before.

"Must be a home run," Wilson said.

Suddenly, the drawbridge dropped, and fearful warriors, servants, the whole of Ur, tried to exit through that doorway. They fell beneath the feet of their friends and family, were knocked into the moat where the crocodiles happily greeted them.

"Drop back," Billy said. "Bad business here."

Hanson jammed a rifle into Wilson's spine, and Wilson, Hanson, and Billy slid back into the jungle, watching this strange spectacle with a kind of awe.

When Jad-bal-ja's wounds were dressed as well as possible, Tarzan extended the pole, and one at a time he pulled his three companions up to the arena box.

Nyama was first. She noted the remains of Kurvandi in one corner, his head smashed like a pottery vase. His beautiful headdress was a bloody ruin.

"So, ends the great Kurvandi," she said. "The lion, I suppose?"

"Yes," Tarzan said, extending the pole down to Jean. "He killed Kurvandi and the black lion. He is very brave. He is my good friend Jad-bal-ja."

"Is he dying?"

"Perhaps."

Jean held the pole as Tarzan, hand over hand, pulled her up. He lowered it for Hunt and soon they all stood in the box, the injured Jad-bal-ja at their feet.

"The lion is a noble warrior," Hunt said. "He was a boon companion."

"He is that," Tarzan said. "There's a litter here for Kurvandi. I will place the lion on it. He is very heavy, but the three of you, if you use it like a travois, you will be able to take him to safety. I want

Nkima to go with you. If you will let him, and he does not become distracted, he can lead you back to safety once you escape Ur."

"What about you?" Jean asked.

"My path lies in another direction," Tarzan said.

"Ebopa?" Nyama said.

"For one," Tarzan said. "Now go, before the crowd reorganizes and decides to elect a new king. Go before you are worse off than before."

Nkima bounced on Tarzan's shoulder and made chittering noises.

"No, Nkima," Tarzan said. "Not this time, old friend. Go with these people and Jad-bal-ja."

Tarzan lifted the lion onto the litter as carefully as he might a kitten. Jad-bal-ja licked his hand. Tarzan spoke to the lion in the language of the jungle. "You will be all right with these tarmangani, old friend. They will take care of you. And if fate and the law of the jungle allows, I will see you and Nkima again."

Hunt shook hands with Tarzan. Jean said, "You are something special, Mr. Tarzan."

"Yes, I am," Tarzan said, and smiled.

"And modest as well," Jean said.

"My greatest trait," Tarzan said.

Nyama and Jean took turns hugging him, then with Hunt's assistance they dragged the litter bearing Jad-bal-ja away. Just before they began carefully descending the stairs that led away from the arena, Jad-bal-ja lifted his bloodied head and looked at the ape-man. His lips curled.

Tarzan thought: Who says a beast cannot smile?

When Hunt, Jean, and Nyama broke into the main courtyard carrying the litter bearing Jad-bal-ja and Nkima, who had hitched a ride, they were amazed at the rush of humanity. There wasn't a hint of civilization amongst the roaring, shoving, pushing crowd. Women, children, the elderly, fell before the frightened and confused masses and were trampled. Seeing their god frightened by an outsider, having it go amok within their own populace had been too much for the Urs' sensibilities.

In their dash to escape death by their god, they had upset lamps and oils and torches. Ur had begun to burn. The fires spread rapidly, and already flames leaped from windows and a smoke thick as wool and dark as pitch rose up above the city and turned the clear blue sky and the snow-white clouds to soot.

Nyama took command immediately. "This way," she shouted, and they bore the litter away from the mass of teeming humanity, and fled back into the flaming building.

"We'll die!" Hunt yelled.

"No," Nyama said. "I know this place. Through the kitchen."

They were almost bowled over by fleeing Urs, but the bulk of the rush was from the main grounds and the arena. This way, they were able to thread their way through the frightened stragglers, and soon they were moving down a long flight of stairs and into the kitchen of the great palace.

They were almost exhausted by the time they reached the kitchen, raced through it, and rushed out the back door and through a courtyard. Warriors, frothing at the mouth as if infected with rabies, pounded past them; the very foundation on which they based their lives had fallen out from beneath them, and now they were all but insane, their one design to get away, to anywhere.

Nyama led her party across the courtyard, and with absolutely no resistance, they moved into the field beyond the great city, and turned wide around the moat toward the jungle that surrounded Ur.

Hanson, Billy, and Wilson watched in amazement from the concealment of the jungle as the people of Ur rushed out of their city. Many tumbled from the drawbridge or were stomped by the populace, but now, for the Urs, a new problem had entered the playing field.

The moat bridge began to collapse due to the great weight it was bearing. It snapped and the lumber leaped high. The frightened masses were dropped into the water with the crocodiles who were having a field day. The water had turned red and slick with blood and the sounds of the wounded and the dying was terrible.

"If Jean was alive," Hanson said. "And inside . . . "

"You don't know that," Billy said.

"I think you can bet on it," Wilson said. "I was you, I'd get me a woman, make another daughter, and head to the house."

Hanson turned and slugged Wilson, knocked him to the ground.

Wilson spat out a tooth and glared at Hanson. "Easy to do with my hands tied."

"Cut him loose, Billy," Hanson said.

"Bwana, I don't know you . . . "

"Cut him loose!" Hanson said.

Billy shook his head, drew his knife, and cut Wilson's hands free.

"I don't like it, Bwana," Billy said.

Wilson stood up. "You ain't gonna like it more when you see what I do here to your boss. Get ready, Hanson. I'm gonna turn your face to hamburger."

There was a break in the foliage, about half the size of a boxing ring, and the two naturally gravitated toward it. Wilson danced and jabbed and Hanson took the blows on his forearms and elbows. Hanson realized immediately that this guy knew what he was doing. Hanson had boxed enough to know that. But Hanson determined that in spite of that, he in fact had the edge. He thought: Wilson doesn't know I know what I know. He doesn't know I've had boxing experience, and if I don't show it up-front, he's going to get overconfident, and when he does . . .

Hanson lowered his guard, purposely. Wilson flashed out a jab, caught Hanson on the forehead. Hanson was able to slip it pretty well, but it was a solid shot. He let Wilson have another. Wilson moved in for the kill.

And then Hanson brought into play what he thought was his best punch. An uppercut. He swung up fast and solid and caught Wilson under the chin, snapping his head back. Wilson wobbled, and Hanson brought in an overhand right, and caught him just above the right eye.

Wilson went down and out.

Breathing heavily, Hanson said, "Tie him up again, Billy."

Billy laughed. "You tough, Bwana. Nobody want to bother you. You tough."

"Right now," Hanson said. "I'm tired."

Tarzan lost sight of Ebopa, but not the scent. The scent was distinct. Carrying the chain, Tarzan tracked Ebopa throughout the arena. He found the beast back in the arena proper, clawing at a wooden door. It looked weak, injured. The wounds he had inflicted on the monster had finally taken their toll. Still, Ebopa clawed so brutally, great sheets of wood peeled off the door and fell around it in strips.

Tarzan was watching from the stands, fifteen feet above the arena. He dropped over the side and into the arena a mere instant after Ebopa managed to shatter the door and enter into the darkness that led deep into the caverns.

Tarzan followed Ebopa into the darkness. The creature was moving rapidly. Tarzan assumed that it had never been hurt in a fight before. No one before had been able to injure it. Tarzan knew it would die, but it would take a long time to die. He must finish it. Even a terrible creature like Ebopa should not be allowed to suffer.

Down, down, down, led only by his sense of smell went Tarzan. Finally his nostrils picked up the aroma of oil. He stretched out his hands and found that there was a trough that ran along the wall of the tunnel, and it was filled with oil. Tarzan grabbed the chain, one end in each hand, and cracked it together. A spark flew. He did it again. He popped it a half dozen times until the spark hit and ignited the oil. Flames charged down the trough and filled the cavern with light.

The tunnel wound down and around and became precarious. Tarzan was overwhelmed by Ebopa's spoor. He was closing in on the creature. A few minutes later he came to a wide cavern. It was dark in there. Tarzan found a row of dry torches jutting out of the wall, and he took one, lit it, and proceeded.

The torchlight played across the rocks and revealed Ebopa. The god of the Urs lay on the floor by an uprise of stone, and on the stone was a greenish, rubbery-looking egg. Ebopa was breathing heavily. One of its claws rested near the egg, protectively. The ceiling dripped dirt, and Tarzan realized this was due not only to the mad rush of humankind above them, but also because part of this cavern was supported by rotten, manmade supports, and the dying Ebopa had fallen against one of them, dislodging it.

Tarzan realized too that Ebopa was not only male, but female. It had impregnated itself. He could see a number of egg-casings lying about, as well as the skeletal remains of adult creatures. Tarzan understood now how Ebopa had lived so long. It had been trapped here many moons ago, but as it aged, it impregnated itself and gave birth to a replacement. There had been many Ebopas.

But there would be no more.

A creature like this, it was not for the upper world.

Tarzan approached Ebopa, the chain ready to strike. But when he was within distance to do the killing, Ebopa's head dropped, the claw scraped over the rock, and Ebopa, The Stick That Walks, the God of the Urs, fell dead.

Tarzan turned his attention to the leather egg. It wobbled. A little hooked claw emerged from the shell, twisted, vibrated.

And above them the earth shifted.

Tarzan looked up. The cavern was starting to collapse. He turned to run, but suddenly the light of the tunnel disappeared behind a curtain of dirt. The stampede of people above, the rotten timbers, the disintegration of the caverns, were all coming into position at once. And the end result was simple.

Destruction.

The ground pitched and rocked. A timber fell toward Tarzan. He caught it, shoved it aside.

Then the world dropped down on him.

TARZAN
The Lost Adventure

XXIII

The Urs, frightened away from the flaming, collapsing city, had primarily taken to the road for their escape route. The time of Ur was finished, for even as Hanson and Billy watched, the city walls began to drop, to fall forward into the moat, revealing the great, burning city.

And then the city itself started to sink. It fell into a massive hole in the earth with an explosion and a burst of dark dust that flared up and mixed with the dark smoke that already coiled above it like a leprous snake.

All that was left of Ur now was a huge dark hole.

"Oh, God," Hanson said. "No one could have lived through that."

"Don't be so sure," Billy said, stepping out from between jungle trees and onto the beginnings of the grassy plain. "Look there."

Coming toward them, bearing a litter, was Hunt and Jean, and a woman they did not recognize.

"My God," Hanson said. "Thank the Lord."

Leaving Wilson bound and unconscious, they bolted across

the grasslands toward the trio.

Jean couldn't believe her eyes. "Father!"

They laid Jad-bal-ja down, and Jean ran to her father and he took her in his arms and covered her face with kisses and hugged her tight. "I thought I had lost you," he said.

"And I, you," she said.

Hunt came forward and shook hands with Hanson and Billy. Billy looked at Nyama. "I do not know you."

"Nor I you," Nyama said. "But you look pretty good."

"So do you."

"That does not mean I will like you," Nyama said. "You looking good."

"No," said Billy, "but it's a better start than thinking I look like back end of zebra."

Jean quickly introduced Nyama to everyone, then said, "We have to watch over Tarzan's lion. He was wounded saving our lives."

Nkima began to bound up and down, making enough noise for a boxcar full of monkeys.

"I think we are neglecting Tarzan's monkey," Hunt said. "He is very spoiled."

"Good monkey," Jean said, and stroked Nkima's head. The little monkey seemed appeased. He leaped to Jean's shoulder and maintained position there.

"And Tarzan?" Hanson asked.

Jean's humor faded. She turned and looked toward where the city of Ur had once been. "I don't know . . . But I doubt he lives."

Billy said: "If anyone lives from such a thing, it is Tarzan. No one else could. But Tarzan could."

"I believe you're right," Hanson said. "At least, I like to think so."

"Let's go home," Jean said. "And forget Ur."

"As far as I'm concerned," Hanson said. "It's still a lost city."

Billy and Hanson helped bear Jad-bal-ja to where Wilson lay unconscious. They treated the lion's wounds again, and when Wilson awoke, they started back the way they had come, looking for the hobbled zebras. It became apparent that some of the fleeing Urs had taken the mounts for themselves, so they continued on foot, little Nkima actually guiding them along on the proper path.

It took them a month, and they had much hardship, but there were positive side effects. Love bloomed between Nyama and Billy, and Jean decided Hunt wasn't quite as stupid and incompetent as she originally thought. At the end of the month, they reached the outskirts of civilization, anxious to turn Wilson over to the authorities and leave the jungle life.

By this time Jad-bal-ja was well and walking, and on the day before Hanson's party would have reached civilization proper, the lion and Nkima simply disappeared. But not before Jad-bal-ja killed a gazelle and left it in camp as a parting gift. Hanson and his party cooked the meat and ate it, and they never saw Tarzan, Nkima, or Jad-bal-ja again.

Down in the dusty bowels of the earth, Tarzan moved. He had lain unconscious for hours, but now he moved. The earth had fallen on him, but like a wave, it had washed him back against a weak tunnel wall and pushed him through it, and finally the wash had stopped and he awoke inside a deep cavern with walls illuminated by phosphorescence, a mound of dirt at his feet.

Tarzan sat up and found next to him the empty leathery shell of Ebopa's egg. The little beast had freed itself.

Tarzan sniffed the air. The creature was heading down the slope of the cavern, toward the earth's center. This route was most likely how the first Ebopa had arrived, and through some freak accident it had been sealed off from its world. Trapped in the caverns. And now, through another freak accident, the newest Ebopa had opened the way for one of its offspring to return to its source.

Tarzan considered trying to reach topside, but it was impossible to go back the way he had come. It was sealed off by tons of dirt and rock and timbers.

And besides. Why should he go back?

He could imagine only one reason. He allowed himself to think momentarily of Jane, and then he thought of her no more. For now such thoughts were useless and distracting. There was no use wishing for what he could not make come true. Perhaps later. What would come would come. He still lived. Tarzan stood up and started following the path of the cavern.

Down, down, down, toward the center of the earth.

Toward Pellucidar, where his kind were timeless and forever king.

THE END

Tarzan Books by Edgar Rice Burroughs

Tarzan of the Apes (1914)
The Return of Tarzan (1915)
The Beasts of Tarzan (1916)
The Son of Tarzan (1917)
Tarzan and the Jewels of Opar (1918)
Jungle Tales of Tarzan (1919)
Tarzan the Untamed (1920)
Tarzan the Terrible (1921)
Tarzan and the Golden Lion (1923)
Tarzan and the Ant Men (1924)
The Tarzan Twins (1927)
Tarzan, Lord of the Jungle (1928)
Tarzan and the Lost Empire (1929)
Tarzan at the Earth's Core (1930)
Tarzan the Invincible (1931)
Tarzan Triumphant (1932)
Tarzan and the City of Gold (1933)
Tarzan and the Lion Man (1934)
Tarzan and the Leopard Men (1935)
Tarzan and the Tarzan Twins
with Jad-Bal-Ja, the Golden Lion (1936)
Tarzan's Quest (1936)
Tarzan and the Forbidden City (1938)
Tarzan the Magnificent (1939)
Tarzan and "The Foreign Legion" (1947)
Tarzan and the Madman* (1964)
Tarzan and the Castaways* (1965)
Tarzan: The Lost Adventure* (1995)

published posthumously